To Nicollo Montserrate

with Best Wishes

Ron Berger

THE
GORGE

A NOVEL

RONALD M. BERGER

Design and Distribution by Bublish, Inc.

Author photo by Lauren Thomas

ISBN: 978-1-64704-188-5 (paperback)
ISBN: 978-1-64704-189-2 (eBook)

This novel is dedicated

To My Grandson,

Leo Martin

ONE

When his truck reached the meadow high above the river, Richard Carlyle quickly began wrapping himself in gear that was supposed to protect him from the bitter cold. The North Country had seen thirty-nine days of below-zero readings this winter and fifty-six days of snow in four months--a hundred twenty inches so far. It was thirty-eight degrees outside. Carlyle would be lucky if the thermometer hit fifty by the time his raft got to the gorge. The sun, when it bothered to appear at all this time of year, rose over the peaks lining the gorge at ten in the morning, and was gone by three.

Carlyle put on a light base layer, a thick pile jacket, and a one-piece dry suit whose waterproof ankle and neck gaskets were meant to keep him dry and reasonably warm. Then he pulled on wool socks, thick river boots, waterproof gloves, and a Kevlar-lined helmet, which guides, when they wanted to impress their girlfriends, called a brain bucket. He clipped an emergency whistle and a six-inch knife to his equipment belt. Once he got to the river, Carlyle would attach a mesh bag holding seventy-five yards of high-tensile rope and five lashing straps to a D-ring next to his seat on the raft.

Carlyle picked up his gear bag, walked over to the top of the path leading to the basin, and watched the river rush down the spillway and into the canyon. During the spring runoff, the Hudson Gorge trip was one of the toughest whitewater runs in the northeast, five hours from beginning to end, almost all of it at the bottom of a cavernous gorge. They would have to pick their way through six or seven difficult rock gardens and a half dozen dangerous rapids. Any two or three of them could kill, given the right combination of bad luck or stupidity.

Alex Betts, who'd worked with Caryle nine years ago when they were both rookies, walked up to him. "I don't get it," Betts said. "From what I hear, you've got a cushy teaching job now, a fat retirement package, and a nice chunk of land outside Albany. Why come up here and freeze your ass off every spring?"

"What can I tell you?" Carlyle said. "I just miss your lovely company."

"Cut the bullshit, Ric. This is a young guy's business. If I was in your boots, I wouldn't be caught dead on the river this time of year."

"Marshall gives me sixty bucks and a steak dinner at the end of the day. Who can resist an offer like that?"

"Well, you better get down there now before he starts bitching at you." Carlyle made his way down an icy path toward the put-in, where he found his former boss, Ryan Marshall, leaning against his boat. "Where's the rookie I'm supposed to check out?" Carlyle said.

Marshall pointed. "Art Sanders, next to the white pine, tall kid with the big grin. Best rookie I've had in years."

"I'll do my report and let DEC decide if it wants to give him a license."

"Carlyle, don't bust my balls."

"Is this his final check run?"

"He starts his career on Wednesday. Once you've cleared him."

"You sure you don't me to wait till all this ice disappears from the river?"

"Nah. He's good-to-go now."

Carlyle walked over and introduced himself to Sanders. "You ready to become a licensed boatman?"

"Mr. Carlyle. Ryan told me all about you."

"Don't believe a word."

"He said you swam an injured guy out of the gorge in '94."

"I was young and stupid. Wouldn't even try it now."

"Mind my asking why you left?"

"I got a gig with benefits. Examining rookies is just a sick hobby, I guess."

"Marshall says you're a professor."

"Don't tell anybody, for Christ's sake. They'd never let me forget it."

"What do you study?"

"Criminals and deviants. People like Betts."

They walked toward six guys in their twenties standing around Sanders's large green raft. "This the kind you're talking about?" Sanders said.

"They'd qualify for a medium-security facility. Go do your talk. I'll just stand here and watch."

Sanders picked up his six-foot guide paddle and faced his crew of clients. "Settle down now. I've got safety information that'll keep you alive today."

"Sure, chief. Just fire away," one of them said.

Sanders ignored the comment. "Rafting can be dangerous. That's why my boss hires guides straight out of rehab. And in case you didn't notice, winter's still hanging around."

It had been snowing since dawn. A dense coating of frost covered the rafts. The dirt surrounding Carlyle's boots was a mixture of mud, stones, and freezing water. Clouds covered the sun, and a bitter wind promised no end of misery.

"Sit three on a side," Sanders said, "feet tucked under those fat tubes in front of you. I need two big guys in front. People who won't puke at the first rapid they see."

"Come on, we're not idiots," the loudmouth said.

"You can prove it when we get to the gorge."

Sanders was at least six-two and must have weighed something north of two thirty. In addition to the standard gear every guide carried—river knife, rope, and lashing straps—Sanders had brought two flares, four carabineers, three feet of climbers' webbing, and one canister of yellow dye. He looked like a castle with arms.

"If you should fall out of the raft, I'll throw you a rope. Grab it right away. We don't want you in the water for more than a minute."

"What happens if we can't reach it?" another client said.

"Then you assume the safe swimmer position—on your back, feet together, legs pointed downstream. But remember this; never stand up in moving water. The river will drive your feet under a rock, bend you over, and force your head below the surface. Then it'll drown you."

Sanders's crew just stared at him.

"If I can't pull you out," Sanders said, "swim for shore, but don't walk away from the river. You're miles from the nearest road. Stay right where you are. Now tighten those chinstraps. Brain buckets don't work if they're not on your head."

Carlyle glanced upstream. He knew that the wall of water surging through the sluice gate at the Abanakee dam and down the spillway would soon wake up this crew.

As Sanders's raft slid into the basin just upstream of the Indian, he said, "All ahead, easy." The raft crawled across the calm water. "Now, give me two quick ones." It leapt forward. "Stop. Back on the right, forward on the left." The raft spun on its axis. "Now reverse it. Keep it going, keep it going. Okay, now stop."

Sitting next to Sanders, Carlyle said, "Don't tire them out. Just make sure they pay attention to your voice."

Sanders told his crew that for the first forty-five minutes of the trip, they would be on the Indian. Then the Hudson, after dropping south through the terrain like a scar, would come barreling in on their left. The combined rivers would plow eastward before cascading into a six-mile gorge.

"The nearest road is three miles away. Those mountains you see right ahead of us? They're with us the whole way down. Once we reach the canyon, the only way out is by this river."

When Ryan Marshall raised his paddle, Sanders yelled, "Here we go! There's no turning back now."

The full snowmelt wasn't expected until mid-April, but the river had already been transformed. Water the consistency of a daiquiri was surging down the Indian, just a sample of what waited for them in the gorge later that morning.

White-tipped waves quickly surrounded the boat as it rushed down the Indian. "Mixmaster's just ahead of us," Sanders said. "It'll swallow this raft if we get too close."

Five hundred yards downstream from the put-in, the boat side-stepped two big waves, plunged over a granite ledge, and headed straight for Mixmaster, a twenty-by-twenty whirlpool lying at the top of Staircase Rapids. Sanders would have been taught to skirt the edge of Mixmaster and pray that his crews didn't panic when they saw what lay in front of them.

The hydraulic could neither be avoided nor finessed. Sanders would have to steer them toward the lip of a wave coming off a boulder and surf the edge of the hole, inches from the thrashing of their lives. Carlyle liked the kid and hoped he'd do well.

Sanders handled his fear of the river by getting into a zone, a co-coon of white noise, as he neared each difficult set of rapids. It was the only way he could cope with the realization of what would happen if he made a mistake.

Knowing that his crew might freak out when they spotted Mixmaster, Sanders leaned out and over the back of his boat and shoved his guide paddle into the Indian to give him better control of the raft.

He looked up for a second and saw they were three feet too far to the left. He could have asked his crew to help him, but they were focused on their fear and paddling clumsily. So he did the only thing he could. He leaned back and extended his arms another six inches over the stern of his boat, letting the current swallow his hands.

He was completely vulnerable now, the top half of his body outside the raft. His left foot, wedged under a six-inch wide piece of webbing, was the only thing securing him to the boat. But in five or six seconds, if everything went as planned, they would be past their first test of the day.

Then, just when he thought he was out of danger, Sanders toppled backward into the Indian, his body doing a cartwheel just before he hit the river.

His ordeal began the moment he tumbled into the enormous hydraulic below Mixmaster. The river scraped his body along the bottom and up toward the boil line on the far side of the hydraulic. Then the recirc wave threw him, like a child in a Kansas tornado, back to the base of the rock. Sanders got recirculated three times in twelve seconds. He was strong and well-trained, grabbed a breath each time he hit light and air, and didn't panic.

Remembering the lessons he learned in rough surf during Seal training at Coronado beach, on his fourth pass through the hydraulic, Sanders lunged for the bottom, under the boil line, and then up to the surface.

Turning on his back to see what lay downstream, he waited for someone to haul him in. But once the Indian had him, it never gave him a chance for redemption. It flushed him downstream another fifty yards, scraping his body across rocks and gravel. Then the current hauled him across a submerged tree, opening a three-inch gash over his left eye and dislocating his right shoulder.

When Sanders thought the Indian could damage him no more, it tossed him toward a boulder, one whose underside had been scraped clean by the spring snowmelt. Then the remainder of his good luck, which had carried him from a shooting war in the Middle East to this unspoiled wilderness, ran out.

As he neared that boulder, Sanders, exhausted and disoriented, attempted to stand up. The river immediately wedged his right foot under the rock as fifteen hundred cubic feet of water a second began working at the back of his thigh like a pit bull on a poodle. Then the Indian grabbed his other leg and pinned that one, too.

Although they appear as disobedient as adolescents, whitewater rivers obey the laws of fluid dynamics: they do their worst damage along the bottom. Sanders was fighting for his life from the moment the Indian fused his feet to that undercut rock.

When he attempted to stand up, the current, enveloping his back like a heavy white concrete blanket, forced him beneath the surface again.

When Sanders could hold his breath no longer, he made one more attempt to grab some air. A burst of ice-cold, frothy water immediately flooded his lungs and his larynx, rebelling against this assault, shut down.

The young guide didn't panic, but when his lungs gave out, he began gasping for air. Placing his hands on the slimy green rock in front of him, he attempted, one final time, to extract his legs from their prison. As his oxygen-starved brain began to shut down, a thin film of darkness spread across his eyes and he began to lose consciousness. Deprived of oxygen, Sanders suffered a seizure. His skin began to turn pale, his body went limp, and within seconds his eyes became fixed and dilated.

Because Carlyle understood what would happen if the crew didn't get to Sanders immediately, he leapt into rescue mode. Grabbing his own guide paddle, he steered the raft into an eddy as the other boats pulled in around him.

Carlyle told Hernandez, "Quick. Get a rope across to the other side and ten yards above him. Betts, go upstream and stop any other boats from coming through here. And tell Nash to run back and contact an EMT crew."

Using hand signals and whistles to coordinate their movements, Hernandez and Keith Nash attempted to lower a dragline to Sanders. They managed to loop the rope between his waist and the boulder six or seven times in four minutes, but they couldn't pull him off the rock. It was like trying to rope a butterfly.

While the crew worked to free the trapped guide, a woman from Marshall's boat rushed toward Carlyle. "How can you just stand there?" she screamed.

"Step back please," Carlyle said without turning to face her.

"Why are you just watching this?"

"Marshall, get her away from me."

"Why don't you go out there?" she said.

"If I do that, I'll lose control of this rescue."

"For Christ's sake, do something."

"We're doing everything we can. Now move away and let us save him."

Unable to free Sanders's legs, Hernandez found a kayaker who managed to attach a line to a small D-ring on the back of Sanders's life vest. Three minutes later they all dragged him from the rock, hauled him to shore, and began CPR and chest compressions.

Lugging their equipment and a stretcher along a muddy path parallel to the Indian, it took an EMT crew half an hour to reach Sanders, begin life support, and carry him back to a chopper waiting near the put-in. Before it lifted off, a paramedic walked up to Carlyle and the other guides. "We'll do what we can. But his vitals don't look that good."

After Marshall rushed off to the Glens Falls Hospital, Carlyle told their clients, "I've seen people survive something like this. The cold water may have protected him." Then he herded them toward the put-in and onto a bus that would take them back to their cars.

Unable to talk about the accident they'd just witnessed, the guides loaded the boats and gear onto a trailer, drove to the South Mountain Lodge, and shut themselves inside the crew room.

Marshall got back at six that evening. "They worked on him for an hour. He was intubated and warmed up. They had lines running in everywhere, but it was no use."

"But an EMT told me he had a pulse," Hernandez said.

"His heart was convulsing, not contracting," Marshall said. "The trauma docs pulled a pint of water from his lungs. The death certificate read 'flush drowning.'" He walked over to his desk and sat down.

"He's dead?" Betts said.

"A nurse said it was a long shot," Marshall said. "He was just submerged too long."

Carlyle said, "Has someone notified his parents?"

"Both dead. They were electrocuted in '95 when a storm dropped power lines on their camper."

"He have any other family?" Nash asked.

Marshall closed his eyes for a long moment. "A wife and two young girls."

After everyone else had cleared out, Marshall turned to Carlyle. "Let's go outside. I need to talk to you."

They left the lodge and walked out onto the bridge spanning the Hudson. Chunks of ice, some the size of small cabins, had turned the river into a chaotic maze. Four-foot waves crashed against rocks scattered across the streambed, and the current pouring downstream obliterated everything in its path. The bridge, a concrete and steel structure supported by four thick pillars, resembled an aircraft carrier wallowing in the ocean.

"How the hell could he fall out of his boat on the Indian?" Marshall said.

"Everything was going fine," Carlyle said. "We slid across the wave coming off Mixmaster, just like we were supposed to. Then the raft slammed into a rock. When I turned around, he was gone."

"Have you ever seen anything like that?"

"No one comes out of a boat that quickly." Carlyle stared down at the Hudson. "He ever make a mistake like that before?"

"Never. He figured out Guide's Hole the first time he saw it. By the end of last season, he was driving boats down the Indian."

"Where are the rafts now?"

"Hernandez said he would take them off the trailer before he left for the night."

"Let's go take a look."

Carlyle and Marshall left the bridge and walked over to a small shed, where Hernandez was stowing equipment.

"You mind showing us Sanders's boat?" Carlyle said.

"What the hell for?" Hernandez said.

"Just do us a favor."

Hernandez reached into the trailer, peeled back two rafts, and found the one Sanders had used.

Carlyle reached for the foot strap, but Hernandez beat him to it and pulled it up. Only one end was attached to the raft. "The piece of shit came apart. We ought to sue the damn company."

"I knew the kid hadn't made a mistake," Marshall said.

"Better leave it," Carlyle said. "A lawyer will want to see the boat."

Carlyle and Marshall walked back toward the lodge.

"You still going ahead with your trip on Wednesday?" Carlyle said.

"DEC says I'm good to go so long as I never have another accident like this one."

"How you going to do that?"

"They told me to find someone qualified to supervise my entire operation. I said you'd do it."

"No way. I only agreed to come up here today to check out Sanders."

"You were right next to him. Why didn't you do something?"

"Are you serious? You know how hard I tried to save that kid."

"Don't you feel any responsibility for what happened?"

"I can't just leave my students this time of year."

"I've got eleven people on my payroll," Marshall said. "If we shut down, they all go on unemployment."

"Nothing doing."

"Are you really going to walk away from us like that?"

Carlyle stopped when he got to the front steps of the lodge. "I've got one condition."

"What's that?"

"You let me handle everything on Wednesday. I mean everything."

"Suit yourself."

"Just to make sure no one gets hurt like this again."

"Fine," Marshall said. "Then you can go back to that desk job of yours."

TWO

H e left his cabin at 3:00 a.m. and drove slowly down a series of switchbacks, past boarded-up ice cream shops and antique barns, past all-night convenience stores and gas stations, past shuttered motels, second homes, and cabins, and finally, when he had left the last town behind, past a half-dozen foreclosed dairy and cattle farms.

Thirty minutes later, just as the right-wing commentators began lashing out at liberals on the local news station, he pulled off into the woods a half-mile past Bell Mountain and started unloading his truck.

If the police discovered that Sanders's death was no accident, he wouldn't be able to launch another attack from anywhere near the Gooley Steps again. The top end of Cedar Ledges, where the Hudson appeared out of the north and overwhelmed the Indian, was his only option now.

They would never expect him to come in from the main road. The area had no trails, not even a decent footpath. It was too remote for the snowmobile guys, people who cruised half-sober all night in terrain that sane people would not approach. There were no houses, backwoods cabins, or ranger outposts where a man could hide or lay over in case he got in trouble. Even hunters, afraid of getting lost in the dense woods south of the river, stayed clear of the region.

But he knew something that even the locals had long forgotten—a single, long-abandoned footpath that ran in from the main road past

Lake Francis and Bad Luck Mountain and ended no more than an eighth of a mile from the Confluence. The route was easy enough in the fall, but at this time of year he would have a three-mile slog through knee-deep snow, a round trip that could take five or six hours.

No one would be out there now. If he broke his femur, slipped down a cliff face, severed an artery with his axe, or lost his way in the nearly impenetrable underbrush, he would die.

With his truck shielding him from the road, he put on knee-high gaiters, two pair of gloves, and a headlamp. His pack contained a twelve-inch saw-toothed knife, twenty-five feet of three-quarter-inch nylon line, a folding snow shovel, duct tape, three large carabineers, four high-strength prussic loops, and spare batteries wrapped in wool. He pulled a pair of backcountry snowshoes from the truck and shoved his boots into the bindings.

If he'd forgotten a single piece of equipment, the map, compass, or pocket thermometer, the four-by-six tarp or the fire starters, candles, water bottle, energy bars, knife or matches, he could be in desperate trouble. Without the extra pair of laces, the glove liners, or a space blanket, he would not survive long. If he turned an ankle, dislocated his shoulder, or fractured a rib, he would be forced to dig his own grave out there. It was a region with no trail markers or reference points to guide him back to the road.

He wouldn't have it any other way.

Three hours later, after following the trees he had notched a week ago and stopping only once to drink hot tea from a thermos, he broke from the woods a hundred-and-fifty yards due east of where the Hudson collided with the Indian. A large sheet of pack ice glided past him, crashed into a submerged granite boulder, and broke into a thousand jagged fragments.

It was 6:55 a.m. Sunlight washed over the summit of Pine Mountain. The snow at his feet went from dull gray to ivory and began to glisten. He would have to be out of here in no more than two hours. He dropped his pack on the snow and went to work.

A thick canopy of pines blocked sunlight from reaching the valley floor. It was thirty-seven degrees, but, breathing hard from his hike, he was still warm. Dangerous as this stunt was, he liked being out here alone. There was no one to order him around, lie about why he was losing his job, or remind him that his family had been outcasts for two generations.

Walking back and forth, he found a rotting sapling eight feet tall and six inches in diameter just ten yards from the water. He dragged it toward the Indian and spent twenty minutes maneuvering it into place. For a brief time, he was forced to place his left foot in the river and the right on a slimy, lichen-covered rock. He refused to think about what would happen if he fell into the water. This job was insanely dangerous, but people like him could not choose what kind of work they took up. They either cut wood, milled logs, or drove a school bus. Better to die like this than in some nursing home.

An hour later, his work done, his tools packed, and his boot prints brushed out of existence, he turned his back on the Hudson. After Marshall and the other outfitters had passed through here, he would come back and erase all evidence of his presence.

After a night with little sleep, Carlyle pulled on a wool hat and gloves and stepped off the front porch of the lodge. It had been snowing since dawn. A storm sweeping in from the west pushed dense gray clouds across the mountains. A half-hour ago, the snow had turned to sleet—a tough, slashing deluge that covered every tree with a thick coating of frost.

As he crossed the yard toward the gear shed, he saw Eric Munck on top of the bus, smacking ice from the rafts with a baseball bat. "Watch yourself up there," Carlyle said.

Munck stopped swinging the bat and turned around. "Listen. Since working for Marshall, I've cracked an elbow, broken a foot, and fractured an eye socket. All that for seventy-five bucks a day. You think he gives a shit what happens to me?"

Munck had been working the occasional weekend as a guide for the past four years. Carlyle had no idea where he lived or what he did when he wasn't pushing boats down the Hudson. Someone said he'd once been an ironworker. The guy certainly looked like he'd been lifting something heavy. He was five-ten, maybe two hundred five pounds, with a torso shaped by bratwurst and lager. He had two scars on his left cheek, both earned in bar fights. Betts called him a train wreck, the only person on this crew Betts went out of his way to avoid.

Munck went to work with the bat on another raft. Ice crystals filled the brittle, white air and fell to the ground. "Seen Marshall this morning?" Carlyle said.

"Just turn around. He's right behind you."

Marshall, clipboard in hand, walked toward them. He looked up at Munck. "Are we all set to go?"

"Have you seen the thermometer?" Munck said.

"I've got eyes. You don't expect me to cancel now, do you?"

The air temperature was 38, the water 34 - two degrees north of a slushie. Carlyle knew that any time those two figures together added up to less than a hundred, Marshall was putting people in harm's way.

The town released water from the big lake west of here ten weeks a year. If Marshall were lucky, he would have a hundred days a year to make a living. If he didn't run boats through the gorge in April, when people were still skiing in the mountains, he would lose his business.

"You sure you want to go through with this trip?" Carlyle said. Neither man wanted to discuss what had happened to Sanders on Saturday. They'd talked themselves out, going over and over the way he'd drowned and wondering if they could have saved him.

"I've got forty-six people standing around the lodge," Marshall said. "We've given them wetsuits, helmets, boots, rain jackets, wool socks, and gloves. You really expect me to march in there and say 'sorry, I changed my mind, my guides screwed up five days ago and I don't think I can keep you safe today?'"

"The state's watching every move you make."

"What's that supposed to mean?"

"I got a call from Karen Raines."

"Who the hell is she?"

"Head of Region Six for DEC. She said she'll let you continue to run trips only if I supervise your operation for the rest of the season."

"No fucking way. This is my business. I'm in charge here."

"You want me to tell her that, just say so."

"All right, what's her bottom line?"

"I make sure nothing goes wrong today. You prove there'll be no more mistakes, and I go back to my classroom life."

Marshall looked up at Munck. "Don't you have something to do in the gear shed?" Munck got off the bus and walked away.

Marshall turned and faced Carlyle. "What do you need me to do?"

"Tell me everything about your plans for the day."

"Nash, my best guide, is running sweep. He'll have the first-aid kit, two seventy-five-foot ropes, and the tag line. You okay with that?"

"Did you check everyone's gear?"

"You ever remember us leaving anything behind?" Guides, who liked to believe they were just as good as Navy Seals, carried all the fancy gear they could lay their hands on: multi-colored prussic loops, heavy-duty climber's webbing, flares, signal mirrors, rescue hooks and pulleys, and carabineers in assorted sizes.

Carlyle thought some of this stuff was nothing more than lucky charms—talismans to ward off danger— but guides, who defended their craft with tenacity, insisted every piece of equipment was vital.

"Did you inspect your boats?" Carlyle said.

"This morning at seven. I guarantee you, none of them have defects."

"Who's on the crew today?"

"Hernandez, Nash, Betts, Chris Blake, and Munck."

"You ever have problems with any of them?"

"Are you crazy? You think I'd put someone out there who'd make me go through a repeat of last week?"

"What about Blake? I've heard he's pretty raw."

"It's only his second season, but he's done nine trips already and he hasn't made a single mistake on any of them."

"Maybe you should think about having a veteran out there with him."

"You really want me to walk up to Blake and tell him to take a hike? Or maybe you're willing to do it."

"Okay, it's on your shoulders." Carlyle looked down at the list in his hand. "What about your boat order?"

"I lead my guys through the gorge. An experienced person usually follows me, but I'm letting Blake run second today."

"You're not serious."

"He deserves a chance to show his stuff."

"Really? Fifty people watched one of your employees drown five days ago. No one will give you a break this time if you make another tragic error."

"I'll tell Blake to stay right behind me. You ride with Nash. The two of you can watch every step he takes if you're so worried about him."

"I had to pull Sanders's body out of the Hudson, remember? Don't make me go through that again."

"When we get back, you can tell Raines I've been a bad boy," Marshall said. "If she wants to punish me, I'll take the whipping. But Blake's riding on my tail." He turned away and walked toward his clients.

Forty-five minutes after boarding the bus that would take them to the river, Marshall's crew turned off the main road running through the valley and drove past a string of gaunt jack pine. Four-foot snowdrifts lapped at the sides of the bus. A bitter wind hurled shards of ice against the windows. To Carlyle's right, thick sheets of water thundered down a steep concrete spillway into a cavernous, boulder-strewn gorge.

A Volvo salesman from Saratoga Springs, a guy who had looked worried all morning, stood up and walked over to Carlyle. "We're really going to go out there with the weather like this?"

"We carry plenty of extra gear. Everything you'll need if you get cold."

"If we get cold?"

"I promise, you'll have a great time."

After his client backed off, Blake turned to Carlyle. "The guy seemed kind of nervous."

"It's a bad sign when they're like that before a trip. Keep an eye on him."

The bus, its wheels churning up snow and mud, rumbled past the dam.

Carlyle said, "Ryan wants you to back him up today."

"You sure about that?"

"Absolutely. Now get ready. We're almost there."

When the bus came to a stop, the six guides, knowing they couldn't let their clients stand around in the cold, rushed out the door. Munck mounted a ladder to the roof and began dropping the boats to outstretched arms.

Carlyle watched the guides corral their people into boats. It was all coming back to him, the excitement and the spectacle at the beginning of each trip, the waiting and the uncertainty, the expectation of what lay ahead.

Marshall shouted, "Come on. Move! We've got to get on this river while the sun's still around."

After the guides had lashed down their gear, Marshall told them to hoist the boats and move toward the path leading down to the Indian. Eight people, who looked like philosophy majors delivering a grand piano, slowly lugged Nash's heavy raft down the mud-slicked trail.

"Anyone ask for a ride back to the lodge?" Carlyle asked Nash. Every week, after realizing they had four or five hours of isolation and misery ahead of them, one or two clients usually jumped ship.

"Not yet. But keep your eyes open."

When all six rafts were lined up at the top of the slope, Marshall yelled, "Hop in, grab a paddle, and pray."

The Volvo dealer grimaced. "What's going on?"

"Do what he says," Carlyle said. "Just get in your boat."

When Marshall yelled, "Now!" Nash put his shoulder against the raft and pushed. They quickly gathered speed, and then began rushing down the trail toward the Indian.

During his rookie season a decade ago, one client told Carlyle, "That stunt on the hill made me think you were all a bunch of madmen."

Using the rafts as bobsleds today was plain stupid. But every trip was a crapshoot. If you eliminated all risk, your clients got bored and didn't sign up again. If you took too many chances, someone ended up in the river.

"I heard you talking to Marshall," Nash said. "I wish Blake were at the three spot, where we all could watch him."

"Marshall never listens to advice." Although the guides were focused on the trip ahead of them, Sanders's death could not have been far from their thoughts. Hernandez, who ran his mouth constantly, had been silent on the bus. Betts, more nervous than usual, had called his clients "stupid mules" on the way down to the basin. Even Nash, who was usually pretty calm, had been chewing on his emergency whistle all morning.

Two minutes after they reached the basin, Marshall's guides began teaching their crews the skills they'd need to survive what lay ahead in the gorge.

As they moved out into the swift current pulling them downstream, Carlyle said to Nash, "Let's keep a close eye on Blake."

"You're the boss," Nash said. "That is, until Marshall tells us he's had enough of you."

As soon as Chris Blake's blunt-nosed raft slid into the Indian, it began to pick up speed. He cut left to avoid two midstream boulders and began teaching his crew how to stay safe in a river running downhill like a herd of stallions. Blake loved this job. The river was one big adrenalin machine, a device designed to make his heart race.

Knowing that he could not take his eyes off the water, that tree roots, rocks, and granite outcrops could appear at any second, Blake tried to imagine what problems lay ahead of him. On his rookie trip, Marshall had said, "Don't focus on what's right in front of your boat. The horizon is your target. That's where the danger is."

Freezing spray coated Blake's eyelids and lashed his face. The numbing cold had begun to penetrate his clothing and his fingers were beginning to cramp up. The Indian was supposed to be a brief overture to what lay ahead, but the early spring runoff this year had transformed the narrow, boulder-strewn current. In the lodge this morning, Betts, who knew that an inch or two of rain could alter a river in minutes, had called this part of their trip "difficult if you're not careful, bloody murder if you not paying attention."

Blake's raft punched through Mixmaster and rushed downstream. For six or seven minutes—an eternity for those who'd never lived through it—his boat careened through Gooley Steps, a frenzied landscape filled with boulders and back-washing waves. As the Indian became steeper, it rumbled rather than screeched, a sign of its volume and speed. Sunlight streaming through the thick canopy of pines on both sides of the river alternately blinded and distracted the young guide.

Twenty minutes later, after a ride that left him stunned by the river's power, Blake cut sharp left and followed Marshall into a large eddy above the confluence with the Hudson.

"You okay?" Marshall said.

Blake wasn't about to admit that he was shocked at the monster the runoff had made of the river. "I've got a great crew. We're fine."

"Don't get too comfortable. You've got another three hours to go."

Blake gave each of his clients a fistful of chocolates, tightened his foot straps, took a swig of water, and waited, his left leg shaking nervously, for the sign to move out.

Marshall leaned toward him. "There's ice all over the river. Stay no more than ten yards behind me. I'm not sure which side of Cedar I'm going to take."

Blake turned to his crew. "You people ready for the best two hours of your lives?"

They raised their arms and cheered.

"Okay, then, let's get ready for some major carnage."

One by one, the six rafts punched through the seething waters at the Confluence, cut diagonally across the swollen, ice-choked crosscurrent, and headed straight for Cedar Ledges.

Blake watched the Hudson pour into the valley from his left and overpower the Indian. For more than a minute, two rivers on a collision course fought for control of his raft.

Blake told his crew to ease up as the Hudson pushed them toward Cedar. Up ahead he saw Marshall, forced to the right to avoid a ten-by-twelve slab of pack ice, enter a narrow, rock-lined channel.

Following his boss into the chute, Blake found himself surrounded by tall pines. Rocks and chunks of ice punctured the current. The sun, pulsing through the trees above his left shoulder, blinded him momentarily. Sighting open water ahead, Blake was anxious to escape the narrow confines of a space that left him almost no room to maneuver.

He never saw the log that struck him in the soft flesh immediately below his right eye. The collision, like a sledgehammer demolishing an over-ripe melon, crushed in his cheek bone, dislodged three molars, and fractured his jaw before sending him into the Hudson. Somersaulting backward, Blake hit the water feet first and disappeared. That's when his real troubles began.

The current carried him ten yards downstream and then, when his foot snagged something for a second, channeled him toward the back wall of a large undercut cave that the Hudson had been carving out since the Pleistocene.

He was only six feet from light and fresh air, but he might as well have been six miles. The chamber, covered in microscopically thin particles of decaying vegetation, was agate smooth. Because the river was focusing its incalculable energy on this single point, the young guide was, for all practical purposes, a hundred feet underwater.

Blake's diligence backfired on him that morning. Five days ago, he'd blown a day's pay on a new life vest. Its thick, rigid panels running from shoulders to hips gave the Hudson a perfect target as it pushed relentlessly against his body. The inexorable pressure enveloped his torso and inch by inch, despite his struggles, shoved him further underwater.

Holding his breath and staring up at the opaque light far above him now, Blake waited to get flushed from the cave. Having run a half-dozen recirculation drills in hydraulics, he knew that rivers could scare the hell out of you, but eventually they released you. Every time he'd done one of these exercises, he'd been told, "Keep your mouth shut and, when your turn comes, swim like hell toward the boil line."

The river was ruthless that day. It crushed Blake's eardrums and dislocated his elbow. It ripped off his helmet and split the gaskets of his dry suit, allowing it to fill with ice-cold water. Then it pushed him closer to the gravel-covered bottom and squeezed the air from his lungs.

While a mediocre student, a sweet goof-off really, Blake was a smart, hardworking, and responsible guide. Though raised by neglectful parents in a community crushed by poverty, he didn't possess two tin cups worth of cynicism, mistrust, or resentment.

The river understood none of this. It did what it was designed to do. It quickly drowned him.

Nash and Carlyle, who were waiting for the rafts ahead of them to clear the chute, pulled up behind Blake's boat thirty seconds later. "What are you all sitting here for?" Nash asked Blake's clients.

"Our boat hit something and just stopped," a young guy said. "When we turned around, our guide was gone."

Just then Munck, Hernandez, and Betts slid up alongside the two other rafts. "What the hell's going on?" Betts said.

"Blake's disappeared."

"We don't have time for this bullshit," Betts said. "Marshall's waiting for us."

Carlyle turned to Blake's crew. "Was everything okay before you entered the chute?"

"He was fine," the guy said. "We were having a great time."

"And you could hear him giving directions?" Carlyle said.

"Yes, of course."

Carlyle stood up in his raft. "He can't have gone far. Hernandez, quick, walk upstream. If another outfit shows up, tell them no one comes through here until we've found our guide."

"Then what?"

"Flag down a safety boater. Have him run back to the basin and alert the authorities."

Just then Marshall, who had parked his boat downstream, emerged from the woods. "What's going on?"

Carlyle grabbed his arm and pulled him aside. "We can't find Blake."

"Are you crazy?" Marshall turned to Nash. "What's he saying?"

"Chris is gone."

Marshall just stared at them.

Carlyle said, "Keith, go downstream. Look along the shore and in the woods. Alex, move his crew to the other boats and get them away from here."

Nash returned three minutes later. "I can't find him anywhere."

Marshall said, "Come on. This makes no sense."

"We need Search and Rescue," Carlyle said. "There's not much time."

As snow dropped from overburdened pines, Marshall walked back and forth along the Hudson. "What are we looking for? Tell me now."

Carlyle said, "Calm down. An EMT squad should be here soon."

Just then they heard three whistle blasts. Carlyle rushed through the woods and found Betts holding onto Blake's body. It was wedged between the bank and tree roots that curled down into the river.

Carlyle said, "Quick. Hand me a line." Stepping carefully across the slick rocks lining the chute, he lowered himself into the current. The water swirled around his thighs, threatening to pull him under. He tied the rope to Blake's life vest, grabbed the boy under his arms and, inch by inch, heaved him out of the water.

Nash bent over the young guide, unsnapped his life vest, and began chest compressions. "Come on," he whispered. "Come on. Come on." Water seeped from Blake's mouth, but he didn't move or breathe.

Carlyle studied his watch as Nash worked on Blake. Finally, he said, "It must be fifteen minutes since he went under. That's enough."

Nash, ignoring Carlyle, continued CPR for another two minutes.

"Keith. He's gone. Stop." Carlyle, his feet numb from the cold, put his right hand on Nash's shoulder. "You did everything you could." Betts picked up a paddle and began abusing a jack pine. His tirade over, he slumped to the ground.

Nash leaned away from Blake but kept his right hand on the body.

"Let me see him," Carlyle said. He bent over and took off Blake's helmet. The right side of the kid's face was stove in. His eye was bloody, the teeth broken and mangled. "How the hell did this happen?"

"Who the hell cares?" Nash said. "He's dead."

"Give me a minute." Carlyle trudged upstream through the forest parallel to the chute, pushing aside low-hanging limbs, for another twenty yards. The Hudson, two steps to his right, roared past him. Dead leaves and branches littered the ground. Sunlight reflecting off the river cast dark shadows on the woods.

Had he had come too far? He stopped, scanned the ground around him, and spotted the trunk of a slender pine lying in the snow. The bottom portion of the tree hung no more than eighteen inches over the current, just enough in the confined space of the chute to have caught an unwary guide or one of his passengers.

Carlyle stared at the tree. He walked around it and kicked at the snow-covered branches. Before leaving, he grabbed one and pulled, but the sapling, frozen to the ground, would not budge.

Carlyle made his way back to Marshall and his crew. "You won't believe this. He hit a log. Come back there with me; I'll show you."

"Are you nuts? We've got forty people sitting over there. A couple of them are hysterical. If we don't get out of here, they'll freeze to death. Let the authorities take care of it."

"DEC is going to demand a full report," Carlyle said.

"Come back tomorrow if you have to," Nash said. "We've got to get everyone back to North River now."

"Then you've got to wait a couple of minutes," Carlyle said. "I need to look at the site again before we leave."

Marshall grabbed his arm. "Get in that boat now."

"We can't leave that log there. What if someone else runs into it?"

"Did you hear me?" Marshall said. "Let the rangers deal with this. It's their problem. They'll move the goddamn tree."

"You're making a big mistake. This is the second death this week. Someone's going to catch hell if we don't do everything we can to explain what just happened."

"I swear I'll leave you here if you don't get going. Now."

Carlyle took two steps toward the log before spotting the DEC raft approaching. Dave Reed, a forest ranger, walked over to Marshall. "We'll handle this now. Move the body into my boat, then get your people out of here."

Two minutes later, a helicopter circled the site and hovered over the gorge. The DEC boat carrying Blake's body in a litter moved into open water and began working its way upstream. As the chopper crew winched the basket up, the blue and gold state police craft, buffeted by cross winds, shuddered. Blake's body grazed the top of a spruce, swayed unsteadily for several seconds, then disappeared into the helicopter's open side door.

Reed's boat worked its way back downstream toward Marshall's group.

"What are they going to do with the body?" Carlyle said.

"He'll go to Glens Falls for the autopsy." Reed turned to Marshall. "We'll meet you at the inn at five. Have your guides there. And get all your papers in order."

"What papers?"

"Your operator's license, insurance documents, training records, and Red Cross certificates. Everything that supports your outfitter application."

Marshall said, "What's going on?"

"Ryan, you've lost two people this week. You can't expect us to ignore that."

"Am I going to lose my license?"

"Just do what Carlyle says."

"For Christ's sake. I can get my people back to North River."

"If you run everything by Carlyle, you've got no problem."

As soon as Marshall and his guides returned to their boats, Carlyle spoke to Blake's crew. "We don't know how this happened. But please, don't ask us to talk about it now. We'll have you off the river in three hours."

A young woman, her hands shaking, said, "Just get us out of here, please."

Carlyle said, "One more thing. DEC and the state police are going to conduct an investigation. If they contact you, tell them everything you remember about the trip, Blake's behavior most of all."

"What should we say?"

"That's up to you. A young guide just died a half-hour ago. I need you to help us understand why that happened."

By the time Marshall's five boats approached North River at three that afternoon, the sun had disappeared behind Black Mountain. It was forty-nine degrees, and a fifteen-mile-an-hour wind was whipping up whitecaps on the Hudson.

Marshall's stunned clients had said little that afternoon. When they reached the beach, they dropped their gear and walked silently up to a waiting bus.

Guides and outfitters from other companies, Marshall's staff, and the media, some fifty people in all, stood in silence on a slight rise overlooking the take-out. Alan Metzger, a reporter from a local paper, shoved a microphone toward Betts's face. "Can you tell us how he died?"

"If you don't get that thing away from me, I'm going to give you a colonoscopy with that mic."

Saying nothing, Carlyle marched past the line of microphones and cameras.

Wearing waterproof boots, a yellow backcountry shell over a pile jacket, and fingerless gloves, Karen Raines was waiting for him near the road. She had a BlackBerry in her left hand. "How the hell did that happen?"

He told her about the accident and his attempt to examine the site. "It's the craziest thing I've even seen."

"Have you ever heard of two fatalities so close together?"

"Never."

"There's going to be an inquiry."

"I'll be glad to tell them what I saw."

"We don't just want your testimony. We want you to lead the investigation."

"Why me?"

"The university says you're this hotshot criminologist. Were they wrong?"

"I'm not a crime-scene investigator. I study the history of crime."

"You were a guide on this river for a decade; you understand this world."

"The state police will be furious if they're not in charge."

"Let me worry about them."

"I told you, I'm no cop."

"We're not looking for a cop. We just need time to decide how to handle all the bad publicity that's coming our way."

"I get it. You're going to sweep this thing under the rug."

"Of course not. DEC wants this problem cleared up so we can get people back on that river."

"If you put me in charge of this thing, I won't stop until I find out what happened out there."

"That's fine. Just be at Marshall's lodge at eight-thirty tomorrow morning. We'll have your witnesses ready."

Carlyle climbed onto the bus and walked to the back to give himself time to think.

Betts dropped into the seat next to him. "You even see anything like those jackals with cameras?"

"Try to stay calm," Carlyle said. "The shit's just beginning for all of us."

At seven that night, when he was sure that no other boats would come down the river, he emerged from the woods. He kicked leaves away from the site and, gripping the long wooden pole in both hands, pried the log into the Indian. He stood there for several minutes to make sure the current carried it clear of the chute. Because it was too late to hike back to the road, he would camp out tonight and return to his truck before dawn, long before the main road would see any traffic.

THREE

The five guides who were on the river when Blake died went their own way after being interviewed by the state police. Betts, Nash, and Hernandez went home to their families and drank beer until they fell asleep. Eric Munck picked up a woman in a bar and stayed with her until four in the morning. Carlyle ate in a restaurant in Warrensburg, then found a room in the lodge. Marshall slept on the couch in his office. When they all got back to Marshall's place on Thursday morning at eight thirty, they found Karen Raines, John Bognor, the county sheriff, and Leo Wells, head of Search and Rescue for the region, waiting for them.

Marshall's lodge sat on a forty-six-acre property surrounded by blue spruce, birch, maple, and flowering crabapple. The main building was a replica of the place Cornelius Vanderbilt had erected a hundred miles north of here a century ago. Sheathed in old-growth cedar, it contained a two-thousand-square-foot conference center, a dining room that could seat fifty, two offices, a guides' lounge, and, around back, a retail shop that sold whitewater gear.

Marshall's father, convinced that it would showcase his plans for the Johnston Mountain Project, had shelled out nearly half a million dollars for the lodge alone. The main room downstairs had a handcrafted stone fireplace, ten-foot mullioned windows, brocade wing chairs, walnut end tables, and oak beams framing a vaulted ceiling.

Each bedroom on the second floor contained a four-poster canopy bed, imitation Tiffany lamps, ship models, bentwood rockers, pack baskets, carvings of owls and loons, and original—if not especially charming—landscape paintings.

Raines opened her purse and took out a BlackBerry and a large manila file. "I just spoke to the commissioner. He wants people back on the river this weekend. If they're not with Marshall, he wants them with another outfitter."

Carlyle sat at the head of the table in the main room downstairs. "There's something else we have to talk about first. The families of these two guides deserve to know why they died."

"The commissioner has another priority: ending the bad publicity and pumping tourist dollars into this region."

"There's a half-dozen fatalities in this county every year," Marshall said. "Why are you laying the blame for these tragedies on me?"

Sheriff Bognor turned in his chair to face Raines. "Karen, Blake's parents have hired a lawyer. You can't ignore the families."

Bognor, age fifty-six, was wearing a plaid shirt, jeans, and scuffed work boots. When asked why he never wore a uniform, he'd said, "I didn't get elected to this job because I look like Smokey the Bear."

"Let's get this investigation over with," Marshall said. "I've got a business to run."

All this talk of profit and loss appalled Carlyle. "DEC will need some reassurance that your people did everything they could to save Blake."

"You can't put the blame for what happened on my crew."

"I'm just trying to make sure this never happens again."

Marshall turned to Raines. "Are you going to let him railroad me like this?"

"Let's just go over yesterday's events and then decide what to do," Raines said.

Carlyle turned to Betts. "Alex, you were with him all morning. Did anything happen before the trip that may have thrown Blake off stride?"

"He had an argument in the parking lot with his crew. They had hangovers and tried to sneak a six-pack of beer onto the bus. None of them had the right gear, naturally."

"What did you do?"

"I took the beer and threw it in the back of my truck."

Betts was six feet tall and nearly two hundred twenty pounds. Unlike Marshall, who wore expensive river gear, Betts adopted the ape-man look: torn wetsuit, ripped river shorts, ragged neoprene boots. Before every trip he strapped a ten-inch diver's knife to his leg with two thick rubber cords. The patch on his life vest read "Paddle or Die."

"Then what happened?" Carlyle said.

"I told them Grace Irwin would sell them gear that would keep them from freezing. I said she made eight bucks an hour, but if they were polite, she'd treat them respectfully."

"Did that end the trouble?" Bognor said.

"You think they were dumb enough to pick a fight with me?"

"That's it?" Carlyle said.

"End of story."

"Let's move on then. Did anything unusual occur between the time you shoved off and when you reached Cedar Ledges?"

Marshall said, "I'd heard that ice had formed on the Indian, but it didn't hold us up yesterday."

Marshall was underestimating the danger of pack ice. Eight years ago, an enormous ice jam had broken up in Cedar Ledges. When it collided with boulders, it sounded like a locomotive plowing through steel bridge girders. They had to work like galley slaves to reach the safety of slow-moving water below Elephant Rock.

"So the only problem was those drunks and the threat of ice?"

Nash cleared his throat. "One other thing. I had a woman turn hypothermic on me almost as soon as we left the basin."

"How'd you handle it?" Carlyle said.

"I gave her dry clothing and hot soup, but she didn't stop shaking until we got her on the bus at North River."

"Okay, then." Carlyle looked over the list of questions he'd made last night. "I think it's time to talk about Blake. Is there anything in Chris's background that we need to know about?"

Betts said, "There's nothing much to say. He was just a great kid. End of story."

"Come on," Carlyle said. "Are you trying to tell us he never screwed up all the time he worked with you?"

Betts fiddled with a set of keys for a minute before answering Carlyle. "He forgot to bring the hypo bag in his boat one time last year. We didn't discover it was missing until we got to the Boreas."

Bognor raised his hand. "You folks mind telling me what a hypo bag is?"

Carlyle said, "A large waterproof container where we put spare clothing—jackets, sweaters, hats, gloves, everything you can imagine—in case someone gets cold."

"We never let him forget it," Betts said. "Jesse Simmons and I made him wear a stupid green and red wool hat, the kind with ear flaps, all spring."

Carlyle, who was writing as Betts talked, looked up. "Jesse Simmons?"

"One of Burton's regulars. He works for us occasionally."

The brutal hazing rookie guides like Blake endured had a single purpose: to remind them that even minor errors could have significant consequences. "You think Blake learned his lesson?"

"He was totally mortified," Betts said. "The kid apologized to all of us the next day at a guide's meeting and swore he'd never do anything that dumb again."

"But he didn't walk away from the job."

"Are you kidding? He grew up in a double-wide in the hills some-where. This was the best gig he'd ever had."

Bognor rocked back in his chair. "I hope you don't mind my saying this, but you all sound like he was some kind of angel."

Betts and Marshall stared at each other for several seconds. Then Betts said, "Blake came to work here when he was seventeen. He had his issues." Betts told them that Blake had dropped out of high school in eleventh grade and spent two years scrubbing pots in a diner in Warrensburg. Then, one January, after three beers, he wrapped his pickup around a telephone pole. "I told him, 'Keep it up and you're going to kill someone.'"

"He tell you to mind your own business?" Carlyle said.

"He admitted he was headed for jail or rehab."

Bognor asked, "Did he stop drinking?"

Marshall nodded. "Absolutely. I offered him a Coors after he passed his written exam. He turned it down. Told me he was going to get a better job at the diner, propose to his girlfriend, and tell his parents that they could stop worrying about him."

Carlyle put down his pen. "How did he do during his apprentice year?"

Betts said, "He watched river videos till his eyes turned red and passed his DEC test just fine."

"Was there ever any sign that he would make a mistake like the one he made yesterday?"

"None at all."

"Come on. He was nineteen."

Betts sneered. "A college professor might not understand why working for eighty bucks a day could be so important to someone like him."

Carlyle ignored the jab. "What about drugs?"

"Never."

"You expect us to believe that?"

"He was a kid. More balls than brains at times, but he swore he didn't do that shit."

"I guess we'll have to take your word for it." Carlyle turned to Marshall. "Think, did anything happen just before the accident that could explain why he ran into that log?"

"You were there, for God's sake. Why make me describe it again?"

"The sheriff and Raines aren't familiar with what we're trying to describe. They need to hear it from someone who was close to Blake."

"I was right in front of him all morning," Marshall said. "He seemed fine when we got to the Confluence."

Carlyle looked down at his notes. "One thing is bothering me. How come you decided to run the chute yesterday?"

"What do you mean?"

"The gauntlet's just fifteen feet wide and filled with boulders. Seems like a pretty risky choice."

"Cedar is often iced over this time of year, but there's always moving water on the right. You know that."

"Are you trying to tell us you never once worried about going in there?" Carlyle said.

"I've spent a decade on that river. You think anything out there's going to surprise me?"

"Let's go back to my earlier question. You got through that chute. Blake didn't. Can you give us any reason why he got hung up?"

Marshall thought for a moment "It was dark in there," he said. "There were trees all around us, my boat was moving like crazy. When I saw the log hanging out over the water I shouted, 'Watch your heads.' I missed it by inches. When we got to the bottom of the chute I made a hard-left turn into the main current. It was all over in seconds."

"There were no other obstacles in there?"

"Just that goddamn log."

Carlyle checked off one line in his two-page list. "Why didn't someone who'd run the chute earlier warn you?"

"We were the first outfit on the river yesterday. You know that."

"How come you didn't let Blake know about the log?"

"Are you completely nuts? By the time I was able to raise my head, we were twenty yards downstream. What was I supposed to do, pull over, run back upstream, and warn him?"

"That doesn't answer the one question we're all wondering about. Why was Blake the only person in his boat who got clobbered?"

Betts said, "You know the answer to that. A guide sits on the back tube, six to nine inches higher than his clients."

"Let me rephrase my question. Why was he the only guide who got hit?"

Betts said, "How the hell would we know that?"

Bognor, who'd been silent for several minutes, said, "Alex, could his crew have screwed up in some way?"

"They were knuckleheads, like I said, but from what I could see, once we got to the river they sobered up fast."

"What happened when they realized he was gone?" Bognor said.

"They thought he was playing some kind of prank on them."

"What did you think?"

Nash answered for Betts. "I knew right away something was wrong."

"Why's that?"

"Guides never leave their boats. It's as simple as that."

"Any idea why his body turned up so soon?" Bognor said.

Nash looked horrified. "Jesus, do I have to answer that?"

"I know how difficult this is Keith," Carlyle said.

Nash shook his head. "I can't explain it. Maybe a block of ice came through and shoved him to the surface."

"We have any idea how long he was under?" Bognor said.

"It couldn't have been more than eight or ten minutes."

"Keith, I have to ask you this," Bognor said. "Can you describe his body?"

Nash leaned back in his chair and closed his eyes for a moment. "The right side of his face was smashed. His left arm was across his chest. His skin was pale. I remember, this is crazy, there was moss under the fingernails of his right hand."

"You did CPR?" Bognor said.

"Of course. You know that extreme cold can prolong survival times."

"But there was no reaction?"

"We must have been past the margin of error."

Bognor turned to Marshall. "Has your dad heard about this yet?"

"He only reads the Philly papers. I'll tell him when he gets back from St. Thomas."

"Let's take a break," Carlyle said. "I'll see you all back here in twenty minutes."

When the others wandered off for coffee, Bognor came up to Carlyle. "You mind coming outside for a minute?"

The two men left the lodge and walked out to the bridge straddling the Hudson. Carlyle buttoned up his jacket and stared down at the river

Bognor pulled a pack of unfiltered Camels from his shirt pocket. "Already had one vein in my leg replaced this year. I suppose this won't help. Let me ask you something. You get the impression Marshall doesn't seem all that fond of his father?"

Carlyle turned his face away from the wind. "The old man put Ryan in a military academy. From what I hear, they still don't speak to each other very often."

Bognor leaned against the bridge railing. "You been doing this job long, tracking down bad guys?"

Carlyle waited while an eighteen-wheel lumber truck downshifted off the mountain and roared past. "God, no. I study crimes, not solve them."

"Then why did they put you on this case?"

"Probably to keep things semi-official and low-profile until DEC decides how they want to handle the two deaths."

"You conducted yourself pretty well in that meeting. I'm told Betts can be hard to keep under control."

"The man has been known to toss furniture when he gets pissed off."

Bognor flipped his cigarette into the wind. "I suppose you understand that no matter what happens, some people will blame you for siding with the authorities."

"I'm not anybody's stalking horse John."

"And I certainly didn't sign up for homicide duty when I moved to a rural county." Bognor straightened up and turned toward the lodge. "I'm just saying, you'd best take cover when the shit starts flying."

Thirty minutes later, just as Carlyle began to wrap up his interrogation of Marshall and the other guides, Caleb Pierce, Bognor's Deputy, walked through the door.

"Caleb, this is a DEC inquiry." Bognor said. "You should be out on patrol."

Pierce sat down and placed a thick file on the table. "Sheriff, this outfit has lost two guides in the past five days. Don't you think we should know why?"

Pierce was five nine and weighed two hundred pounds, most of it muscle. He carried a Glock and a three-foot club on his hip belt.

Leo Wells stared at Pierce. "You heard the sheriff. This meeting is none of your business."

"Leo, I don't see how you can mind if I ask a few questions." Although Pierce must have been on duty since early morning, his dark gray uniform was still laundry crisp.

"Make it quick then," Wells said.

Pierce opened his file and began arranging the papers in front of him. "First, I'd like to know why someone didn't remove that log before you all entered that particular section of the river."

Wells said, "How the hell were they supposed to know it was there?"

Pierce stared at his short, thick fingers and immaculately trimmed nails. "Watch your language, please."

Debbie, Marshall's wife, opened the door. "The reporters want to know what the Deputy is doing here."

Bognor said, "Tell them to hold on. I'll be out shortly."

When Debbie left, Pierce said, "I'll accept that for the moment. My next question is this: What do we really know about this kid?"

Carlyle passed a folder over to Pierce. "We pulled Blake's complete file from Fish and Game. There's not much to go on."

"Are you sure about that?" Pierce said. Everyone in the room turned toward him.

"If you've got some information," Carlyle said, "Let's have it."

Pierce held up a file. "Let's see now. This is a state police report. It says he flipped his truck last February 15. It was eight in the evening and snowing. Blake was driving too fast for conditions. No one got hurt, but it does seem kind of reckless, wouldn't you say?"

"What does that prove?" Marshall said. "Everybody here has had an accident on these roads."

"Hold on, I didn't say I'd finished, did I?" He turned the page. "Blake's had three other moving violations. Turning right without stopping at a red light, drifting over the double yellow twice, and, more seriously, side-swiping a kid on a bicycle." Pierce looked up and stared at Marshall. "Your employee wasn't exactly a choir boy, was he now?"

Betts stood up. "Wait a minute. Who the hell made you the district attorney around here?"

"Alex, don't take this personally. I'm just trying to assist this investigation."

"Bullshit! You want to make this kid responsible for what happened yesterday."

While Betts and Pierce continued yelling at each other, Carlyle began drawing a diagram of the chute where Blake died. He estimated that it was at least a hundred yards long, maybe fifteen wide. He put an X where Blake hit the log, a second X where he fell overboard, and another ten yards downstream where Nash found the body. Ignoring the sound of Betts's voice, he stared at the page in front of him. When there was a break in the argument, Carlyle looked up. "Caleb, is there anything else in that file?"

Pierce looked through the papers in front of him. "Not much. Birth certificate, high school graduation records, application for the job here, and two letters of recommendation."

"That's it?"

"No, there's one more thing. His DEC file with his test scores and a copy of his driver's license."

Carlyle leaned forward. "Anything unusual on the license?"

"Not that I can see. Home address, DOB, date issued, and expiration. It says he had brown eyes and was five foot nine."

While Pierce was examining Blake's permit, Carlyle reached into his back pocket and pulled his own license from his wallet. "Look all the way down on page one of the Xerox copy in front of you and tell us what's there."

"A letter—R."

"And it says what?"

"See other side."

"Now look at the next page, bottom right, under Restrictions."

"Got it." Pierce sat up straight. "Christ. You're not going to believe this."

"Read it."

"Subject has no sight: right eye."

Marshall stood up. "I told you Blake's accident wasn't our fault. Now let's get out of here and back to work."

When Carlyle left the lodge ten minutes later, he found Bognor leaning against his patrol car, a beat-up, metallic blue '97 Dodge Charger. "Is Pierce always so belligerent?"

"You have no idea. His first day at work, I told him he didn't have to shave his scalp to show how tough he was, that people around here would respect the badge and the uniform. He said he'd been hired to arrest people, not make friends."

Carlyle shoved his hands into his pockets. "I suppose he's had his share of run-ins with guides."

Bognor laughed. "Oh, my God, has he ever. Pierce once tried to evict Munck for failure to pay his back rent. When Munck refused to leave his cabin, Pierce pepper sprayed him and then threw him in the county jail overnight."

"Apart from the strong-arm stuff, how's he done his job?"

"In his first three months, he cited a local teacher for doing seven over the fifty-five limit and a widow on food stamps for driving with a busted headlamp. He's harassed grieving families on their way to funerals, teenagers who park in the woods, and pensioners caught without fishing licenses."

"You ever ask him to explain his storm trooper act?"

"I did say I got the feeling he didn't especially like poor folk."

Carlyle shuffled his feet to keep warm. "How did he take it?"

"He said he'd grown up on white bread and margarine sandwiches. His parents spent half their lives in court defending themselves against the charge of being unemployed. He wanted people around here to understand the legal system was stacked against them."

"Any formal complaints against him?"

"I don't think anyone would risk it."

"He and Betts have a history?"

"Pierce has a thing about long-haired types. I'm surprised they haven't come to blows."

Carlyle opened his note pad. "What do you think about what happened in the lodge just now?"

"Blake's death is a damn shame, but it isn't a case for the authorities." Carlyle said nothing. "You don't see it that way?" Bognor asked.

"I think it may be too early to close the books on this one yet."

"Are you serious? The kid was blind in one eye."

"I've read all the accident statistics. There's never been two fatalities a week apart on the same river."

"What are you saying, Ric?"

"Marshall runs a professional operation. His people are well-trained. They go to rescue clinics and have a two-day refresher course every season."

"They never make mistakes?"

"Hardly ever."

"What about Sanders? That was pure bad luck?"

"Sanders didn't screw up in Mixmaster. Some clients have no business on that river, but the guides know what they're doing." Carlyle shut his note pad. "And I don't believe that what happened is just terrible luck."

"Doesn't it seem like Blake shouldn't have been out there at all."

"But he worked for almost two years without any trouble," Carlyle said. "How did that log just happen to fall right where it was guaranteed to clobber someone? Are we missing some underlying pattern here?"

"Where are you going to start?" Bognor said.

Carlyle turned toward his truck. "I guess I'll have to go back to the gorge. Where everything's gone wrong so far."

FOUR

An hour past dawn on Friday morning, needing time to decide how he would handle Gus Burton, the outfitter he was riding with today, Carlyle pulled off the road a dozen miles west of Warrensburg. He shut off the engine, left his truck, and crossed the road to an embankment overlooking the Hudson.

Although unleashed from the six-mile canyon, the Hudson was still an impressive river. Unable to contain all the rain and snowmelt that poured into its tributaries, the river crashed against mid-stream boulders and overflowed both banks. Blocks of snow and ice, leftovers from a five-month winter, were strewn haphazardly up and down the valley.

Just as he finished his coffee, Carlyle heard a car pull up behind him. A voice cut through the air. "Sir. Please go back to your vehicle." Carlyle turned away from the embankment and spotted a sheriff's green and white sedan parked behind his truck.

The voice became more persistent. "I said, step this way, please."

Carlyle crossed the road and walked toward the cruiser.

"Do not approach me. Go to your vehicle and wait for my instructions."

Three minutes later, Caleb Pierce appeared next to Carlyle's truck. He was wearing a crisp green uniform, tinted aviator glasses, and a thick Sam Browne belt holding a Maglite, a Glock, and pepper spray. "May I ask what in hell you were doing just now, sir?"

"Caleb, what's going on?"

Pierce placed his left hand on the roof of Carlyle's truck. "Do you realize that if someone had hit a patch of ice a minute ago, the paramedics would have had to peel you off the guard rail?"

"You can't be serious?"

Ignoring Carlyle, Pierce stared at the notes in his booking log. "State records say that you committed a serious moving violation some time ago."

"They keep records going back ten years?" Carlyle's violation, a four-point speeding charge, had been his first traffic stop ever.

"Just hand over your license and registration, please."

Carlyle pulled both documents from his wallet.

"I thought we'd seen the last of you yesterday," Pierce said. He handed Carlyle's license and registration back through the open window. "These roads can be treacherous. You'll want to be more careful next time you leave Albany." He turned and walked back to his patrol car.

As Carlyle pulled onto the road, he looked back and saw Pierce entering the details of their encounter into the State Motor Vehicle Complaint Data Base.

When Carlyle drove into the parking lot of the Silver River Outfitters twenty minutes later, he saw Burton shouting orders to his crew. Carlyle left his truck and the two men shook hands. "I just ran into Pierce," Carlyle said.

"So, you finally met the Dentist."

"The Dentist?"

Burton said that ten months ago, Pierce, on DUI patrol, had arrested Michael Shillings, a married father of two little girls. "Shillings mouthed off, and Pierce used his baton to remove the guy's front teeth."

"He's a piece of work all right." Carlyle pulled his gear from his truck. "Thanks for letting me ride with your outfit today."

"If Mussolini had a hundred bucks, I'd sell him a ticket. I told Molly you'll be with Jesse Simmons. Go inside and see her."

Carlyle entered a small A-frame, crossed a screened front porch, and walked up to a desk covered in river rescue videos and outdoor magazines. "I'd like to sign up for the trip," he said to the middle-aged woman standing in front of him.

"Could have fooled me, sweetheart," Molly Carson said. "I thought you were on your way to a photo shoot."

The woman had some tough miles on her. Years of smoking unfiltered cigarettes had creased her face. There was a portable oxygen tank somewhere in her future.

"Stay around after the trip," Carson said. "I'd like to show my old man what purdy looks like."

She was five foot eight and a bit under a hundred and ten. Her tight jeans, wool shirt, and pile vest were tattered. Carlyle guessed ex-fashion model, Midwest born, fed up with New York City, living on twenty acres planted with alfalfa and high-quality weed.

Carlyle laughed. "Sorry, I'm spoken for, ma'am."

"Course you are. I haven't had the pick of the litter for years." She handed Carlyle a registration form. "Done this before?"

"Years ago. I brought my own gear."

"Good for you. We get rookies wearing cotton and fancy new mesh sandals. They get cold real quick. Twenty minutes into the trip, their nuts are so small you can hardly see 'em."

Carlyle laughed. "No problem for me there."

Carson pushed a generic one-page release of liability form across the desk. "Sign here. This tells your family and your goddamn lawyer that we warned you this was a life-threatening activity and you were too dumb to take it seriously."

Carlyle signed the waiver form and handed it back. "Where do I find Jesse Simmons?"

"Outside somewhere. Find the guy who looks like he was put together by a backhoe. If he's red in the face and swearing like he stepped on a nail, that's him."

"Sounds like a real sweetheart."

"Do not get that man angry. He means well, but he's got more rough edges than a young bull on his way to the knife. You mind my asking why you're riding with Simmons?"

"I'm told he's the best guide you've got."

"He'll keep you safe, but he's no Gandhi, that's for sure. Now get the hell out of here. I've got a bunch of flatlanders coming in any second."

Carlyle walked outside and saw twenty or thirty clients milling around the front yard. Silent, clutching their gear, a few looked like they'd just learned the Hudson was filled with barracuda. The rest, guys in their twenties, were swearing, telling filthy stories, or terrorizing their more timid companions. When Carlyle had worked up here, he'd watch these people, all mouth and no guts, freak out once they hit the gorge. Everyone, he'd learned after a year or two, is gutsy in the abstract.

Carlyle spotted Simmons immediately. He was medium height, not an ounce of it fat. He carried three flares, a river knife strapped to his right thigh, a string of carabineers, a rescue belt containing seventy-five feet of high-tensile rope, a diver's watch, a high-definition whistle, several prussic loops, and z-drag equipment.

Three men and three women, their eyes fixed on the ground, stood silently around him.

Carlyle walked up to Simmons. "Got room for one more in your boat today? I'm Burton's guest."

"You're late." Simmons turned his back on Carlyle and addressed his crew. "This isn't some Disney World ride. There's no guarantee you'll come back with all your fuckin' teeth in the right place. But if you do exactly what I tell you, I may be able to keep you safe today."

An hour after they dropped their raft into the Indian, Simmons's belligerence, which had been designed to drive the timid ones back to the bus, quickly vanished. Using both precise paddle strokes and brute force, he waltzed his boat around obstacles that seemed likely to send his people into the river. When he couldn't avoid hydraulics completely, he allowed himself to take the full brunt of the freezing water that exploded into their boat.

Halfway down Indian Head Rapids, he shouted, "We've got to go around these fucking boulders, people, not bounce off them!"

Simmons never became the least bit pleasant that day. "Pay attention now," he growled just above Guide's Hole. When the crew got lazy a few minutes later, he said, "You will follow my instructions or you will die, goddammit."

Carlyle knew that the river had climbed to five feet this morning, a foot higher than it had been last week. Almost three thousand cubic feet of water per second was now rushing toward the gorge. Waves erupted all around the raft as it hurled down the Indian. By the time they got to the Narrows, with a dozen tributaries disgorging snowmelt into the canyon, Burton's clients would have a month's worth of stories that wouldn't need to be exaggerated.

Carlyle, meanwhile, kept a close eye on Simmons while scanning ahead for unfamiliar hazards and anything that seemed out of place.

Freezing spray, the kind that turns exposed flesh white, filled the air and made Carlyle's lungs seize up. The river's numbing cold penetrated his dry suit and all three layers of wool, pile, and polypro underneath. He couldn't imagine what the others in their boat, who wore only cotton gloves and thin wetsuits, were feeling.

When they stopped to rest for a minute, Carlyle noticed that Simmons wasn't wearing neoprene gloves. "Aren't you cold?"

Simmons stared at his hands. "Nah, not really."

"Your fingers are white."

"They always look that way after a manicure."

Carlyle knew you had to be a bit crazy to do this kind of work. Most guides, especially those who had thought they were too talented to be carpenters or roofers, began their careers in macho mode. But once they'd seen teeth lying around their boats like spilled Chiclets, even the most belligerent guides settled into the arduous task of learning this demanding profession.

Simmons resumed his Captain America act as soon as they hit the river again. "Pay attention, now. I get docked ten bucks every time a client drowns." A couple of minutes later, he said, "If you paddle like pansies, I'll spank you." Although Carlyle didn't like Simmons's attitude, he understood that it had a single purpose: to keep his inexperienced clients reasonably dry and out of danger.

For six or seven minutes—an eternity for those who'd never been down a river like this one—the boat careened down through Gooley Steps, a chaotic landscape of boulders and backwashing waves.

After they punched through the strong current where the Hudson joined the Indian, Carlyle asked Simmons to take a break just above Cedar Ledges and let him get out for a few minutes.

Simmons smirked. "You got a weak bladder?"

"What did Burton tell you about cooperating with me?"

Simmons slewed the raft toward the right side of the river. "Let's take five, ladies."

Carlyle stepped out onto the bank, ducked under the yellow DEC tape and, watching for anything out of the ordinary, slowly walked downstream toward the spot where Blake had died. When he reached it, he looked for the log he'd come to examine but couldn't find it. He glanced around. Was he in the wrong place? The rocks, the sloping forest floor—this was the only place along the chute it could have been. But where was the log?

He studied the ground where he had last seen it. Clumps of snow fallen from trees obscured any tracks or drag marks that might have been there. When he brushed away a patch of snow, he found a thick layer of dead leaves still there. He turned and, for a good two minutes, studied the forested hillside.

He then walked down to where they had pulled Blake out, found nothing new, and headed back to the raft.

It took Simmons and his crew thirty minutes to go from Cedar Ledges to Entrance Rapid. When they reached the gorge itself, Simmons said, "Two hundred yards downstream, there's an Everest-sized boulder on your left. Don't ask me what happens if we hit it. Immediately after that, you'll see six huge waves in front of you. Let me do the thinking.

Just keep your heads down and paddle like this is the fucking Zambezi and the river is filled with snakes."

As they entered the Narrows, Carlyle, his eyes fixed on Simmons, knew he was watching a performer at the top of his game. Simmons was like one of those stocky, thick-fingered Russian pianists, both self-confident and agile, bull-rushing his way through a Brahms piano concerto. He sat on the edge of the back tube, his upper body arched out over the water, perilously close to thrashing waves, the weight of his entire body secured to the raft by a narrow foot strap. Every time the boat threatened to drop into a hydraulic, he plunged his guide paddle a bit deeper into the agitated whitewater surrounding their raft.

After their sprint through Carter's Rapid—another four minutes of neck-snapping maneuvers—Simmons, breathing heavily, pointed his boat toward an eddy on the river's right side.

This rest stop couldn't possibly revive the clients, thought Carlyle. The thermometer on his jacket read forty-nine degrees. Snow falling from the trees settled on his helmet and shoulders. His feet were sitting in ice-cold water that sloshed back and forth across the bottom of the raft. The crew, aware they still had over an hour until this ordeal ended, must be wondering how much longer they could endure these conditions.

Simmons ran the final two miles of the gorge without mishap. Because it was too dangerous to approach Greyhound today, they skirted the two-foot trench and let the current push them slowly south, past a deserted garnet mine, derelict cabins, and an abandoned railroad trestle running over the river, while Simmons explained to his clients why this region had, as he said, "fallen into the shitter."

In the past ten days, two of Marshall's better guides had made fatal errors, but Simmons, a part-timer, had performed flawlessly today in harsh conditions.

Burton's entire crew, exhilarated after a day battling whitewater, pulled into North River at three that afternoon. Carlyle thanked Simmons and Burton for their help, and hurriedly changed into street clothes. Looking for a place where he could think quietly for an hour, he drove to a barbeque joint overlooking the Hudson just outside of North River.

Grateful that nobody in the restaurant recognized him, Carlyle found a table in a deserted corner of the raucous dining room, pulled a laptop from his briefcase, and entered the details of his trip with Simmons. Still, other than the missing log, nothing stood out. Nothing unexpected had happened in the rafting itself, not even a minor mishap or close shave.

He reread his notes for Sanders's and Blake's last trips. Reliving the morning of the first accident, he imagined Sanders to his right, sitting on the back tube, and tried to recall the interval between the time he'd last felt the young guide next to him and when he'd heard him hit the water. Sanders hadn't simply fallen out of the boat, he'd exploded out. If the frayed strap had unraveled, Sanders's foot would have merely slipped out of it and he'd have probably ended up on his ass in the cockpit, not in the river.

His mind churning, Carlyle next wrote the names "Sanders" and "Blake" in separate columns on his evidence list. He then tried to visualize every detail of the events the morning each man died. Thinking of what might have caused their deaths, he wrote *equipment failure, unpredictable weather, inadequate training, unexpectedly high river levels, alcohol or drugs, crew error,* and *poor judgment.*

Then, tuning out the noise from a group of fishermen who'd just come into the restaurant, he closed his eyes for several seconds and visualized both convoys of rafts as if next to each other. His eyes popped open and a chill swept through his body. He added *boat order* to his list, threw a sawbuck on the table, grabbed his stuff, and bolted out of the restaurant.

Carlyle raced over to the South Mountain Lodge and, without knocking, marched into Marshall's office. "We have to talk."

"Can't you see I'm busy?" Maps, DEC files, account books, and aerial photographs of the gorge covered Marshall's desk. A picture of his mother, standing outside a ski lodge in Switzerland, was on the wall behind his head.

Ignoring his comment, Carlyle pulled out a chair and sat down. "Think back. Did you switch boats with Sanders at the last minute?"

Marshall sat up straight. "How'd you know that?"

"What raft was he supposed to be in?"

"The green monster."

"Why wasn't he driving it then?"

"There was a ton of ice on the river on Saturday. His boat's a real pig, so I gave him mine. It's much more maneuverable."

"The one with the defective foot strap."

Marshall hesitated for a moment. "So what?"

"Did anyone see him fall out that morning?"

"Betts was right behind the two of you. He said Sanders did a high brace when he came up to Mixmaster, back arched, extended out over the end of the boat, inches from the river, steering like crazy. Then, bam, he just disappeared."

"Where's the boat now?" Carlyle said.

"Somewhere out back."

"Show it to me."

"I haven't got time for this shit. Why don't you go pester Bognor or that fascist deputy of his."

"If you don't cooperate, I'll let Raines take over this investigation."

Marshall pointed a finger at Carlyle. "Are you threatening me?"

"Of course not. Just show me that damned raft."

Marshall stood up. "Five minutes. Then I want you out of here."

The two men walked across the yard in the fading light and stood looking down at the remains of Sanders's raft, buried under a foot of snow.

Without bothering to put gloves on, Carlyle went down on his hands and knees and dug at the hard, crusty snow until he'd uncovered the raft. "You mind giving me a hand?" Both men bent over, dragged the boat away from the shed, and unfolded it.

"What the hell are you looking for?" Marshall said.

Carlyle turned over the raft, reached into the two-by-three-foot cockpit and, like a blind person searching for his house keys, moved his fingers slowly over the restraining strap's coarse rubber fabric.

Carlyle exhaled and sat back on his knees. "Look at it. Carefully."

Marshall stared at the strap. "It's broken. What about it?"

"It didn't break. It's been cut." Carlyle brought the two ends of the strap together. "If it had worn out or Sanders had simply over-stressed it, it would have ragged edges. The first four inches are perfectly smooth. Only a knife could have done that. It looks like a single stroke. Whoever did this left just enough for the strap to hold until Sanders really needed it."

Marshall didn't take his eyes off the raft.

"Since he was such a big kid," Carlyle said, "I assumed it had pulled away or split."

"What made you change your mind?"

"Two deaths in five days? I couldn't accept they were both accidents."

"But how can you connect Blake's death to the first one?"

"At the hearing yesterday, you said how close you came to being hit. That log wasn't meant for Blake."

"What are you talking about?"

"You were supposed to be driving this raft, and then on Wednesday, in the first raft, you narrowly missed the log that got Blake."

"How can you be so sure that Blake's death was no accident?"

"I had Simmons stop at Cedar this afternoon. The log is gone."

"It must have gotten washed out of the chute."

"A year's worth of dead leaves are still there."

"An outfitter probably dumped it in the river to make sure nobody else ran into it."

"After we left Cedar Ledges yesterday, DEC blocked the entrance to the chute with yellow tape. And besides, if the tree had simply fallen, why would the stump end of it have been out over the river instead of the treetop?"

Marshall leaned heavily against the boat shed. "You're saying my guides were murdered?"

"But they weren't the targets. You were."

Marshall stood up and began shoving the raft close to the shed. Carlyle pulled him away. "Don't touch it; it's a crucial piece of evidence."

"What do we do now?"

"We call Bognor and Raines. They'll contact the state police."

"If news gets around that my two guides were murdered, I won't have another booking for years."

Carlyle stuffed his cold hands into his jacket. "This isn't just some business deal gone bad. Someone may be trying to kill you."

"Me? Are you crazy?"

"Do you have another explanation?"

Marshall took two steps away from the shed. "What are we going to do now?"

"I'll drive over to Gus Burton's place first thing tomorrow."

"Why Burton?

"He's the biggest outfitter around here. Maybe he knows something that can help us."

"Burton's got no reason to help me out."

"He'll talk once he figures out his empire will fall apart if DEC shuts down this river."

He had concealed himself on the north side of the Hudson directly across from the lodge in a grove of ice-covered pine trees. From where he stood, he could see Marshall and Carlyle move toward the shed and begin examining the remains of Sanders's raft.

If the two men discovered the strap had been slit, they'd immediately understand why Sanders had fallen out of his boat. Carlyle would then notify the sheriff, the state police, and lab technicians. Within hours, the region would be crawling with cops. As Carlyle turned over the raft, it was clear why the authorities had brought in a former guide to help them figure out what had caused these two fatal accidents.

The sun dropped behind Crane Mountain and dark shadows began to creep across the valley. When Marshall and Carlyle went back inside the lodge, he hiked up the hill to his truck and drove off. He didn't need anyone wandering down this road and wondering what he was doing out here at this time of day. Besides, there was still some daylight and he had more work to do.

FIVE

When Carlyle drove up to Warrensburg the next morning, he found Burton smoking a cigar on the second-story balcony of the house he'd just had built.

"You ever think of calling first?" Burton said.

A decade ago, after a trip down the Colorado, Carlyle realized that driving a raft had to be better than spending the rest of his life teaching college students how to do regression analysis. When he got back to Albany, he'd called Burton. "How about letting me train as a guide?"

"I tried a professor once," Burton had said. "He wasn't worth shit."

Marshall, who'd just opened his business and was looking for cheap help, had agreed to hire Carlyle, but Burton never stopped referring to him as "that professor."

"Since when did you start requiring invitations?" Carlyle said.

"Since your storm troopers started crawling all over this goddamn valley. What the hell do you want now?"

"Ten minutes of your precious time."

"The front door is unlocked. Don't forget to wipe your feet."

Carlyle walked into the kitchen, where three books sat on the counter: *The Flame Thrower in World War I*, *The World's Most Dangerous Snakes*, and *History of the Guillotine*. "That's quite some library you've got."

"Bedtime reading." Burton was forty-nine years old and still hadn't an ounce of belly fat.

"You look in great shape."

"Don't ever listen to doctors. Human growth hormone works just fine."

Carlyle wandered over to a huge picture window looking out over the Screaming Eagle Ski Resort and, in the distance, the Mackenzie Range. "Jesus, this is some place."

"It took me three years to buy the hundred-and-fifty acres. The house is four-thousand square feet, with three bedrooms, one for each of my failed marriages. There's a large bunkroom for my kids, who never show up, a sauna, and weight room. You should see the garage."

"Why's that?"

"You ever see a Ducati motorcycle, a '56 lime green Fairlane, a brand-new Range Rover, and a Toyota Land Cruiser all lined up?" Burton glanced down at his watch. "But you didn't come this far to admire the architecture."

"I want to talk to you about what's happened to Marshall."

"The answer's no."

"How do you know what I'm going to ask?"

"A fat guy with a badge on his chest stopped by last night. He said you wanted my cooperation. I told him no, too, goddammit."

Carlyle decided to remain calm. He enjoyed watching an uncontrolled eruption now and then, as long as he wasn't its target. "You don't even know what this is about."

"Let me guess. You want me to let cops ride in my boats."

"No."

"Encourage my guides to snitch?"

"Sorry, no."

"You want me to tell you why someone would be attacking Marshall."

"Not that either."

"Then why the hell are you wasting my time?"

Carlyle told Burton about the foot strap that had been sliced. "I want you to help me find out who killed those kids."

"You're completely nuts. If it was murder—and, by the way, I think your evidence stinks—I want this person hung in chains as much as you do. But the answer is still no."

"You mind telling me why?"

"Sure, if it'll get you out of here. First, it's none of my business why someone's taking out his rage on Marshall. And second, I don't want my people involved in a witch hunt in this valley. It can only hurt my business." Burton stood up, picked up a fly swatter, and slammed it against the picture window.

"I'll keep my mouth shut."

"Bullshit. You'll ask my employees who hates Marshall and they'll say that some competitor was behind it, meaning me."

"Don't be silly. They're too afraid of you to say that."

"Okay, then, how's this? You're not a cop or a lawyer. How am I going to sue your ass off when you drive all my clients away?"

"You still haven't heard what I'm asking for."

Burton glanced at his watch. "You've got ten minutes left."

"I want some background on the people who work for you. Guides, kitchen crew, bus drivers, maids, and cooks."

"Absolutely not."

"Then let us put a park ranger, incognito of course, in one of your boats."

"Never. It would make me a target for that asshole you're chasing."

"Then do us a favor. Hire Marshall's guides. You already know them all."

"Sure. If Ryan pays, I'd love to have them in my boats."

Carlyle ignored the insult. "Let me interview your guides. When I'm done, much as I'd like to avoid this place like the plague, I'll tell you what I've found."

Burton shook his head. "People around here still haven't forgotten how you let them down. Why should I help you now?"

Carlyle had begun driving rafts through the Hudson Gorge a decade ago. Wanting to make his new colleagues look good, he wrote an article for one of those glossy second-home magazines on the glamorous lives of whitewater guides. He listed all the risks they faced, unpredictable river levels, treacherous rapids, hypothermia, severe weather, and clients who didn't know a paddle from a pisspot, and then sat back waiting for the letters of congratulations to come pouring in.

When his story was published, Burton was the first to call him. "What the hell were you thinking?" he yelled. "You made those trips seem like just one endless ordeal. We get just ten weeks in the spring to make enough to last until skiing season. Are you trying to ruin all that?"

Carlyle had felt like a fool. Instead of winning the respect of people he admired, he'd made them think he was naïve and disloyal.

"Your clients aren't risking their lives for the scenery," he'd said. "They go because it's the most demanding thing they'll ever do."

"What are you talking about?"

"They say they only feel really alive when they're on that river. And want to come as close to death as they can without flinching."

"Are you nuts?" Burton had said.

"You should emphasize the hardship."

"It's our goddamn livelihood," Burton had said that day almost ten years ago. "You can write whatever you want when you really understand what we're up against."

"I apologized for that article," Carlyle said.

"Makes no difference. People around here'll crucify me if I cooperate with you."

"Get serious. You own a fleet of school buses, three convenience stores, two sporting-goods shops, a pizza palace, a twenty-four-unit motel, and a two-bay gas station. Who's going to crucify you?"

Burton hurled a book against the wall. "Listen to me. My father died in a paint factory fire when I was two years old. When my mother recovered from a nervous breakdown, she dumped me on her relatives for a year. I worked every summer on a potato farm and ran away from home a half-dozen times. So stop bitching about Marshall's problems. I've got my own shit to deal with."

As Carlyle listened to Burton's life story, he remembered how little empathy the guy had. One April four years after Carlyle had retired from the business, Burton had invited him up to Warrensburg to run the Hudson Gorge one final time. It had rained for three straight days and the snowpack, unable to absorb another soaking, had begun pouring off the slopes. When Burton's crew took off, the river was at near-record levels.

When he heard that he would be in a raft with a rookie guide, Carlyle knew he should have backed out, but admitting his fear in front of Burton and his former colleagues was unimaginable.

His luck ran out in Mile-Long Rapid. When he got caught in the backwash pouring off Big Nasty, his raft hit a huge boulder sitting midstream just east of the Narrows, flipped, and dumped him into the middle of the longest continuous Class IV-rapid on the East Coast.

The thirty-four-degree water and unstoppable waves quickly overwhelmed him. Unable to pull himself into an eddy, he was swept downstream like a rag doll in a tornado. His dry suit came apart and water just this side of slush turned his skin blue. Tumbling downstream and caught in the trough in a seemingly endless series of waves, Carlyle realized that unless help came soon, he was going to drown.

Leo Wells, who'd been waiting at the bottom of Mile-Long, managed to snag Carlyle just as he was about to plunge into another set of rapids. Two hours later, shivering uncontrollably and unable to believe he was still alive, Carlyle found himself back at the take-out in North River.

As he was about to get in his car, Burton walked up. "I heard you decided to swim the Narrows. Pretty ballsy move for a guy your age."

Carlyle was almost speechless with fury. "You have any idea at all how long I was in that fucking river?"

"Oh, please. We've all gone through shit like that. Don't get all weepy on me. We were watching your clown act the whole time. You had nothing to be afraid of. My insurance policy discourages me from letting my employees drown."

Carlyle now said, "Listen, are you going to help Marshall, or not?"

"Not a chance. Guess who's going to buy up his seat licenses if he goes under?"

"His guides are living in trailers and unheated cabins. If we don't stop this person, they'll all be out of work for good."

"Not my people. They'll always have jobs."

"I hate to ruin your dream of a motel and laundromat empire, but if one more person gets hurt on that river, the DEC and the police are going to close down every operation up here. Including yours."

"You think they're going to tangle with someone who creates almost two hundred jobs in this county?"

"Do you have any idea what's really been going on just ten miles from here?" Carlyle told Burton that Marshall's father had spent the past five years buying up pretty near all of Johnston Mountain. Private investors and hedge funds were supporting his plan to turn the place into a ski area that would rival anything that could be found in Utah. They'd begun evicting locals and bulldozing the valley so they could put up a huge base lodge, thirty shops, a golf course, and several hundred town homes and condos. The development would transform the economy of the entire region. "These guys are thinking Las Vegas plus snow. The last thing they want is headlines about some murderer running around loose in these woods. If I were you, I'd do everything I could to catch this guy."

"No one's going to push me out of here," Burton said.

"Do you seriously believe that if the Governor wants this project built, and he knows that logging interests and the unions are backing it, he'll let people like you stand in his way?" Carlyle walked over to the large window that dominated Burton's living room. "What do you think will happen once they discover there isn't enough natural snow up there to generate the kind of profits they require? Phil Marshall and his partners have plans to throw up a dam across the Narrows that'll divert ten thousand cubic feet of water a second into a holding pond for their snow guns. They've already submitted a permit to DEC and the federal government. Do you know what will happen to the rafting business if it gets in the way of a two-hundred-million-dollar project for that mountain?"

"Where'd you find this out?" Burton said.

"Bognor handed me a copy of the building permit applications and the environmental impact statements."

"How much time do I have?"

"A day, maybe a bit more."

"What's the goddamn rush?"

"Betts called me last night. He said that Marshall had two other serious incidents last season that went unreported. If the press gets hold of that story, they'll claim that a serial killer is on the loose in this region. And then everyone's reservations, including yours, will simply vanish."

Burton reached into a refrigerator and tore the top off a can of Bud. "You've got one week to interview my people. Then you leave me alone." He started to take a gulp of beer and suddenly stopped, slopping a little onto the floor. "But not the guides. You don't go near them."

"I need to talk to the guides more than anyone."

"Stay away from them. If I let you chase all my guides away, I might as well close up shop right now. Now get the hell out. I've got to fire two cooks and a waitress who've been stealing me blind."

An hour and a half later, Carlyle jogged across the desolate central plaza of the university. Albany's traditional architects, tenacious defenders of the Romanesque, had labeled the campus "a modernist nightmare" when it was built thirty years ago. Three decades later, after weathering two dozen ice storms, the concrete-clad buildings were beginning to resemble the Chernobyl reactor. Four ten-story student dormitories, each surrounded by soulless glass and steel "teaching and learning centers," stood guard over the bleak, nearly treeless campus.

The political hack who designed the university had never given much thought to what it would be like to work here during the brutal, five-month upstate winters. Unprotected corridors between buildings funneled Arctic storms into fierce whirlwinds. Faculty and students were forced to sprint between classes in the poorly lit, dust-chocked subterranean tunnels rather than brave exposed, ice-coated walkways.

After picking up his mail, Carlyle went to his office, made coffee, and waited for his first appointment of the day. He'd come in this afternoon for one reason only—to terminate the career of a diligent but poorly prepared graduate student.

Two weeks ago, Adrian Long had failed his PhD qualifying examinations in criminal justice for the second—and final—time. A four-person dissertation committee, anxious to weed out students who might tarnish the reputation of the department, had decided that Long would have to leave the program at the end of the current semester. Although Carlyle knew his student would take this news badly, he had to give him notice in person.

Carlyle watched snow blanket the trees outside his office window. The sun had not appeared for more than an hour or two since early November. It began snowing just after Thanksgiving. At first it was just a couple of inches every few days. Then, in late December, major storms began arriving, nor'easters that brought six or seven inches every two weeks or so. By late January, the days began growing longer, but fierce Canadian winds, dubbed Alberta Clippers by some wise guy on a Montreal radio station, brought afternoons when the temperature struggled to reach ten degrees. The misery had continued until early April. Then, as if some weary meteorologist had finally had enough and had thrown a magic switch, the thermometer started climbing.

Carlyle looked around his office. Bookshelves and filing cabinets lined two walls. Law reports were stacked two-feet deep on the floor. His computer contained the final draft of a manuscript that he hoped would get him lifetime employment and financial security. He'd spent six years on the project, reading legal cases and scholarly studies, interviewing judges, lawyers, and prison officials, but the book was still years from completion. His department chair, Jason Pawa, kept reminding Carlyle that he had been hired to churn out academic papers describing the complex motives driving people to commit homicide, reports that would bring huge grants to the university. The Dean said, "No one gets tenure without a well-reviewed book," but it was, as Carlyle knew, the way things worked in his department.

Carlyle's next-door colleague, Bill Majors, described what would happen if Carlyle's publishing career stalled. "Pawa will come into your office acting all apologetic of course. 'Ric,' he'll say, 'we know how hard you've worked. The teaching's been great and those two small grants helped, but the Committee on Tenure and Promotion has said that without that book contract, we can't offer you continuing employment.' Then he'll saunter back to his office and flush your career down the toilet."

Five minutes after Carlyle sat down there was a knock at the door. Before he could get up, Adrian Long walked into the office. Long had served two tours with the Marines in Iraq before doing a ten-year stretch with the state police. He still looked like a grunt: a jarhead scalp, thick biceps, and stiff demeanor that could turn mean in a heartbeat.

"Doc, I got your message," Long said. "What's up?"

"Adrian, we have to talk about your exams."

"I failed again, didn't I?"

"Three out of four parts."

"Your questions, too?" Long was no longer smiling, but still oblivious to what was about to happen.

"Mine, too. I'm sorry." This was not the first time Carlyle had washed someone out of the program. A few students, unwilling to let two or three years of tuition and sweat go down the toilet, pleaded for a second chance. Most left silently, however, dragging behind them bitterness that they would never wash from their souls.

"Where do I go from here?" Long said.

"I don't follow you."

"How do I prepare now? Make sure I don't fail again."

"Adrian, this isn't like the state police. Even if you pass next time, you'll still have to do a year's worth of calculus and statistics, then take a twelve-hour written exam and a two-hour oral."

"I'll bust my butt, you know that."

"Do you really want to spend the rest of your life writing academic articles and teaching indifferent undergraduates?"

Despite his request that students turn off their cell phones, stop text messaging, and keep the whispering down to a dull roar, Carlyle could no longer control his two-hundred-seat undergrad lecture class. One student, a tall blond woman, came late to class every morning, never took notes, and didn't hide her boredom. A mediocre student, she seemed to take pleasure in her ability to distract Carlyle by picking at the tangled strands of her long hair.

"I'd really like another chance," Long said.

"The Committee won't go for it."

"What are my options, then?"

Carlyle stared at the late winter clouds massing in the distance. "You haven't read the graduate student guidelines, have you?"

"No, sir."

"A student has only two chances to take the qualifying exams."

"Who do I write, then?"

"Write?"

"To petition for another opportunity."

"We almost never grant waivers."

"That's it? I'm out?" Long looked incredulous.

"You may have a better shot with another department. Sociology might really want someone with your background." No other unit would take Long once he'd failed his exams twice. He would probably end up with the state police again or as a military recruiter. Even though he'd put three years into the program, his academic career was probably over.

Carlyle heard a door open and close down the hall and hoped that someone headed to his office would interrupt this conversation.

"You're really telling me I'm finished?"

"Adrian, maybe this career wasn't a good fit. You're a talented guy. There must be plenty of jobs you qualify for now that you've got additional training."

Long picked up his briefcase. "The state police do this differently. They don't just wash you out. Everybody leaves the barracks proud."

"Adrian, stay in touch. I'd like to hear how things turn out." Embarrassed that he had to force a deserving student from the program, Carlyle secretly hoped he'd never have to face Long again.

"Stay in touch. Sure. Let's do that." Long got up, stared at his professor for a moment, then walked out into the hallway.

Anxious to drive the discussion with Long out of his mind, Carlyle began to read an essay claiming that while the country was at war, evidence gathered from torture would be upheld by the Supreme Court. He then sent an email to the Dean of the College saying that although he had been forced to terminate Adrian Long's graduate scholarship, "Something tells me he is one of those students who will not go quietly."

At 6:00 p.m., Carlyle called his wife. He told her he was stuck in his office but promised to be home in an hour.

To prepare for the investigation that would take place tomorrow in Warrensburg, he retrieved several books from the bookshelves lining the walls of his office, brought them to his desk, and began poring through them.

At 7:30 p.m., he walked down a dimly lit hallway and out into what he hoped was the last winter storm of the year.

His wife, Beth, was waiting for him when he got home thirty minutes later. She'd heard about the deaths of the two guides who worked for Marshall. Carlyle now told her he was almost certain they'd been murdered.

She picked up one of the books he'd brought home with him, a study of psychopaths. "Does this mean you've got a madman on the loose up there?"

"Too early to say. But possibly."

"He must be insane."

"Psychopaths are impulsive. They commit crimes because it gives them pleasure and they don't care about the impact on other people."

"My god. So he *is* a psychopath."

"Not necessarily. The person we're after, from what I've seen so far, is disciplined and deliberate. Maybe he just has a grievance against Ryan."

Beth picked up the other book Carlyle had brought home. "What's this got to do with the investigation?"

Carlyle said, "It's about the fanatic who detonated a bomb in downtown Atlanta during the Summer Olympics in 1996. He spent five years on the run in the mountains of western North Carolina before finally being captured. Our guy's a lot like him. He hits us when we're vulnerable and then, using techniques they teach in the military, disappears into the wilderness surrounding the gorge."

Beth stared at her husband. "Are you telling me you're going to be involved in a manhunt for a maniac?"

"The police might ask me for some help. It should be over in a week. Two at most."

"What about your job?"

"I have a hunch the university's going to love the fact that one of their faculty is helping the cops chase down a killer. It can't hurt my tenure chances."

SIX

The parking lot of the lodge was nearly deserted when Carlyle drove in at eight thirty on Sunday morning. He shut off the engine, finished his coffee, and cracked the window. The sun wouldn't appear over the ridge to his left for another hour. He could hear the Hudson tearing at the ice down the slope in the valley. In a week, the thermometer would top fifty degrees, the spring rafting season would begin in earnest and the area would be filled with people anxious to challenge the river.

Carlyle turned off the radio and rested his head against the back of the seat. Two guides had died in the past eight days. Reporters from all over upstate were now on the story. They had camped out in Warrensburg and were spending their time pulling rumors from every local willing to face a microphone or a camera.

He glanced over at the lodge. Nine years ago, when he first began work here, it had been just a five-room, single-story clapboard house with a living room, kitchen, office, and three tiny bedrooms in back. The first time he broke his arm in the gorge, he'd slept on a couch after returning from the emergency room in Glens Falls. A fractured eye socket, sprained knee, and three broken ribs later, Carlyle decided he'd had enough. It was time to finish his PhD and get a real job, one with a steady paycheck and benefits, minus the overnight hospital trips.

Marshall walked down the hill from his house, stopped next to Carlyle's truck, and rapped his knuckles on the door. "You going to sit there all day? I thought you were here to examine the way I run my business."

"Have your guides showed up yet?"

Marshall counted the vehicles in his lot. "Looks like they're inside. The Sheriff said he'd be here any minute. You absolutely sure we've got to do this?"

"DEC heard rumors that you had two clients injured last season. They're thinking that it might be connected to what happened to Sanders and Blake."

"My guys don't like the idea of defending themselves like this. What am I supposed to tell them?"

"The truth. This isn't a trial. We're just trying to understand why Sanders and Blake died and keep anything like it from happening again."

Marshall kicked mud from his boots. "You think being honest will make my employees feel better?"

"What other choice do you have?"

"I see. We do it your way or my business closes. Let's get this over with then."

Betts, Nash, and Hernandez sat around the conference table in the lodge, drinking coffee, staring at their hands, saying little. Bob Ashcroft, the part-time guide who was involved in an accident last October, sat by himself along the back wall of the room. Bognor and Pierce came in a minute later and sat down at the far end of the table.

"Let's get started." Carlyle gestured toward an empty seat near him. "Bob, nobody's on trial here. Join us."

Pierce pulled a small wireless tape recorder and a note pad from his briefcase.

"Don't tell me you're going to record this inquisition," Betts said.

"This conversation's off the record," Pierce said, "but a transcript might be of some use in the future."

"Bullshit," Betts said. "Is this a legal thing or not?"

Bognor held out his hands in a calming gesture. "We're not the enemy, Alex. Let's just hear everyone's testimony and determine if it helps our investigation."

"Why don't you first tell us why we're here," Hernandez said.

Carlyle said, "We want to see if what happened to Ashcroft can be connected to the deaths of Sanders and Blake."

"A dozen things can go wrong on these trips," Betts said. "How the hell are we supposed to know if they're sabotage or not?"

"Just answer a few questions. We'll decide what might be relevant." Carlyle pulled a small, red, spiral-bound notebook from his briefcase. "Ryan, I'd like to get some background first."

"Fine. Let's get this over with."

"Have you fired anyone in the last couple of years?"

"No, but I should have."

"Have you added anyone to your crew lately who you hadn't checked out fully?"

"Are you serious?"

"I meant anyone inexperienced."

"Why the hell would I do that?"

"Understood. Had any quarrels with an employee over pay?"

"No."

Betts laughed and gave Marshall the finger.

"Have you had any arguments with other outfitters?"

"Other than Burton? No."

"What about the time that idiot working for Eastern Rivers collided with one of our boats?" Nash said.

"He apologized," Marshall said. "End of story."

Carlyle wrote "collision" in his notepad. "Any trespassers on your property lately? Hunters or snowmobilers who ignored your posted signs?"

"My father's got someone patrolling the grounds. No one goes near this place who doesn't have a reason to be here."

"What about contractors? Someone annoyed because they weren't paid for work on the lodge?"

"I never see those bills. They go directly to Philip Marshall's accountants."

"Your guides ever get into bar fights?"

"Not recently."

"Sleep with someone else's wife?"

Betts said, "You counting one-night stands?"

"He's talking about human females, Betts," Nash said.

"That's enough. Let's move on. Ryan, what about that accident one of your clients had last season?"

"We thought it was just bad luck at the time."

"We need to hear what happened. Everything you can remember."

Ashcroft looked up. "The kid was in my boat and I made a mistake in Cedar."

"I warned you about getting careless," Betts said. "If someone falls out of your boat, you've got real trouble."

"For Christ's sake," Ashcroft said. "I know that."

"You think I'm being too tough on you?" Betts said. "Just wait till some lawyer hits you with a wrongful-death suit."

"You don't have to give me shit in front of everyone when I screw up."

Carlyle rapped the table with his right hand. "Stuff happens out there all the time. Why was this incident so unusual?"

Betts shook his head. "Just wait till you hear what happened."

"I was running third that morning," Ashcroft said. "Every seat in my boat was filled." At fifty-two, Ashcroft was the oldest guide on the river and, by his own admission, no longer able to simply muscle a raft out of trouble. A guy with scrawny arms and a comb-over, Carlyle wondered why Marshall had hired him in the first place.

"You remember much about your crew?"

Ashcroft stared at his former employer. "Marshall dumped a bunch of teenage boys on me. The little bastards goofed around during my safety talk, jumping up and down on the boat, and never shut up."

Pierce said, "Why didn't you come down hard on them right then and there?"

"I laid into them and didn't hold back, dammit."

Pierce shook his head. "Telling kids to behave is like asking crows to stop shitting on your car. You've got to make people afraid of you."

"Caleb," Carlyle said, "why don't you let me ask the questions?" He turned to Ashcroft. "You explained all about strainers and foot entrapment, right?"

"It's the first thing we do every trip."

"But it didn't do any good. Then what did you say?"

"I told them that if we hit a boulder they had to jump to the high side or the raft would pin."

"Go on."

"They refused to pay attention to me, but I figured that by the time we reached the gorge, they would have wised up."

Betts slapped his palms onto the table. "Just tell him what happened, for Christ's sake."

"Two hundred yards from the Basin, they started rocking the boat, smacking their paddles on the water, jumping up and down on the thwarts."

"I was right behind him," Betts said. "They staggered down the Indian like a blind man on roller skates, colliding with tree stumps and boulders. His boat was completely out of control."

"It wasn't like that at all," Ashcroft said.

"Tell him about the kid," Betts said. "See what he thinks then."

"Jeff Katz, the one who got hurt, went kind of nuts. He began waving his paddle like a sword and yelling like a madman. That's when we hit the rock and Katz did a backflip into the Indian."

"Neil Armstrong could have seen that rock from the moon," Betts said.

"It was below the surface. How was I supposed to know it was there?

"That wasn't the end of your problems that morning was it?

"No. Just as I was about to warn Katz again, we hit a rock.

"How long was he under water?" Carlyle said.

"Three or four seconds. He came up right next to us, choking, with a terrified look on his face. I grabbed his vest and heaved him into the boat."

"You read him the riot act finally?"

"I said the next time I might not be able to save him."

"If you were having so much trouble with Katz, why didn't you ask Betts to take him?"

"Ask Betts? Are you kidding? Look at him now. He'd just laugh at me. So would the others."

Carlyle looked away from Ashcroft, then down at his notes. "Go on with your story."

"By then, my arms felt like lead weights. There was ice everywhere. We even saw a couple of whole trees coming down from up north. I thought I still had some time to turn them into a decent crew, but Katz began horsing around again. He punched the kid next to him and bounced around on the front tube like a madman."

Pierce leaned forward. "Did it ever occur to you at that point to finally put him in someone else's boat?"

"How was I supposed to do that while we were surfing down Cedar?"

"You could have ordered him to stop his bullshit."

Betts laughed. "Why didn't I think of that? We could carry hand-cuffs and clubs in our rafts next time."

"People do what they're told if they're frightened enough," Pierce said.

"Alex, just let Bob continue," Carlyle said.

Ashcroft slouched with his head bent forward like a disgraced monk. "We came rushing up on Entrance. You all know how quickly everything turns bad there. One second, you're floating past Virgin Falls, then you turn the corner and you see the river boiling." He stopped and took a breath. "The boat hit a rock and Katz went airborne." Ashcroft's voice was hollow, as though he was describing a movie he'd seen. "When Katz tumbled over the side, his left leg got tangled in the chicken line."

"For how long?"

"Thirty seconds or so. I couldn't drop my paddle until we'd moved away from the worst hydraulics. Then I ran up the side of the raft, grabbed his life vest, and hauled him in. He lay in the bottom of the raft, thrashing around, grabbing the back of his leg, and screaming." Ashcroft, head down, stared at his hands. "I can't talk about this anymore."

Carlyle looked at Marshall. "Ryan?"

Marshall scowled. "When we slid into Blue Ledge basin, Bob yelled that he needed some help. I grabbed the First Aid Kit, ran over, and sliced open the left leg of the kid's wetsuit with a pair of scissors. I saw right away that it had begun to swell. And his foot had already turned white. People in the other boats could hear him crying." The room was silent for a few moments.

"What then?" Carlyle said.

"I had Nash there. He'd been an EMT in the army for three years and had seen more blunt force trauma and open fractures than most surgeons deal with in a lifetime."

"Keith, what about the kid's leg?"

"The knee was dislocated, but that wasn't what really worried me. I thought there was a chance that Katz had ruptured an artery in the back of his leg."

"And that's a real emergency?"

"If you don't stabilize the leg and get the patient to a hospital immediately, there's a good chance you get paralysis or worse."

"Worse?"

"Gangrene. We had no way of getting back to the put-in, and North River was at least two hours away. Since we were just five hundred yards from Virgin Falls, I told Betts to run back upstream and grab the backboard we'd stowed there. It was in a stand of cedar ten yards from the river."

"For the record, say how you knew this."

Marshall leaned back. "Every rafting company puts backboards below each major rapid. They're wrapped in plastic, bound with duct tape, and lashed upright."

"How long was Betts gone?" Carlyle said.

"Five, ten minutes at the most. But when he got back, he said there was no backboard at Virgin."

"You knew that couldn't be true."

"Of course not. We put that thing there three weeks earlier. Right before the season began. I marked the tree with orange surveyor's tape myself."

"You're absolutely sure about where it was?"

"If you ask me that one more time, this interview's over."

"What did you do then?"

"Keith fixed up a splint using a spare paddle. It would do until we got down to Osprey where there was another board."

Carlyle put down his pen. "I'm going to take a guess. That one was missing too."

Marshall looked suspicious. "How did you know?"

"We know Sanders and Blake were murdered."

The room erupted. Carlyle quieted them down and briefly told them about the foot strap and missing log. "It seems reasonable to suspect that if the murderer failed to get your attention earlier, he would try something else, and two guides died. But why didn't you follow up on the missing backboards?"

"I had a kid going crazy. My major concern was getting him out of there safely."

"What did you do once you found out the second board was missing?"

"We sent Hernandez ahead to North Creek to call in a Medevac crew to the small meadow just east of the Boreas." Marshall stood up and walked to a large topo map pinned to the wall. "They picked him up there. Right where the abandoned railway trestle crosses the Hudson."

"But you never suspected sabotage?"

"Why the hell should I? Who goes out in those woods and steals a goddamn backboard? Ashcroft may have made a mistake, but there's an insane person out there. Why keep blaming us?"

"DEC, the state police, and lawyers are going to ask you to go over all this again," Carlyle said. "I'm just getting you ready for their questions."

"You don't sound like you're on my side."

"DEC asked me to help you out. Your season may be over, but I can't save your business if you don't come clean."

"Let's just get this over with."

"I only have one more question," Carlyle said. "What happened to Katz?"

"Alex and I went to the hospital as soon as the trip ended. His doctor said that Nash was correct; the boy had a severed artery in the back of his knee. Gangrene was a possibility. He advised us to leave before the parents got there."

"When did you replace the missing boards?" Bognor said.

"The next day Alex wrapped bright orange surveyor tape around the trees to mark the spot. Then we went over to the other side of the river and put more tape there just to be sure we could locate it."

Carlyle looked at his watch. "Sanders's memorial begins in an hour. After that, we've got the other incident to discuss. I'd like you all back here by two thirty."

The Methodist church stood at the far end of a cul-de-sac on the north end of the village where Sanders had grown up. It was an Arts and Crafts building covered in dark-brown shingles, with a steeply pitched roof and half a dozen blue, green, and red stained-glass windows lining the central aisle. Sitting at the top of a small hill, surrounded on three sides by a forest of jack pine and juniper, the structure had been built by lumber barons who wanted no part of the Roman Catholic theology their workers followed.

Insisting that everyone present at the funeral could be in danger, Caleb Pierce had placed his cruiser at the entrance to the cul-de-sac.

Unwilling to increase his deputy's paranoia, Bognor hadn't told Pierce that a state police sniper from the Syracuse Barracks had been stationed across the street at the second-floor window of the parish hall.

Mourners filled every pew. Sanders's family, friends, and immediate neighbors sat in the first two rows. Seated behind them were members of the volunteer fire company, employees of the nursing home where Sanders's mom had worked, his colleagues and students from the local high school, all eight members of the Village Council, and the town highway crew from where his father had been employed. Karen Raines, furious that her BlackBerry would not function in the mountains, sat alone at the end of the second row. Two dozen Hudson River guides sat behind her. Six state police detectives disguised as pallbearers stood along the back wall of the church.

At the end of the hour-long service, Carlyle and Bognor walked across a gravel parking lot toward their vehicles. Clouds, gathering energy and moisture as they passed over the mountains, turned dark gray. Lightning and heavy rain would roll in later this afternoon, a typical Adirondack thunderstorm that locals called the two o'clock express.

Deep creases lined Bognor's face. "Can you imagine drowning like that?" Carlyle had been forced to describe Sanders's death a half-dozen times in the past week and had no stomach for going over it again. Bognor leaned against his cruiser. "Any chance this backboard thing could have been a prank? Teenagers running wild in the woods?"

"Kids around here know better than to tamper with rafting equipment. Guides are heroes; every teenage boy would die to work on the river. And who would take a hike like that for a prank?"

"Could one of his competitors have done it?"

"Absolutely not. Outfitters don't have much love for each other, but they're not crazy enough to steal lifesaving gear."

"What about those jackasses out at the Mt. Rushmore Club? They'd love to evict the rafting crowd."

Carlyle shook his head. "They're too busy getting drunk and killing fish to worry about a couple of dozen rafts on the weekend."

"Suppose some nut case got drunk one night and decided to raise hell. That could account for those missing backboards."

"How would he know where Marshall had hidden them?"

Sanders's wife, propped up by her parents, walked silently out of the church.

Bognor said, "No matter how this turns out, Marshall's finished. Can you imagine anyone trusting his operation again?"

Carlyle reached for the door of his truck. "Did Marshall have any enemies that you know of?"

"I've never had any trouble with him, but others have. He buys up every seat permit that hits the market and fires employees for no reason. But who could hate him enough to do something like this?"

The crowd had begun to thin out. Two black limousines carrying grieving family members left the church and headed toward the grave-yard on the far side of the village.

"What really scares me," Carlyle said, "is that the guy who killed those two guides may not be finished."

"What are you saying?"

Carlyle opened the door of his truck. "There's three possibilities. He thinks he's got a damn good reason for harassing Marshall, he's started to enjoy watching the carnage, or he won't stop until Marshall is dead."

SEVEN

Carlyle was standing in the conference room of the lodge at 2:00 p.m. studying a stack of computer printouts when Marshall walked in. "What the hell's all that?"

"DEC accident reports going back two years."

"What do you expect to find there?"

"To see if you're the only outfitter he's after." Carlyle, known as a quant guy by his colleagues, had earned his reputation through a meticulous analysis of crime statistics.

"You going to keep me waiting for an answer?"

"So far, looks like you're his only target." Carlyle dropped the files into his briefcase and sat down at the head of the table. "By the way, what ever happened to Katz?"

Marshall sat to Carlyle's left. "He had two operations on his leg, but the infection spread. They had to amputate just below his knee."

The door opened and Nash, Hernandez, and Betts came in, followed by Bognor and Pierce.

Carlyle looked across the table. "Ryan, you said something else happened last fall."

"I never said it was connected to Sanders and Blake."

"Why don't you let us decide that?" Bognor said. The sheriff still had a black mourning band wrapped around the left arm of his uniform.

Marshall pushed his chair back. "It was the third week in September. Betts called me on Saturday at dawn to say the Hudson had erupted

— 77 —

overnight. It was up to 8.5 and he wanted to know if I was going to cancel the trip."

"And?"

"I told him to mind his own business. He knows I don't cancel trips."

"Why didn't you change your plans once you heard that the Hudson was busting loose?" Carlyle said.

"We'd filled eight boats. I can't afford to turn people away in my busy season. I told Betts that if he was afraid to do his job, Nash could run sweep."

Bognor made several entries in a small spiral notebook. "Anything else you remember about that morning?" Carlyle said.

"Blake had just begun his second year with us. He said he wasn't sure he could get a boat through Mile-Long when the river was near flood stage."

"What did you tell him?"

"I said this business is about guts, not brains."

"You really let inexperienced people go out there like that?"

"That's how we train rookies. They either survive or they look someplace else for excitement."

Carlyle knew that Marshall, not understanding that his comments would get him in trouble later, was showing off in front of Bognor. "Anybody in particular give you problems that day?"

"There were six people I was keeping my eye on," Marshall said. "They were butting helmets and pounding their paddles into the ground like year-old bulls. The usual macho shit, but there was something about them that I didn't like."

"Was that the end of their shenanigans?"

"I wish. One of them, a dude wearing a tricked-out new wetsuit, asked me what to do if he had to take a leak when he was out on the river."

"And you told him the usual?"

"Right. I said we get two kinds of people here. Those who piss in their wetsuits and those who lie about it."

Bognor said, "Since you thought that they might make trouble, what did you do?"

"I put them in Hernandez's boat. He would never take any shit from people like that."

"You regularly let troublemakers like that on the river?"

"If we turned away every asshole who showed up, we'd have no clients."

"Anyone else in that bunch give you problems?" Carlyle asked.

"A tall dude," Marshall said, "maybe six-two, six-three, dressed like the Terminator. Expensive wraparound sunglasses, new wetsuit, black diver's watch, and a knife fixed to his life vest. You don't see that often."

"How do you remember all this?"

"If you hold on a minute, I'll tell you. As we walked toward our bus, I said I didn't think he'd need that knife today. He says, 'I needed it on the Rogue. You can never tell when you're going to get into trouble.'"

"That's it? Just a guy with a big mouth?"

Marshall shook his head. "He had another knife strapped to his leg. Bigger than the first one."

When Carlyle had worked here, he'd carried a small, black, saw-toothed Spyderco on his life vest, but he'd never seen a client wear a knife. "You remember the guy's name?"

"I knew you'd ask, so I looked it up. Morgan Price. A Wall Street big shot with an attitude--paid cash for his entire posse. He started mouthing off again when our bus broke down on the way to Indian Lake."

"You remember your driver that day?"

"Ben Albert, a cook with the school district. Been with me for a decade. Nothing wrong there except he smokes and is seriously overweight. His wife died of emphysema recently. Lives on a half-acre just outside of town."

"You get along with him?"

"He drives just fine. But last December, he asked for two hundred and fifty bucks because he was short on rent money. I turned him down."

"You think he might hold that against you?"

"What if he did? He couldn't be involved in all this."

"Why's that?" Carlyle said.

"Ben Albert can hardly walk a hundred feet."

"So what happened when the bus finally got going again that morning?"

"Price interrupted my safety talk. I'd just warned everyone that if they fell out, they should assume the safe swimmer position—on their backs and feet together. He shouted, 'Come on, skip the pussy stuff.'"

"And you told him what?"

"I walked back to where he was sitting and told him this talk was for his own good. He said, 'I'm not looking for someone to hold my hand.' After his buddies stopped laughing, I gave them the never-stand-up-in-moving-water lecture and said their guide would give them specific instructions when they got to the Indian. And I made the usual joke about my spiel being part of our parole agreement with New York State."

"Price continued to give you trouble?" Bognor said.

"Ryan put that bunch in my boat," Hernandez said. "I had trouble with them from the get-go." For the next ten minutes, Hernandez continued to recite instances of Price's arrogance and disregard for safety rules.

Hernandez had a reputation as a flake. On the coldest days, while handing out chocolate to his people, he would shut his right eye, turn his fist into a claw and bellow, "Energy for the gorge, me hearties, energy for the gorge." He also had a withering sense of humor. One morning, he spotted a woman smoking near his raft. "I'd put that out if I were you."

"Why's that?"

"We fill those things with hydrogen. You ever hear of the Hindenburg?"

Hernandez was deadly serious about this job, however. He pored over videos of whitewater accidents and pestered the most experienced guides with technical questions.

"Did Price's comment piss you off?" Carlyle said.

"Nah. I just told them that story about Elisha Belden to calm them down. I'm sure you used it when you worked here." Belden, a fur trapper, unable to make it back to his cabin when a snowstorm hit the region in 1937, had his feet turn black from frostbite. A doctor sawed off all his toes, and Belden had to attach snowshoes to his stumps in order to stand upright. From then on, he made his living by going around to taverns, making drunks pay to watch rattlers bite him.

Hernandez's crew had come alive in Cedar when they saw the Hudson working itself into a frenzy. "I pointed out the undercut ledges all along there and told them they were really dangerous, which they lapped up. Because the Hudson had doubled in size, we'd begun picking up speed. When the river turned right and began to collide with boulders, my crew went nuts, yelling and swearing, the typical macho bullshit."

Carlyle leaned forward. "How did Price react?"

"As we turned the corner at the top of Entrance, we could see Blue Ledges up ahead and a lot of turbulence. It's like a minefield, rocks everywhere. Then he did something really weird."

"Like what?"

"He took off his sunglasses and put them in the mesh pocket of his life vest." Hernandez swallowed some coffee. "Just as we got into the middle of all that turbulence, Price, the paddle in his left hand, leaned out over the side, just like guides do. When he put all his weight on the thwart—he was really close to the water at that point—the floor strap on his side tore away."

Everybody was looking at Hernandez, whose hands were shaking.

"I know this is difficult," Carlyle said, "but tell us everything you remember."

"He just flew backward out of the boat. Christ, it was awful. He tumbled through Entrance, head over heels, submerged most of the time, ten or fifteen feet behind us. Then I heard him scream. That's when he must have done it—dislocated his shoulder."

Bognor said, "There was no way you could help him?"

"I was too busy keeping us upright to throw him a rope. He tumbled down through a rock-lined chute and straight into another hydraulic. He must have been recirced four times at least before he finally flushed out."

Carlyle said, "Was there any way for him to swim to shore?"

"His right arm wasn't working. Every time he came up for air, he screamed."

"How'd you get to him, finally?"

"At Blue Ledge basin, Alex pulled up real close, grabbed his vest, and hauled him in. Then we all hurried into an eddy."

"What about his arm?"

"I guess this is where I take over," Nash said. "Since it had come out of the socket, I put him face down across my raft and popped it back in place. It's a pretty routine technique."

"Let's stop here for a minute," Carlyle said. "Did anyone happen to take a look at the thwart?"

Marshall said, "That's the first thing we did when we got back to the lodge. I saw right away that a four-by-six piece holding the crosspiece in place had let go."

"Is the boat outside?"

"It's with the manufacturer," Marshall said. "They claimed that it wasn't under warranty and not their fault."

"Why's it still with them?"

"My father's lawyer is planning to sue."

Carlyle put down his pen and leaned back in his chair. "From what we've heard so far, my guess is that our guy probably used a box cutter or an Exacto knife on the boat. Just like he did to Sanders's foot strap."

Marshall looked stunned. "What the hell did we do to deserve this?"

"We'll get to that later. How did Price make out?"

"I bound his arm to his side," Nash said. "Then I wrapped his bleeding hand in gauze. It looked like hamburger."

"You've done these procedures before?"

"Dozens of times. In the army, out on the river, you name it."

Marshall said, "What do I do now?"

"First, we run a check on Price," Carlyle said.

"I don't think he blames us," Hernandez said.

"Why not?"

"Before he left he handed me an envelope. There were five bills in it. All hundreds."

Marshall glared at Carlyle. "I suppose you're going to let DEC know about these two incidents."

"Do I have a choice?"

After Marshall and his guides left, Bognor fished in his pockets. "You mind if we go outside? I need a smoke." When they reached the bottom step of the lodge, he said, "Any idea why Marshall didn't report those incidents earlier?"

Carlyle leaned against the sheriff's cruiser. "He probably didn't know it was sabotage."

"You think there were other events like these two?"

"Could be, but he may have covered them up. Wouldn't you, if you were in this business?"

"Can't we just ask him straight out what else has gone wrong recently?"

"There may be a pattern he's not aware of. Little things like a bus that won't start or a frayed rope that fails at a critical time."

Bognor began coughing.

Carlyle said, "You want to go in and sit down?"

"If I can't stand up, what good am I to this job?"

"No one's going to push you out, John. You've helped more families around here than all the social workers in the county."

It was 5:00 p.m. Mist began rising from the river. A string of cars filled with city-bound tourists, their ski weekends finished, rushed past the lodge. On the far side of the valley, shadows began to engulf a grove of slender mountain aspen. The air in the gorge turned cold again. The inn was dark, seemingly abandoned.

"What next?" Bognor said.

"We interview anyone who might provide us with information, like that guy who works the floodgates at the dam."

"Jimmy Clark? Why him?"

"He's at the river every day, right?"

"He is, but he just sits in that beat-up green pickup of his, tinted windows rolled up in all weather."

"You ever see him leave that truck?"

"No. He opens the sluice gate before the outfitters arrive and closes it after they take off. Never says a word to anyone."

"What do we know about him?"

"Not a lot. Works for the Water Department. Been there thirty years. Sad little guy, I hear."

"You ever ask him if he's seen anyone suspicious poking around the dam?"

"Ric, when people see the sheriff coming, they clam up."

"Can you think of anyone who might have a grudge against Marshall?"

"What kind of person are we looking for?"

"Single white males to start with."

"My jail's filled with idiots like that every weekend."

"Let me narrow it down. Anyone with a history of causing trouble for their neighbors."

"Ric, people up here carry guns, build fences around their property, and keep their shades drawn. You can be damn sure they don't report their personal grudges to me."

"This is someone who believes he's not being treated fairly and has a history of being a pain in the ass."

"Can you be more specific?"

"A person who doesn't cut his lawn or threatens deer hunters who stray onto his property. That kind of thing."

Bognor laughed.

"That narrows it down to about fifty people I've been in contact with lately. You got any other hints for me?"

"Because of the way he plans these attacks, I'd say this guy is meticulous and highly organized."

"God in Christ. I don't know what we'll do if we have a maniac loose in these mountains."

"Don't panic yet."

"Why in hell not?"

"Because Marshall may be his only target."

Bognor turned to look at the woods. "Mind if I ask you something? You've got a great job now. There's no need to be up here anymore, freezing your ass off in a raft, chasing a madman. So why have you come back?"

"I had an accident right before I left here. One of Burton's guides made a mistake and I nearly drowned. I swore I'd never get in a raft again. Some people believe it shows I wasn't meant for this work. I guess I'm trying to prove them wrong."

"You'll see this investigation through to the end, then."

"As long as you need me." Carlyle pulled a bunch of keys from his pocket. "One more thing. You mind if I ask Leo Wells to help me out? If I have to look for this guy in the backcountry, there's no better person to have around."

"Go ahead. But make sure Wells stays away from cliffs. The guy has a reckless streak in him."

EIGHT

He woke at 5:00 a.m., threw a log in the woodstove, and made a pot of coffee. He walked back and forth in the semidarkness, the bitter cold clawing at his bones. How was he supposed to have known that Sanders would do something as stupid as stand up in a moving river, and that his goddamn buddies would be too inept to rescue him? The kid's death was not his fault, but he could not put it out of his mind. Light began to pour in from the single, east-facing window. Those incompetent bastards who worked for Marshall could have saved Blake, too, if they knew what they were doing.

The cabin was small but immaculate. Lining one wall were three bookcases filled with county histories, surveyor's maps, state law reports, photographs of the region as it existed a century ago, and deeds to properties scattered all over the mountain. An eight-by-ten sleeping loft mounted on four hand-hewn beams hovered over the single room. A cast-iron woodstove and a cane rocker sat in the center of the room. His collection of logging tools, their blades recently honed, stood against the back wall.

He cracked open the front door and stared out at the row of red spruce along the road that guarded his privacy. A two-story, pine-clad barn sat just uphill and to his left. His nearest neighbor, a widow whose husband had died in a mine accident thirty years ago, lived a mile away. Working nights and weekends for two years, his parents had built this cabin halfway up a slope leading to the summit of the mountain. The eighty-foot trees guarding his property were more than a century old. Surrounded on all sides by thick foliage, the house received sunlight only an hour or two either side of noon.

Locals never came near his cabin. Everyone knew he patrolled his property, owned guns, and would enforce the no trespassing signs that he'd posted. No one ever visited the place now that his parents had passed on.

He went inside, threw another log in the stove, and collected his gear. Although he planned to be away from his truck for only five or six hours, his backpack contained everything he would need should he get stranded in the gorge: snowshoes, ten-point crampons, an ice axe, a lightweight GPS unit, fifty yards of high-tensile rope, a tarp, a thermos filled with black coffee, and ten MREs. He wrapped a 10X spotting scope in flannel and placed it in the vest pocket of his parka.

After pulling on a pair of waterproof boots, he hoisted his pack and locked the front door behind him. This conflict with the Marshalls was about more than his family's grievances. An entire community, people who had carved their dreams from this soil, was at risk. He walked across the yard, chained up his eight-year-old yellow lab, threw his gear in the truck, and drove slowly down the mountain toward Indian Lake.

After twenty minutes on the two-lane, he turned onto Parkerville Road and drove south for three-quarters of a mile. Soon after the pavement ended, he pulled off into the woods thirty yards from the small pond where that ten-year-old girl, the one running from her father, had drowned a year ago.

He was not afraid of being pulled over by the cops. No one around here would look twice at a guy driving a battered pickup while wearing a Jets cap and a brown-and-white camo jacket.

These disguises made him feel invisible. During the past three weeks, he'd stood unnoticed along the Indian while hikers, forest rangers, and outfitters passed within fifty yards of his campsite. To minimize the risk of getting caught, he'd driven to New Jersey to purchase full-body camouflage outfits, to Plattsburg for non-glare binoculars, to Albany for knee-high gaiters, and then to Freeport, Maine for what LL Bean called its Pine Forest Camouflage Backpack.

Ice crystals as delicate as Christmas ornaments glistened in the sunlight. He pulled on a pair of thick wool gloves, reached into the back seat for his pack, and got out of the truck. After sweeping a Scotch pine branch across his tire tracks, he jogged across the road and disappeared into the woods just as the sun broke the horizon.

At 7:00 a.m., Carlyle watched Marshall's new red Toyota 4x4 pull off the main road and bounce down the gravel trail toward the meadow perched above the Indian. Betts, in a rusting, decade-old pickup, arrived three minutes later. Nash, driving a Jeep tricked out with an emergency light bar and a winch, was just behind him.

On weekends during the rafting season, the scene at the meadow was chaotic. Hundreds of boisterous clients milled around, churning the ground into mud while outfitters attempted to corral them into boats at the foot of the hill.

The meadow was empty and almost silent this morning. It had snowed for several hours last night. Carlyle's thermometer read forty-two degrees. The ground was still frozen and would not turn to slush until the sun appeared over the tree line.

The four men exchanged handshakes and finished their coffee. Betts stared down at the basin. "So, what's this all about?"

"What does it look like?" Carlyle said. "We're taking a little trip."

"Yeah? Where to?"

"Cedar Ledges."

Betts threw his coffee cup into the woods. "Why make us go through Blake's death again?"

"We need to find out how this son of a bitch moves around without anyone seeing him."

Nash said, "How are we supposed to do that?"

"If we do a meticulous search of the chute and the ground all around it, we may find something that the cops overlooked."

"Like what?" Nash said.

"No matter what you've heard, criminals aren't the smartest people in the world. If you know what you're looking for, you can always find something out of place."

Nash zipped up his life vest. "You mind telling me why it was necessary to leave at dawn?"

"I didn't want reporters following us. We need time to examine the site without anyone looking over our shoulders. The sooner we leave, the less chance there is we'll be interrupted."

Marshall peered down toward the water. "Is that my raft down there?"

"I took it from the shed two hours ago."

"What the hell have you been doing since five in the morning?"

"Deciding how I was going to convince you to come with me today."

"Screw it," Betts said. "Let's just get this over with."

The four men inched down the hill and dropped their gear into the boat. "You can examine whatever the hell you want," Marshall said to Carlyle, "but I'm in charge of this crew today."

Betts picked up a paddle. "Can we please get going before I kill both of you?"

It took them twenty minutes to reach the Gooley Steps. Carlyle paddled in silence, staring at the Indian and the woods. Although it was mid-April already, the forest was still in the grip of winter, the maples and birch without leaves, the white pine, spruce, and hemlock dull green.

No outfitter ran midweek trips until the end of the month, and DEC, fearing another incident, had warned the kayak crowd to stay off the water. If they were attacked today, Carlyle and the others would be three hours from the nearest road and unable to call in for help.

Ignoring the bitter cold and the piercing wind, the four men quickly worked their way down the ice-choked Indian River. At 8:20 a. m., they pulled into an eddy halfway down Cedar, fifteen yards upstream from where they'd found Blake's body six days ago. They tied the boat up and waded through snow and mud across a narrow peninsula to the cheat chute.

Nash said, "You have any idea what we're looking for?"

Carlyle stopped to catch his breath. "Two things. Evidence of how he dropped the log right where he wanted it, and where he was that morning while we were trying to revive Blake."

Carlyle ducked under the flimsy police tape and began pacing the area, stopping every few seconds to measure the distance between the chute and the tree line. "To get his ambush to work, the tree had to be facing upstream, just about here." He pointed to a bare spot in the snow. Carlyle turned around and walked twenty feet into the woods. "Break off a branch, stay ten feet apart, and sweep the ground."

"We're supposed to find what?" Betts said.

"Come on, Alex," Carlyle said. "We're looking for the tree stump."

The four men, bent over at the waist like peasant farmers in some Third World country, began swiping at the snow with their makeshift pine brooms. After twenty minutes, they'd found nothing.

Marshall threw his branch down. "Okay, Sherlock, we struck out. This is a dead end."

Carlyle stood up. "It's too early to say that. We saw the log. It had to be at least eight feet long. He couldn't have brought it far. That means we haven't found it yet or he was able to dispose of it."

"What happens if we don't find it?" Nash said.

Carlyle thought a moment. "We know something else about him already. This guy was no amateur. We already knew he was familiar enough with rafting to sabotage your operation. He also knew exactly how to drop that pine so it wouldn't get hung up or he had some kind of tool that let him drag it to the river."

Carlyle pulled a small black digital camera from his pocket and, circling the site, took two dozen pictures.

"The log's gone," Marshall said. "Let's get the hell out of here."

Carlyle wiped the sweat from his forehead. "Not so fast. There's one more thing. Where was he hiding? You don't just come all this way, spend a couple of hours preparing a trap, and take a cab home."

"What are you saying?" Marshall said.

"You're not going to like this."

"I haven't liked anything you've ever told me, so it can't get any worse."

"The killer needed six or seven hours to get here, drop the tree, and disappear before we came down Cedar that morning. He had to lay over someplace."

"He stayed out here after we left?" Nash said.

"How else could he do it?" Pushing aside branches, Carlyle walked back and forth along the chute. "There's another thing. You know how pyromaniacs like to watch their buildings burn to the ground? It's like that with some criminals."

"Jesus," Betts said. "Are you saying he stayed here and watched Blake die?"

"It's more than likely."

"What do you do," Marshall said, "lay in bed at night and dream up these sick ideas?"

Betts clenched his fists. "Are you telling me this asshole has a place somewhere out here?"

"And could be around here right now?" Nash said.

Carlyle took a couple of steps toward the Hudson, turned, and walked back to where they were standing. "I think we should fan out, within earshot of each other, and walk a thousand yards out from the river. You've each got a whistle. Use it if you find anything."

The four men turned away from the Hudson and began slogging through the snow. Carlyle, on the upstream end of the uneven line, stared straight in front of him. Quickly losing sight of the others, he could hear little besides the sound of his own labored breathing. Perspiring heavily, he wiped sweat from his eyes.

Several minutes later, Carlyle heard a series of sharp blasts, like the pinging of a nuclear submarine homing in on a target. Following the sound, he made his way through the woods to his left and found Nash, with Betts and Marshall next to him, standing in front of a small cabin.

Weathered gray boards covered the derelict structure. It had a single window in the front wall and a brick chimney projecting through a partially collapsed gray metal roof. Four stairs led up to a porch. A cane rocker hemorrhaging green mold stood next to a front door covered in peeling red paint.

Nash turned when he heard Carlyle walk up behind him. "How'd you know we'd find this?"

"There were hundreds, maybe thousands of these structures all over the backcountry. Loggers driving horse-drawn sleds couldn't leave the woods every night. It stands to reason our guy found one of them around here."

Betts began to make his way up the stairs. "What are we waiting for? Let's look inside."

Carlyle reached out a hand to stop him. "Stay away from that door, it could be booby-trapped."

"There's nothing but a rusting goddamn hasp." Betts planted his foot on the door and drove it off its hinges.

"If you keep destroying evidence," Carlyle said, "we'll never catch the guy."

Betts started through the door. "We're here. Might as well have a quick peek."

Carlyle followed Betts up the stairs. "For Christ's sake, go in slowly."

The cabin looked like it hadn't been used since Teddy Roosevelt hiked through these woods a century ago. An inch of mouse droppings lay on the floor. Green and white mold covered an eight-foot-long plank table, several wood and canvas chairs, and four bunk beds along one wall. A cast-iron stove, its vent pipe lying in pieces on the floor, sat in the center of the room.

Betts moved toward the table and leaned over to read a single sheet of paper that had been taped to its surface. His shoulders sagged. "Come over here. But don't get too near me."

When Carlyle edged close, Betts lifted the note from the table and handed it back to him. "What do I do now?"

I warned you to leave me alone but you didn't listen. You're standing on a pressure-sensitive detonator attached to three sticks of dynamite. Now figure out how you're going to get yourself out of this one.

"Don't move or touch anything," Carlyle said. "Let me think for a second." He took a couple of deep breaths and slowly took off his gloves, backpack, and jacket and set them on the floor. "Keith, Ryan. Don't ask any questions. Do exactly as I tell you."

"What did it say?" Nash said.

Carlyle read the note aloud.

"What should we do?" Nash said.

"Pick up the stove and move it toward Alex."

Nash and Marshall each grabbed one end of the stove and slid it across the rough plank floor.

"Good," Carlyle said. "Set it down slowly next to his left foot." He then waved them away.

Once Nash and Marshall had backed off, Carlyle said, "You better get out of here now."

"I'm staying," Nash said. "You might need my help."

Marshall, who didn't take his eyes off Betts, said nothing.

"That's stupid," Carlyle said. "Leave now and wait outside for us."

When Nash and Marshall had left the cabin, Carlyle said, "Okay, then, we're all set. You ready?"

Betts said, "Will you please just get this over with?"

Carlyle inched toward the table and put his hand on Betts's shoulder. "Pick up your left foot and put it down six inches behind you."

Betts straightened up. "Where exactly?"

"Right next to the front leg of the stove."

Betts whispered, "How do you know this is going to work?"

"You trigger a detonator when you remove weight. I think we've neutralized it."

Betts, sweating profusely, lifted up his left heel and slid his foot away from the table.

"Now the right one. That's it. When I say so, shift your weight toward me and, one step at a time, move back slowly."

Within seconds, both men were eight feet away from the table.

Betts leaned against the wall. Sweat dripped from his chin. He was breathing heavily, his face white, eyes unfocused. "Christ. We did it."

Carlyle picked up his gear and exhaled loudly. "Okay, let's get the hell out of here." He paused for a final look around and saw another note taped to the back of the front door.

Next time, you won't be warned. Stay away from this place. And leave the gorge for good.

Carlyle and Betts walked through the door and down the steps. When he was ten yards away from the cabin, Betts stepped over to a tree and vomited.

Carlyle said, "The bastard's had his fun, but I still think there's a camp somewhere around here."

"Will you stop this bullshit?" Marshall said. "Let's go."

"He can't pull this stuff without having a place to hide."

Marshall stepped close to Carlyle. "The only thing we're going to find is another booby trap and really get our asses handed to us."

Carlyle shook his head. "We can't stop looking now."

"No? I say we cut the crap and get back to Warrensburg."

"Boss," Nash said. "We've gone this far."

"One hour," Marshall said. "Then I'm taking my boat out of here."

"We should move another thousand yards into the woods," Carlyle said. "I'll take the right flank again. Our guy feels at home here. Look for any place he could construct a shelter."

The four men began hiking slowly away from the cabin.

Carlyle, never moving on until he was certain that he had covered an area completely, was staring at the base of a granite cliff face ten minutes later when he saw an irregular opening in the rock, screened from view by a stand of black maple. He blew his whistle three times and the others came running up.

"I think this may be it."

Nash said, "You're not going in there, are you?"

"Not any farther than I have to." Carlyle bent down and crawled toward the open space in the rock. The site was little more than a bed of pine needles with a half-dozen small, granite boulders surrounding a fire pit filled with gray ash. But, as a place to remain concealed, it was almost perfect. He crawled to the back of the cave, turned around, and faced the others. Sitting in near darkness he said, "You'd never just stumble across this in a dozen years."

Betts stuck his head in. "He could get caught out in a snowstorm and survive for a week in there."

Carlyle marveled at the camp's placement. The sound of the Hudson crashing downstream would muffle footsteps. The sun, even if directly overhead, would hardly be visible.

He crawled out of the cave and walked slowly around the site, moving his eyes back and forth between the granite overhang and the river. "He must know every foot of this gorge."

"That's all we've got from this expedition of yours?" Marshall said.

"I've learned something else about him."

"What's that?"

"The person we're looking for just doesn't let himself get sidetracked."

"So, we're finally done here?" Betts said.

Carlyle picked up his backpack. "There's one more thing we've got to do."

"Christ," Betts said. "What now?"

"We've got to find that log. It may tell us how he killed Blake."

"You're nuts," Betts said. "There's only one way to get rid of something that weighs several hundred pounds."

"I know that." Carlyle dragged a map of the Hudson from his pack. "The snowmelt probably flushed it through the gorge. What if it got hung up somewhere?" Carlyle pointed to a spot on the map as the others looked over his shoulder. "The logging industry used the spring flood to bring timber down to Glens Falls. But just downstream from here, the Hudson makes two S-turns in a quarter mile. If it's anywhere, it's there, stuck in a strainer."

"Even if we find it," Marshall said, "what would that prove? We already know this guy's a psychopath."

"We can't be sure about anything yet. That's why we need all the evidence we can get our hands on."

"So, what do we do now?" Betts said.

"Retrace our steps to the river, examine that strainer, then get back to the lodge."

"It's about time," Marshall said.

Carlyle said, "You all go ahead. I want to take another quick look around."

Twenty minutes later, as he neared the Hudson, he heard Betts yell, "Fuck! Can you believe this?"

Running through ankle-deep snow, Carlyle found Betts, Nash, and Marshall standing around the raft. "What's going on?"

Marshall's raft had been dragged from the river and tied to a tree. The side tubes and thwarts had been sliced clean through. It lay there, gray and immobile, like a decaying elephant carcass.

"How could he have gotten here without us seeing him?" Nash said.

"He must have come by in a kayak or canoe while we were at the cabin," Carlyle said. "Or maybe he's been hiding out overnight. Who knows?"

Nash said, "Why destroy the raft, then?"

"To teach us a lesson," Carlyle said.

"About what?"

"I'm guessing he's telling us that we're trespassing on his territory."

"How can you be so sure?" Marshall said. "And why do you keep staring at my boat?"

Carlyle put down his pack. "This stunt's more proof we're not dealing with a maniac. He doesn't blow people up or commit horrific acts. That would only make the cops furious. I'm more certain than ever that he's got a plan for what he wants to achieve and he's not going to let us sidetrack him."

"That's terrific," Betts said. "But we're forgetting one thing."

"What's that?" Marshall said.

"How the hell do we get out of here?"

MONDAY AFTERNOON

As soon as Karen Raines had finished reading Carlyle's twelve-page report on the deaths of Sanders and Blake, she reached for her phone. "Have Elliot call me," she told his secretary. "No, Marcy, not when he's available, the minute he's back from lunch."

Raines walked toward a row of floor-to-ceiling windows overlooking Albany and the Hudson. To her left were the four intricately carved Gothic towers of the Richardson-designed State Legislature. Directly across the street was Rockefeller Plaza, the Brasilia knock-off the former Governor had erected over the rubble of an immigrant neighborhood that had stood there for over a century.

Raines, a twenty-year DEC employee who'd clawed her way up the ranks from summer intern to Deputy Director of Communications, returned to the conference table and leafed through the last four pages of Carlyle's report. He had examined all three volumes of the American Canoe Association's River Safety Report and concluded that while there were often a half-dozen serious accidents a year on stretches as difficult as the Hudson Gorge, "two guides had never died in the same year."

The phone rang. "It's Elliot. What's up?"

"I'm in the Executive Conference Room. It's the only place that's not bugged." The room had cost a quarter of a million to trick out. It had an eighteen-foot teak conference table, a mahogany credenza, three overhead projectors, two computer-linked light screens, a plasma TV, and a state-of-the-art lectern with video-conferencing capabilities. It had been completely renovated because some up-and-coming young bureaucrat had wanted to demonstrate his loyalty to the new Republican regime.

Abel Elliot marched in five minutes later. He was dressed like a Deputy Commissioner: pale gray suit, yellow tie, off-white shirt, and tan, hand-stitched loafers. Someone in DEC's field staff thought he was gay, but two former secretaries, now exiled to an office in Buffalo, knew better.

"I'm sorry to hear about your guides," he said. "Where did it happen?"

"On the Indian River."

"Where's that?"

"A hundred miles north of here and twenty west of Warrensburg."

Elliot was a policy guy who did everything he could to avoid "walking through muck" as he called it. After picking up his Yale law degree, he'd gotten this job because he'd spent over a decade running campaigns for the state Republican Party.

He grabbed the phone. "Send in two coffees, please. Black." He turned to Raines. "Who's running the preliminary investigation?"

"Guy named Richard Carlyle. He's a former guide but now a criminologist at the university."

"Seems like a strange choice."

"It lets us show the environmental crowd we're on their side."

"Come on, Karen. They're not paying us to protect birds. We're the firewall between the timber people and the tree huggers. The only thing we're preserving is the governor's ability to win the next election."

"Carlyle's just our point man for now." She gestured to the folder on the desk. "You want to see his credentials?"

"You handle the case. Leave me out of it." Elliot glanced at his daily schedule. "Any chance these accidents will cause problems for us or the Commissioner?"

"I don't see how. Our forest rangers in District Four were doing their jobs and the guides had both passed their licensing exams."

"Any way we can lay these quote-unquote unfortunate events on the outfitter?"

"Probably not. He has a spotless record. His father may be a problem, however. He's got political connections all over the state and in Washington. You know the drill. We give him permits to build those malls of his and he makes financial contributions, through third parties of course, to our candidates."

"We can't seem helpless." Elliot pushed his coffee away. "Wagner, the Congressman for that district, says tourism's dropping."

"I promise. The news will not get more toxic."

"When will this mess get cleared up?"

"A crew is checking out the site of the second death today. They should be able to give us some answers soon."

"Is Carlyle going with them?"

"We had to convince the university to set him free for a few days."

"What's his angle in all this?"

"He was sitting right next to the first guide who died."

"Let me know as soon as you get some news."

Raines knew she was being set up. If the department were held responsible for these two deaths, Elliot would demand her resignation.

He stood up and walked to the door. "The paper said it took that first one forever to drown."

"That's not the worst part. Fifty people watched it happen. You want to go up there and examine the site?"

"I'm not a river person, Karen. You know that."

"What do we do if the investigation shows that the department is at fault?"

"We make Carlyle the fall guy. He's the common denominator, a person who goes on only two trips the whole year, and a guide dies on both of them."

"If it comes to that," Raines said, "it could work."

NINE

"He cut your boat to ribbons?" Leo Wells asked.

"Into little pieces is more like it," Carlyle said. "I thought we'd have to spend the night out there."

"What finally happened?"

"Two DEC rangers found us. They were pissed as hell that we didn't tell them what we were doing."

Carlyle was sitting across from Wells in the Acropolis Diner in Albany's derelict port district, a maze of food warehouses, scrap metal yards, body shops, and oil storage tanks.

The Acropolis was all brushed aluminum and fake leather, but since cops had begun stopping by every four hours, street kids quit robbing the place at knifepoint.

Gus "Teddy" Theodorakis, the owner, thought of himself as a comic running this joint only until his breakthrough moment on the "Tonight Show." "This menu," he told his customers, "is my masterpiece." He'd named the lamb kebob "El Greco" and claimed that the Greek salad would put huge stones on Michelangelo's David.

Because he was due back at the ranger station in Ray Brook at noon, Wells was wearing work clothes: a Gore-Tex parka, down vest, plaid shirt, and hard-shell plastic mountain boots.

"I like your gold-rimmed glasses," Carlyle said.

"It's the existential look. Women find it irresistible."

"You look beat. What the hell's going on?"

"I've been up all night with Jack." Wells's father had been diagnosed with dementia five years ago.

"How long's he been in a nursing home?"

"Three years. He went from an appellate lawyer to a ghost overnight."

"Jesus."

"Let's drop it." Wells dumped three sugars in his coffee. "You and Beth still in the city?"

"We've got a place outside of town now." Carlyle wiped his glasses. "How come you stopped guiding?"

"I got fed up hauling idiots through the gorge." Wells was now head of Search and Rescue in the northern district, an occupation that ful-filled his depression-driven need to flirt with death.

"Your shoulder any better?"

Wells had ripped his arm from the socket while pulling a teenager off a cliff face. "It only took two operations and six months of rehab."

The waitress came over to their table. "Leo. What'll it be?"

"We'll both have Greek salads. But don't tell Gus that we didn't order lamb."

"Boss!" she yelled. "Leo and his girlfriend want the Special. Better put in extra olives."

After the laughter died down, Wells said, "How's that cop thing going? You sure the kid's death wasn't accidental?"

"No question about it."

"Marshall's father must be livid."

"He thinks all this bad publicity will ruin his Johnston Mountain project."

"I have a hunch his kid is blaming you for what went wrong."

"He thinks I could have saved Sanders."

"He's never been a fan of yours."

Despite Carlyle's spotless safety record, Marshall and his guides had never stopped treating him like a middle-aged professor masquerading as an experienced guide. During his training a decade ago, Betts had told Carlyle, "We want to see if you crack under pressure. So you won't do it with people in your boat."

The harassment never stopped. One Saturday morning in early May several years ago, Carlyle had let his boat stray too near a massive hydraulic. When they got back to the inn that afternoon, Marshall had screamed, "One more mistake and you're gone!"

"Now they're all depending on you to save their jobs."

"The only thing I care about is finding this maniac."

When the waitress passed their table, Wells pointed to his coffee cup. After she left, he said, "What's next, then?"

"We start by looking for people with a history of petty crimes."

"This isn't suburbia. That shit's pretty common around here."

"Not if it leads us to a person who's starting to come apart."

"You mind explaining just what that means?"

"When someone has a run-in with the law or a violent argument with his wife or girlfriend, it may predict more serious trouble down the road."

"You think he's really angry enough to kill a couple of guides?"

"It's way beyond anger now. He may have started off with a chip on his shoulder, but, for whatever reason, his grievances have mushroomed."

"What are we talking about?"

Carlyle said, "If whatever has been gnawing at him is still there, he could eventually erupt. And if he's really been screwed over and can't forget or forgive whatever's happened to him...."

"What do you do then?"

"If this guy's rage becomes uncontrollable, he may not stop with Marshall."

"Then what?"

"We'll need an army to get him."

"Why don't you leave it to professionals? They'll bring in dogs and trackers."

"This guy's like Rambo. He'll ambush any cop we send in there, and then we'll have a massacre on our hands."

Wells sipped his coffee and watched Carlyle silently for a minute. "You mind my asking what's got you so lit up about this case?"

"I've spent my entire career trying to explain why people commit violent crimes. This is my chance to prove I haven't wasted my time."

"This is more than just some academic exercise, isn't it?"

"I feel responsible for finding out who did this. That doesn't change anything."

"Like hell it doesn't. You're personally involved in this case and you'll take more risks than you should."

"I won't do anything stupid."

Wells laughed. "With a sliced and diced raft? You already have."

"If he never intended those two deaths, we may be able to negotiate with him."

"What if he catches you alone and doesn't want to negotiate?"

"I won't be alone. You're coming with me."

Wells shook his head. "I saved your ass once in Mile-Long. Now you're asking me to do it again?"

"Okay, I'll get Pierce to help me. He'd love telling everyone he was protecting a hotshot professor."

Wells's pager went off. "I've got an emergency on Santanoni Peak. Gotta go." He paid the check, pinched the waitress on his way out, and drove out of the parking lot.

Theodorakis walked over to Carlyle's table. "What's the matter with Leo? He doesn't like my food?"

Later that afternoon, the heavy oak barn door slid open, and Beth, Carlyle's wife, stepped in. He was standing over a workbench. His waterproof dry suit, thick neoprene boots, plastic helmet, and heavy guide paddle sat in a pile in front of him. All of his rescue equipment—prussic loops, high-tensile rope, throw bags, strobe lights, tow lines, and Z-drag kit—were neatly arranged on a pegboard to his right. Although he had lit a tall white propane stove an hour ago, it was still bitterly cold in the barn.

"Why are you working on this stuff now?" Beth said.

"I'm hiking into the canyon tomorrow morning."

Carlyle had told her about the investigation, but not that the authorities had asked him to assist them in the search for the person responsible for the murders.

"Shouldn't you let the police handle it?"

"I'll have a cop with me," Carlyle said. "We'll be fine."

"Why do you have to get involved in this?"

"I was right there when they died. Marshall and the other guides are expecting me to help them through this."

"You had your first accident on the Indian, didn't you?"

One September morning nine years ago, when he had just started his career on the Hudson, Carlyle allowed his raft to drift into a boulder garden. The river was bone dry, a minefield of rocks strewn across the current. As his boat rushed downstream, the sun disappeared behind a layer of gray clouds. Two minutes later, the raft plunged over a steep ledge and the stern heaved upward and to the left. Unprepared for the backlash, Carlyle flew across the back tube and into the river.

"This is completely different. Someone sabotaged Sanders's raft. I was just green and unlucky back then."

"But your accident was near where that boy died."

"I was in the water for less than a minute. It was my first day as a guide. Everyone pulls a dumb stunt once."

"But you came out of your boat, too, just like he did."

"Sanders didn't have an accident. He was murdered." Although he'd never been in real danger that morning a decade ago, Carlyle thought he understood what Sanders and Blake must have been thinking as they were pulled underwater by a river indifferent to their pleas for help.

"You're ten years older now. Should you still be doing something like this?"

"Beth, I promise. I'll be fine."

She was right. It was the worst time of the season to be on that river. The snowmelt would let loose any day now. In a week or two, the

Hudson would resemble a wall of liquid concrete rather than a mountain stream. A series of boat-eating hydraulics would litter the gorge all the way from Blue Ledges to the Boreas. What if the killer decided to go after Marshall and his clients again? Preoccupied with keeping their boats upright, guides would be defenseless, their clients confused and terrified. With roads nonexistent and communication with the outside impossible, any rescue would take hours.

Beth stared at him as he sorted through the equipment on the workbench. "How long will you be away this time?"

"The investigation's just beginning. I don't know where it's headed, but I promise I'll come home once we've arrested someone."

"What about your work at the university? They can't just cancel your classes."

"I'll get a teaching assistant to take over the undergrads for a week or two. Believe me, those kids will be delighted I won't be around to give them more work at the end of the semester."

"You're not thinking about giving up your job in Albany, are you?"

"The endless committee meetings are driving me crazy. This investigation will give me a break from that."

"Do the other guides know you're a professor now?"

"They don't care what I do. They're just desperate for help."

"I don't understand why you're risking your life again."

"Karen Raines at DEC said I know the river as well as anyone and the guides trust me. I can't just walk away."

"What about your book? It's almost done. You can't abandon it now."

Carlyle began packing up his gear. "I'll get back to it this summer."

"I won't be able to stop you, will I?"

"Please don't put it that way."

"It's freezing in here." Beth zipped up her jacket and left the barn.

Just after dark, Carlyle loaded his pickup, moved his tractor into the barn, and walked toward the house. A heavy, wind-driven snow began to envelop the tulip beds Beth had put in last year. The branches of a newly planted white birch, unable to bear the storm's weight, were bent near to the ground. Walking up the path, Carlyle slipped on a small patch of ice. Near the porch swing sat eight or nine large cardboard boxes tightly wrapped with packing tape.

Beth didn't turn around when Carlyle entered the kitchen. Every square inch of the room was filled with pottery, pressed flowers, dried mushrooms, garlic stalks, tiny herb jars, bits of multi-colored tile, and plants in tan clay pots. A reproduction of Matisse's *Two Girls in a Yellow and Red Interior* hung on the wall next to an eight-foot oak trestle dining table.

Beth put out barley soup, slices of dark bread, strong sheep cheese, and salad. Carlyle set the table and poured coffee.

Her sketchbook was on a side table. "What are you working on?" he asked.

"I spent all day waiting for the clouds to lift over the escarpment, but the sun never once broke through." A series of landscapes begun months ago sat unfinished in her studio.

They'd met four years ago during a late afternoon reception at the Dean's house. Beth appeared at the front door with a streak of light-gray paint on her forehead. Tall, thin, blond, and disheveled, she spent nearly an hour walking alone through the downstairs rooms of the ornate red brick Tudor mansion.

They met in front of a nineteenth-century portrait of a merchant's family. She told him she was an artist, teaching part-time at the university. Her eyes were light blue and pale. They talked briefly, mostly about her career. She stared at her hands the entire time but smiled when he asked her out for dinner.

Six months later, after many afternoons hiking the hills surrounding Albany, they were married.

"I'm sorry your day was ruined," Carlyle said. "Maybe tomorrow."

It was dark now. Wind rattled the house and made the candles on the table flicker.

"What's in the boxes out front?" Carlyle said as they began to eat.

"One of your students brought over some books. He said he didn't need them any longer."

Carlyle broke off a piece of bread and reached for the coffee. "What did he look like?"

"Tall, mid-twenties. A grad student, I think."

"Big guy, shaved head?"

"Yes and very polite. He kept apologizing for disturbing me."

"What time did he get here?"

"Around two, I think. His truck just appeared in the drive."

"How did he find us?"

"I don't know. He told me he wanted you to have his books."

"Did he leave a message?"

"No. He just said to wish you well."

"How long was he here?"

"A half-hour or so."

Carlyle told her about his meeting with Long and that he had been asked to leave the program. "He knows he's not supposed to come here without an invitation."

"Ric, he didn't cause me any problems."

Carlyle began clearing the dishes. "I've got to put a stop to this. Call me if he shows up again."

"Aren't you exaggerating? What harm can he do?" Beth stood up and began to clear the table. "Will you at least let someone know where you're going tomorrow?"

"I'll leave a note on my truck to say what route we're taking."

"A note on your truck. How will that help if something happens to you?"

TEN

The Town of Indian Lake, never crowded since the logging industry packed up and left fifty years ago, was deserted at 4:00 a.m. on Wednesday morning. He drove down Main Street past the Central Mountain Bank, Dutcher's Hardware, and Steve's All Night Convenience Store. When he reached the lake, a half-mile west of town, he pulled off the road next to Al's Bait and Tackle and stopped. Caleb Pierce, known to lie in wait for speeders even at this hour, was nowhere to be seen. Circling back three minutes later, he turned right off the main east-west road onto Route 30, and parked behind the Upstate Garage.

He pulled a small ice axe from his truck and made his way through boot-high snow to the back of the Elijah J. Mayhew Local History Museum, a turreted two-story, yellow brick structure. Using the axe blade, he forced open the back door and entered the building. After switching on his headlamp, he walked down the main hall past rows of glass cages filled with the preserved remains of black bears, martens, badgers, wolves, beaver, and moose.

Halfway down the central corridor of the main hall, past rooms labeled Director, Administration, Taxidermy, Staff Lounge, and Friends of the Museum, he found the Archives.

He'd been here twenty years ago, on a high school field trip with his sophomore class. The room had changed little in two decades. To his right, just inside the unlocked door, was a small black safe. The desk of the sixty-two-year-old volunteer librarian, Mary Smith, sat to his left. Portraits of the Museum's former trustees, logging barons and hotel developers who had made the wilderness safe for industry and tourism, were hanging behind the desk. Floor-to-ceiling bookcases covered both side walls. Two ten-foot-long oak tables ran down the center of the room. A row of ten gray filing cabinets sat against the far wall.

The archives had not a single piece of equipment found in up-to-date libraries—no Xerox or fax machines, no white cotton gloves or glassine envelopes for handling rare documents and photographs, no magnifying glasses, up-to-date reference works, microfilm readers, or Internet ports, and, most crucial, no guide to the holdings of the collection. He knew, however, where to find the one file drawer that contained something crucial—a piece of his past and a map that would keep him out of prison.

Careful not to touch any exposed surfaces, he walked down the center of the room toward the filing cabinets. Each one was devoted to a single decade, beginning in 1910 and ending in 1999. He pulled open the second drawer of the first cabinet. It took him only six minutes to find what he was looking for—a thick manila folder labelled Pasco.

He placed the packet of documents on the nearest table, removed its elastic strap, and rifled through its contents: photographs of the three towns where the tragic events took place; articles clipped from the *Warrensburg Times* from 1930 to 1934; a seventeen-page report from the state police, the agency that had coordinated the search for the fugitives; the yellowed telegraph message from Governor Herbert H. Lehman to Sheriff Thomas Davies, pledging his full support for the apprehension of the killers; copies of the four local and regional magazines that had covered the manhunt and trial; letters from relatives of victims and from defenders of the two accused men; a detailed summary of the autopsy conducted by Dr. Philander J. Adams at the Glens Falls Hospital; a bill for $17.50 for the services of two men and a trained bloodhound for two days; and a single sheet of paper entitled *Catalogue of Evidence: The Pasco Affair*.

He found what he had come for near the back of the folder: a rough, hand-drawn map of the gorge on a tissue-thin piece of eight-by-eleven paper that had been folded in half and placed in a plastic sleeve. Drawn in pencil, its edges in tatters, he could see by the slender but intense light of his headlamp seven tiny X's and the faint corresponding lines between the interior and the river's edge. There were two from the vicinity of the Gooley Steps, one each from the Confluence and Blue Ledges, and three between the Narrows and the Boreas, the far end of the gorge. After making a rough copy of the location of those trails, he slid the map back into its plastic sleeve, secured the folder, and returned it to the filing cabinet.

Twenty-four minutes after he'd entered the building, having wiped clean each flat surface and doorknob he might have touched, he exited the museum. Sweeping his tracks in the snow with a broom he'd taken from the hallway, he backed his truck onto the road and, keeping an eye out for Caleb Pierce, left town.

Just after nine thirty that morning, Carlyle turned off the two-lane road that paralleled the gorge and wrestled his truck down a dirt path. After a thousand yards, occasionally sinking axel-deep in mud, he and Pierce reached the Indian Lake dam.

Carlyle shut off the engine. "You ready?"

"Let's go. I can't be playing nursemaid for you every day, now, can I?"

Carlyle scrawled a note and dropped it on the dashboard.

Pierce picked it up. "What's this for?"

"Backup. In case we get into trouble."

"We'll be frozen stiff by the time someone discovers that thing." Pierce grabbed his twelve-gauge. "Here's my backup." He cracked his door open. "You sure we're not going on some wild-goose chase?"

"We've got to find out where Marshall's vulnerable. That means examining every foot of ground from the put-in to the Confluence."

"You have no idea where this idiot's going to attack next, do you?"

"I'm pretty sure he'll come back to the west bank of the Indian."

"How can you know that?"

"It's the only place accessible by road."

"Come on, admit it. You're guessing."

"Then tell me why he hasn't moved to another spot on the river."

Pierce ran a soft cloth along the barrel of his shotgun "What makes you sure he'll attack again, anyway?"

"What makes you so sure he won't?"

"I'm glad one of us had the good sense to carry a weapon today."

Carlyle grabbed his day pack from the truck and set it on the ground. "You really think that gun's going to save us if we get in trouble?"

"What would you do, throw a book at him?"

The two men shouldered their packs and headed north-west along a path that would bring them to the Confluence.

To their right, Carlyle could see the lake that, for a few months a year, turned the Indian into a navigable river. Just below the dam, he watched torrents of water plunging down Beaver Creek.

"Last month," Pierce said, "two teenagers tried to run the creek in inner tubes. Search and Rescue found their bodies a week later underneath a pile of logs and brush a half-mile downstream."

"What happened to the warning sign at the dam?"

"Someone tore it out."

"You think our guy was responsible?" Carlyle said.

"Probably not. The coroner said those kids had been drinking. But now, I'm not so sure."

Two minutes later, they came to a truck sitting just off the road. The door panel read Town of Indian Lake Water Department.

"I'm going to ask the guy if he's seen anything unusual," Carlyle said.

"Him? He won't talk to outsiders."

"Can't hurt to try."

"Go ahead. I can't wait to see what happens."

Carlyle walked up to the gray Ford F150 and knocked on the window. A rack of blue and white emergency lights ran along the top of the cab. A half-dozen orange traffic cones and a load of wood sat in back of the truck. Its occupant rolled down his window part way. "We're hiking out to the Confluence," Carlyle said. "Mind if we leave our vehicle here?"

"Suit yourself."

"Can I ask you a question?"

"Shoot."

"Have you seen much foot traffic on this road?"

Cigarette smoke drifted out of the cab. "Like what?"

"People you didn't recognize."

"Other than yourself? No, sir."

"No strangers at all?"

"Flatlanders have bought up land on both sides of the river. Locals hardly ever come by here now."

"What about when those two guides died?"

"I was out hunting rabbits."

"So you've seen nothing unusual."

"No, sir, I haven't."

"Thanks for your time."

The truck's occupant simply nodded and rolled up the window.

Carlyle walked back to where the Deputy was standing. "Okay, you were right."

Pierce laughed. "I take it you've never seen *Deliverance*?"

"Come on, Caleb. People around here aren't idiots."

"No? You just wait and see."

They continued moving toward the Confluence, mud and wet snow sucking at their boots.

"Let me ask you something," Pierce said. "Most people can't wait to get away from this place. Why the hell did you come back?"

"It's pretty easy to get hooked on this work when you've spent nearly ten years running boats through the gorge."

Carlyle would never forget the first time he'd driven clients through the Narrows. The power and velocity of the Hudson as it spilled downhill out of the mountains astonished him. Afraid of making a rookie mistake, he'd willed his crew to punch through those six huge waves that threatened to capsize their raft. He'd never lost his respect for the river, but he'd gradually realized that if he could overcome that anxiety, nothing else would ever terrify him again.

A half-mile beyond the dam, Carlyle stopped and pulled a pair of thick green mittens and a down sweater from his pack. "You think that accident at Givenny's last April could be something he was responsible for?" Carlyle said.

Twelve months ago, a sixty-five-year-old insurance agent from Chicago, trying to throw himself a birthday party he would never forget, had a fatal heart attack after somersaulting through Soup Strainer.

"You mean the dude who got tossed from his raft? The asshole should never have been out there in the first place. It's a shame everyone had to watch the paramedics doing chest compressions on him, but it was his own damn fault."

"I didn't know the incident touched you so deeply," Carlyle said. "Sorry I brought it up."

An hour after leaving the basin, they came to a barrier mounted on iron poles: *Private Property Ahead. Trespassers will be prosecuted to the Full Extent of the Law.* Pierce walked around the sign. "I guess I'm the law, right?"

"Does anyone ever go back in here?" Carlyle said.

"You saw that sign. Who'd risk it?"

"Then we'll have the place to ourselves."

"You better hope so," Pierce said.

Carlyle stared up at the jack pine, their rough bark glowing red in the morning light. His thermometer said it was forty-four degrees. Wind lashed his face. Knowing they had to get back to the main road before sunset, he pushed on toward the Confluence.

After another mile, the trail, which had paralleled a thirty-foot cliff face, began to drop toward the valley floor. Carlyle could hear the Indian rushing through a series of granite boulder gardens off to his right.

As they rounded a bend in the trail, a rust-red retriever and a large brown mutt with a metal-studded choke collar broke from the woods and, barking furiously, rushed toward them.

A couple trailed after the animals. The woman, trying to conceal a limp, was about five-three, maybe maybe a hundred and forty pounds. She wore a brown coat with ragged sleeves, a thin wool hat, and ankle high boots despite the deep, wet snow. When she reached the growling dogs, now standing still, she grabbed the retriever by its collar. "Quiet. Don't you move now."

The man, a shade under six feet and lean, was smoking a hand-rolled cigarette and wore a thick denim jacket and underneath it a tee-shirt that read, *Watch Your Damn Head. NYS Logging Association.* His red beard was untrimmed, his wrists and face sunburned, the knuckles of both hands raw. A green bandana encircled his head. "These animals scare you?"

Carlyle said, "No. I'm fine with dogs. Thanks for asking."

"I guess some people must hate them."

"Why do you say that?"

"We had one mutt shot recently."

"Where was that?"

"Near the main road. He ran off, chasing a rabbit I suspect. We found him in the woods next day. Dead, of course."

"You ever learn who did it?" Carlyle said.

"No. But if I catch the bastard, he won't shoot no more dogs." He glanced at the shotgun on Pierce's arm. "You out here on official business?"

"You could say that," Pierce said.

The woman, eyes red as if from crying, edged closer to her husband. Her right arm dangled at her side, the hand clenched as if in a permanent spasm. She held a handkerchief in her left hand.

Odd the couple was out walking on a weekday in such bitter weather. "You have any idea how far the Mt. Rushmore Club is?" Carlyle said.

"About two miles," the man said. "But I'd pay attention to their no-trespassing sign if I was you. The people who stay in those big cabins don't appreciate unannounced visitors."

"We'll stay off their property," Carlyle said. "I hope you don't mind my asking. Do you come down this road often?"

"Nearly every day for the past week now."

"Every day?" Carlyle said. "It can't be easy for you this time of year."

"It's hard on her, but we have to come see where our boy died."

"Your son?"

"Chris Blake. Our only child." The man turned around briefly to stare at the river. "He drowned out there a week ago this past Wednesday while working for one of the outfitters. We can only make it to the end of the trail, but the accident happened farther out, just east of where the Hudson comes in to meet the Indian."

The woman, who had begun to weep, wiped her eyes and turned away from the men.

"There's nothing I can say except we're sorry for your loss." Carlyle glanced at Pierce who stood, shotgun clutched to his chest, staring at the parents. Carlyle hoped Pierce wouldn't tell the couple that Carlyle had been the one who had pulled their son's body from the Hudson.

Blake's father put his arm around his wife's shoulder. "We appreciate your words. Sorry to have kept you."

The dogs, desperate to run now that they were off a chain, began whimpering.

"My wife's exhausted and cold," the man said. "We best be going."

The two grieving parents turned and walked down the trail, the woman first, dragging her right leg, the man two steps behind her. A minute later they were fifty yards away, haltingly mounting the next crest in the road.

Carlyle dropped his pack on the ground. "Jesus Christ."

"Their kid was earning eighty bucks a day when he was murdered," Pierce said. "And you wonder why the guides resent Marshall?" He leaned his shotgun on his shoulder and began walking. "Let's get moving before we freeze to death."

Somewhere to their right, down a steep embankment choked with dense undergrowth, thorn bushes, shrubs, and stunted pines, the Indian was gathering speed and power as it rushed through the valley.

After a mile of snow, stagnant water, and thick red mud, the trail began to rise. Five minutes later, Carlyle reached the crest of a hill and stared down at the river. Sunlight reflecting off a single, never-ending wave train flooded the air with blue-white brilliance. A long, pencil-thin island, little more than a collection of rocks and tangled vegetation, bisected the current.

Pierce spat toward the river. "So this is where he's been operating."

"A month from now," Carlyle said, "once the snowpack melts and the current drops, he'll be able to get at us from both sides of the gorge." He stared at the forest encircling them. "When those trees leaf out, it'll be almost dark at ground level and impossible to track him."

"Don't worry," Pierce said. "We won't have to go looking for him. He'll find us."

A half-hour later, they reached a wood-and-pipe barrier topped by a sign: *Mt. Rushmore Club. Members Only.*

Rather than face harassment by a six-man security staff that patrolled the property, they turned off the road and slogged through knee-deep snow, bushwhacking toward the Indian. Fallen trees, boulders, and rotting logs blocked the path. Plowing through snowdrifts and bending low to avoid overhanging branches, they continued to move north.

From the sound of it, the Indian was now no more than two-hundred and fifty yards away. Attempting to sidestep a boulder, Carlyle placed his right foot on rough ground, turned his ankle, and fell forward. Up to his elbows in snow, he hauled himself to his knees, then pushed himself into a standing position.

"You okay?" Pierce said.

"I fell just like that cross-country skiing eight years ago. Dislocated my left shoulder. Three snowmobilers found me and brought me back to the road. Had to wait an hour for an ambulance to arrive." Despite two layers of protective gear, Carlyle's hands had turned white with cold. Snow had invaded his boots. "You bring any coffee in that thermos?"

"I did."

"I'll have some of it when we reach the river."

Pierce stared at the trees around them. "Finding our way back is going to be a bitch."

"No it won't. Just turn around. See your footsteps coming down from the escarpment? No matter where we go, we'll know that the road's right up there. If we head for that ridge, we can't get lost. Meanwhile, keep your eyes open. This would be a great spot for a hideout with a view of the river."

A twenty-mile-an-hour wind rushed through the narrow gorge and the temperature began to drop as they closed in on the Indian. Ten minutes later, shoving their way through waist-high thorn bushes, the two men reached the river.

"I know now why you people love this forest," Pierce said.

"No one's ever going to clear-cut these woods again, that's for sure."

Pierce pulled the thermos from his pack. When they'd finished the coffee and started walking again, he said, "I don't understand how he gets in here without someone coming across him."

"He stays off well-used trails during the day and hides out somewhere at night."

"Why not bring in equipment to track the bastard?"

"Helicopters and heat-seeking radar don't work in dense undergrowth. We have to understand his behavior, see if patterns emerge, and anticipate his next move. Then, if he makes just one dumb mistake, we can take him down."

Pierce shook his head. "I bet you think all criminals are just misguided souls. They're not. The majority are vicious assholes. Robbing and mayhem give them power or pleasure."

"Then that shotgun of yours is useless. This person will never let himself get caught. But if we can figure out what he wants, we may be able to negotiate with him."

Pierce, who never took his eyes off the woods, laughed. "Negotiate with this guy?"

"You don't believe people can change?"

"I don't have time for psychology; I'm too busy dealing with robbers and drunks. That's why I carry this Glock and a shotgun, because the people I have to arrest think weapons will solve all their problems."

Carlyle peeled back his sleeve and glanced at his watch. "It's two. We better start back. It'll take us almost three hours to get back to the truck." When they'd reached the Indian, they'd moved right, to the north-west, to avoid a thick line of trees and bushes. Then they'd clambered over several rocks and crossed a large stretch of ice. The sun had been over their left shoulders when they started out; now it was high in the sky and to their right.

"This way." Carlyle made a new set of postholes in the heavy fresh snow as he plodded up the hill, constantly scanning the terrain. He stopped for a second to catch his breath and pointed to a blank space in the cliff face above them. "See that?"

"What the hell are you looking at?"

Carlyle grabbed the branch of a yearling pine with his left hand and pointed with his right. "The boulder to our left. About one o'clock. It's just above that. Let's take a closer look."

Carlyle bent down on all fours and crawled up through dense undergrowth. When he stopped, he saw a cave, larger than the one he and the other guides had come across in Cedar Ledges.

"Must be a bear," Pierce said.

Carlyle dug a headlamp from his pack, switched it on, and began to crawl inside. "If it is a bear, now's the time to put some shells in that shotgun."

As his eyes adjusted to the cold white beam of his light, he could see a space six feet high by eight wide, the back wall hidden in shadows.

"What the hell is this?" Pierce said.

"The answer to our question."

"Which one is that?"

"Where he hides out at night."

Balsam fir shavings littered the cave floor. A rough plank bed covered by a gray woolen blanket sat against the left wall. Resting on the bed was a pair of wool gloves and hobnailed leather boots. A tin plate, knife and fork, and an earthen jug lay on a low shelf. A hiking stick and a cane pack basket with leather straps leaned against the right wall.

Pierce pointed to a tall wooden tool topped by a curved metal hook. "What's that?"

Carlyle pulled it toward him. "I've seen pictures of this thing. It's a pike pole."

"What the hell's it for?"

"When these woods were worked by hand, it was used to unpack logjams during spring river drives."

"How long ago was that?"

"Seventy, eighty years."

"You're kidding me."

Carlyle placed the pole on the ground and swept his light along the far wall. Four thin lines, each several inches high, had been carved into the rock with a blade. "Jesus Christ."

"What are those?"

"He sabotaged Marshall's crew twice last year and killed two guides this season. I think he's keeping score."

Pierce looked around the cave. "You only see these things in junk shops and flea markets. What the hell's all of it doing out here?"

When Carlyle had begun working on the Hudson, he learned that he'd have to tell his clients stories about how explorers and guides took control of the backcountry. Haunting used bookstores and libraries, he'd studied histories of the region and collected old photographs and postcards. The second he crawled inside this cave, he remembered he'd seen something like it before.

"It's a replica of the bunk room in a logging camp. Or the cabin of someone who spent his winters alone in the woods. A caretaker maybe, or just some poor unemployed bastard who had nowhere else to go."

"Why would someone take the time to lug this stuff into the backcountry?"

"Good question," Carlyle said. "But we've got one answer to our problem at least."

"What's that?"

"How he can move around undetected. You can't see it from up above or from the river. He hikes in at night, holes up here till dawn, and lays a trap for us. Then he comes back and waits until our boats have passed."

Carlyle took another look around the cave. "This changes everything. If he has this place, he's got others. Each one gives him access to a different stretch of the river."

Pierce bent down and began backing out of the cave. "I've seen enough. Let's get out of here."

Carlyle grabbed his shoulder. "Stop. Now move back slowly toward me."

Pierce inched into the cave while Carlyle reached over him and lifted something from his pack. "Okay. Now stay low and crawl out."

When both were back in sunlight, Pierce said, "What the hell were you doing?"

"You were caught on a thin wire." Carlyle stood up and took a deep breath. "It wasn't attached to a device, though."

"That crazy bastard."

"He just rigged it up to scare the hell out of anyone who found this place."

"This guy is certifiable. We'll need a hundred men to find him."

"An army won't help us out here," Carlyle said. "He's as good as Rambo. And you know what happened to the morons who tried to stop that lunatic."

Carlyle turned his back on the cave and, following a switchback in the cliff face, scrambled up toward the road. After several minutes of pushing through thorn bushes, he was able to make his way to level ground.

"I nearly got blown up because of you," Pierce said, "and we still don't know shit about this guy."

"We know he's some kind of history buff—"

"History freak is more like it. Can't you give me something more specific to go on, for Christ's sake?"

"—and probably a local with longtime ties to the region. We have the names, prison records, and life histories of everyone in this county who's committed a felony going back a hundred years. If criminal behavior runs in families, we may be able to narrow down our list of suspects."

"That's it?"

Carlyle shouldered his pack. "Our best bet is to keep exploring his vendetta against the Marshalls."

"We're still at square one. Any idea what our next step is?"

"These woods are his territory, a place he knows and feels safe. We have to figure out some way to lure him out of here."

"How do you do that?"

"Use bait he won't be able to resist," Carlyle said.

Ten minutes later, the two men walked up to Carlyle's truck. A second note lay on top of the one Carlyle had left. He brushed off the snow and read it.

"It's from Bognor. He says DEC has given Marshall permission to take clients back to the Hudson."

"When's this supposed to happen?"

"Tomorrow."

"You going with them?"

"I have to," Carlyle said. "My name's on the permit."

ELEVEN

At 5:00 a.m. on Thursday, an hour before sunrise, he wrestled the canoe into the bone chilling water. The sky was black, the trees mere stick figures, the river deafening. He could not risk buying the Grumman from someone local, so he'd taken the ferry to Vermont yesterday and hauled the boat back after dark. He might die if he made a mistake out here today, but vengeance has its costs. People might call him a madman, but privately they would be amazed by his audacity.

The heavy canoe moved sluggishly in the current. The headlamp strapped to his helmet washed over the boulders lining his path. He'd never felt such cold. Although wrapped in thick gloves, his hands were already numb, his fingers inflexible.

Moving slowly through mist blanketing the Indian, he picked his way downstream. Working almost sightless, he was seconds from disaster.

Forty-five minutes later, just as the sun broke over the horizon, he slithered down the left side of Cedar Ledges and straight into Entrance, where he simply abandoned himself to the boulder-strewn rapid.

Knowing he could not do the next stretch in semidarkness, he lined the boat down along the shore through the Narrows. Too exhausted to think straight, he trusted his instincts and experience to get him through Mile-Long. Having forgotten what warmth felt like, it took him another hour to reach his target at the bottom of Harris.

He wished he could see their faces when they realized he'd run the gorge in the dark. At first they'd simply deny that anyone could pull off such a stunt. He had accomplices, they would say, or he'd brought the boat in overland. Anything to deny him credit for daring and perseverance.

Bognor and the others might discover who he was and why he was doing this, but he would never give up, never disappoint his grandfather, never let Marshall's old man get his way with the property on Johnston Mountain.

In Harris, the pain was beyond words. He had to stand in the freezing current, his feet and legs turning to stone, aware that he could be swept downstream any second. It took him nearly thirty minutes to find a place to put the boat and to secure the bow and stern with lashing straps.

By the time his work was done, ice hung from his helmet and he could feel nothing from the waist down. His left arm, the one he had broken two years ago, hung limp at his side. The skin on his face and hands felt as fragile as ancient parchment.

When he was sure the canoe wouldn't be discovered until it was too late, he dragged himself from the water, hid his gear under thick brush, and turned his back on the river. Following the route he had marked two days ago, he scrambled up the embankment, made his way across the iron and oak trestle, and disappeared into the woods.

Carlyle awoke just after dawn. Beth was already sitting in a chair underneath the window.

"What are you doing today?" he said.

"I was planning to work on the garden."

He put his right hand on her shoulder. "I'll help when I get back this afternoon."

"If you're here before dark, sure. I'd like that."

Carlyle went downstairs and made coffee. Fog shrouded the pond, and gray clouds enveloped the escarpment as he drove away from the house. Taking narrow, meandering back roads east to the Hudson, he turned left onto the highway that bordered the river, and, avoiding the city, headed north.

Elevated highway ramps carved their way through the industrial landscape. Plastic bags and refuse littered the roadside. It took Carlyle half an hour to put the junkyards, tank farms, derelict piers, cement plants, railroad sidings, and abandoned factories behind him.

At 7:00 a.m., thirty minutes before the other guides arrived, Carlyle found Grace Irwin on her hands and knees in the living room of the lodge, surrounded by crushed beer cans, crumpled pizza boxes, and overflowing ashtrays.

"You would think," she said, "that grown men wouldn't leave their shit around where other people, namely me, would have to pick it up."

Carlyle bent down and began helping her corral the garbage. "Grace, how's my favorite goat farmer?"

"Sherlock. You near to catching that madman yet?"

"We've got half the state police out looking for him."

"How many cops does it take to find one dumb schmuck?"

"If your neighbors would help us, it might be over sooner."

"People around here are of two minds," she said. "They hate what that killer's doing, but they can't stand Marshall's father."

A black pickup turned into the parking lot. "Well, well," Grace said. "Tarzan's here."

"Betts?"

"Who else would drive a gas guzzler like that?"

Ten minutes later, after Carlyle had inspected the rafts they'd be using today, he found Hernandez, Nash, and Betts standing quietly around the coffee pot. "What's going on?" Carlyle said.

"Burton had two boats flip in the Narrows yesterday," Hernandez said. "He had people and equipment scattered all up and down the river."

"It wasn't our guy," Carlyle said, "if that's what you're thinking."

"How can you be so sure?" Nash said.

"He's only after Marshall."

"It's true," Hernandez said. "When they picked up the crew and their clients downstream from Osprey, his guides apologized for making a dumb mistake."

Nash finished his coffee and put the cup into the sink. "Why hasn't Marshall's father taken care of this mess yet?"

"Apparently, there are limits," Carlyle said, "even for millionaires."

Marshall stomped out of his office. "You see the damned weather report?"

The snowmelt usually began pouring into the gorge in mid-April, but the jet stream parked itself over the Adirondacks at the beginning of the month and late afternoon thunderstorms had never let up.

"The gauge is already up to 7.9," Marshall said. "By the time we get there, the Narrows is going to be a bitch." He looked at his clipboard. "You know the routine. I'll run first. Betts and Hernandez follow me. Keith will be our sweep."

"Hold on a second," Carlyle said. "You mind if I make a suggestion?"

Marshall glared at him. "About what?"

Carlyle pulled a small yellow card from his pocket and studied it. "Why don't you have Keith lead us through the gorge. Betts will follow him. Hernandez takes the three spot. You can run sweep."

"What are you talking about?" Marshall said.

"If we run into trouble, we can count on you to pick up the pieces."

Marshall checked his watch. "You have any idea how long I've been running my operation this way?"

"Why don't you ask the others what they think?"

Marshall turned to Nash. "Is this the first time you've heard of his plan?"

"Of course."

"You agree with him?"

"What can you lose?"

Marshall put his clipboard down on the dining room table and stared at Carlyle. "You got any more advice for me this morning?"

Carlyle checked his list. "We should leave twenty yards between boats, not ten."

"Why's that?"

"It'll give us more time to react in case there's an accident."

"And what makes you so sure he'll hit us again?"

"Until we know what this guy is after, another attack may be unavoidable."

"Is that it, then?" Marshall said.

"One more thing. I want to choose the people who go in Keith's boat."

Marshall grabbed the list in Carlyle's hand and tore it up. "You've certainly got some balls. But just remember this. Once we get back here, I'm taking over this outfit again."

"I'm not asking you to give up control of anything," Carlyle said. "Let's just try it my way this time. See how things turn out."

Marshall slammed down his coffee cup and walked into his office.

Carlyle passed Grace on the way out of the lodge. She was selling use-it-and-toss-it rain gear and souvenir t-shirts to three women who'd just pulled into the parking lot. "Excuse me a moment, will you?" she said to her clients. "I've got to pick a fight with one of our guides." She walked out from behind her desk and pulled Carlyle aside. "Sherlock. Hold on a minute."

Carlyle dropped his gear bag on the ground. "I've got a trip to run."

She grabbed the sleeve of his dry suit. "I just heard what went on in there. Are you serious? Talking to him like that?"

"The storm will pass, don't worry."

"When are you going to realize he doesn't like getting sandbagged in front of his employees?"

"He's running out of options. What choice does he have?"

She shook her head. "You've been reading too many of them school-books, Carlyle. He'll never forget this."

An hour later, while walking from their bus to the headwaters of the Indian, Betts spotted Pierce standing next to an unmarked patrol car. "What's that asshole doing here?"

Carlyle nodded to the Deputy but said nothing to him. "Pierce may not be the only cop on duty today."

"That's just what we need right now, a shoot-out on the river." Betts, who was carrying a large jug of water in his right hand, shifted it to his left. "By the way, you see these clients? A couple of them look like ads for human growth hormone."

"Don't complain. We may just need all that muscle."

The light rain turned into a steady downpour as Carlyle and Betts slid down the muddy slope to the put-in. Hernandez, who looked relieved to have a strong crew for once, kept busy rearranging the equipment in his boat. Marshall, at the back of the line, sat tight-lipped, waiting for the trip to begin.

"You better prepare yourself for one huge river today," Betts said.

"What are you talking about?" Carlyle said.

"The guy at the sluice was told to keep the gate wide open all morning. The town's worried about upstream flooding."

"You sure?"

"Absolutely. It'll add another foot to what we have already. By the time this is over, Marshall may wish for once that he'd cancelled a trip."

As they waited for the go-ahead signal from Nash, Betts gave his standard "paddle or die" speech to their crew. He sounded like one of those shipwrecked Arctic explorers, tight-lipped and grim in the face of an approaching calamity. After he'd finished putting the fear of God into them, he turned to Carlyle. "Now we're supposed to just sit here and wait like fish in a barrel?"

"Keep it down, will you? Let's just follow Keith and stay out of trouble."

"Stay out of trouble?" Betts said. "Why the fuck didn't I think of that?"

Nash, with a crew working like galley slaves, led the four-boat convoy quickly through the first series of staircase rapids. They reached the eddy at the bottom of Gooley Steps in twenty minutes and pulled over for a quick break.

Water poured off Betts's helmet. "If this rain doesn't let up soon, we could be in deep shit."

"You've seen it worse than this." Carlyle knew, however, that they'd be trapped in the gorge between sheer granite walls for at least two hours. If this madman had figured out how to attack them in Mile-Long or Givenny's, their boats would be scattered all up and down the river, like rabbits in a cornfield, ready to be picked off.

Despite Carlyle's concern about another attack, Marshall's outfit made it from the Confluence to Blue Ledge Basin in one piece.

After his crew went off to stretch their legs, Betts said, "What if I told you this might be my last season?" He was also eyeing the three men and three women in Nash's raft who, instead of goofing around, as most clients did, were examining their gear and talking quietly.

Carlyle pulled a small thermos of coffee from his dry bag. "You're bailing out on us?"

"You know what it's like having a bull's-eye on your back every time you get on this river?"

"We're going to catch this guy."

"You think you'll still be around to see that day?"

"What do you mean?"

Betts rose from his seat in the cockpit. "Marshall's terminally pissed. You made him look like an idiot this morning with that boat-order stunt."

"He can't get rid of me just yet."

"I wouldn't turn my back on him." Betts walked away from the raft. "I better get these schmucks back here. Nash looks like he's getting ready to shove off."

Despite a current that had grown in size and velocity as they got closer to the gorge, Marshall's four boats made it safely through the Narrows and Mile Long Rapid. Around 1:30, with Nash providing hand signals to warn them of obstacles, they picked their way through two rock-lined channels in Gunsight Rapids. When their boat made a hard-right-hand turn at the end of Gunsight, Carlyle could see the top end of Harris Rift and, in the distance, the derelict wood and steel trestle spanning the Hudson.

Nash was fifty yards ahead of them when Carlyle leaned toward Betts. "Get going, will you. We need to stay close to him."

"What's the rush?"

"I told you all this morning. I want us within hailing distance. Just move the boat."

Betts stood up on the back tube of their raft. "He's almost over the edge. We'll never get near him now."

Avoiding a half-dozen recircs and hydraulics, Betts and Carlyle rushed down the right side of Harris. Four minutes later, they found Nash sitting in tall grass, holding a pressure bandage to his forehead. Blood ran down his face and hands. His life vest was gone and vomit was splattered across the front of his dry suit.

Carlyle jumped from his raft and rushed over to him. "What the hell happened?" he said, kneeling down in front of Nash.

"Everything was going fine, then just as I maneuvered us between those two boulders, we ran into something and, bam, we turned over. I got trapped under the boat, my right foot caught between the floor of the raft and the thwart."

While Nash described his ordeal, two people from his crew, standing in current up to their knees, hooked a line to a D-ring on his raft and pulled it from the water.

Nash tried to stand up. "They're not supposed to do that," he said. "Get them out of there, will you?"

"I'll take care of it in a second," Carlyle said, "You have any idea how long you were under?"

"Long enough to think about how Blake died." Nash took a couple of deep breaths and winced.

"How'd you get out?" Carlyle said.

Nash pointed to one of the women wearing a green and blue wetsuit standing next to the Hudson. "She slipped into the current, fought her way down to me, and slit the thwart. That freed my foot." He looked straight at Carlyle. "How the hell did she know to do that?"

Carlyle turned and stared at the woman.

Nash's hands would not stop shaking. "You also mind telling me why she happens to be carrying a six-inch knife?"

The woman who'd saved Nash was speaking quietly to the other members of her crew. The guy to her left began taking notes of their conversation.

"What's going on?" Nash said. "They look like commandos, for fuck's sake."

"First tell me what you ran into down there," Carlyle said.

"Look for yourself."

Carlyle walked to the edge of the river. Looking down, he could see the shimmering outline of an aluminum canoe, like some huge silver marlin, wedged between two boulders.

Hernandez and then Marshall pulled into an eddy five yards upstream and rushed over. "Why'd you stop?" Marshall yelled. "What's going on?"

"He did it again," Carlyle said. "Laid a trap for us."

"Tell him about the woman," Nash said. "The commando, or whatever the hell she is, who saved me."

"What about her?" Marshall said.

"You're not going to like this," Carlyle said. "She's a cop."

Marshall's face turned red and he threw his guide paddle into the grass. "What's a cop doing here?"

"Calm down," Carlyle said. "Once DEC approved this trip, I convinced the agency that we needed people who could handle an emergency. Then I made sure they were in the lead raft with Nash. The one that would get hit first."

"Are you telling me you knew about all this?"

"We were pretty sure that if our guy heard you were going out today, he wouldn't pass up the chance to attack again."

"Who approved this goddamn plan of yours?"

"DEC, Bognor, and the state police. They all signed off on it."

"That's why you changed the boat order this morning?" Marshall said.

"I wanted our best crew up front."

"How many cops are with us?" Nash said.

"They're all cops. Six are from a Coxsackie dive team, eight are detectives from Albany, and five are EPB."

Nash looked confused. "EP what?"

"Executive Protection Bureau. The Governor's bodyguard."

"You used us as guinea pigs?" Nash said.

"No, I surrounded you with the best people we had."

Betts stood up and adjusted the clasp on his helmet. "Don't let me interrupt your little tea party."

"What the hell are you doing?" Carlyle said.

"If some other boat comes through here, we could have another shit storm." He dragged his raft closer to the submerged canoe.

Carlyle grabbed Betts's arm. "Leave it for the dive team."

"Get your hand off me. Someone could drown while you stand around." He shrugged off his life vest, took a deep breath, and slid over the side of his raft into the water.

Nash stood up. "That's crazy. He doesn't have to do that."

"Betts does what's necessary, not what's logical," Carlyle said.

Betts fought his way down to the canoe, pulled a knife from his leg sheath, and cut through the lashing straps wrapped around the two boulders. When the canoe burst to the surface, he shoved it out of the current and dragged himself into the cockpit of his raft.

"Your right hand's bleeding," Carlyle said. "Let Marshall take care of it."

"I'll bandage it later."

Carlyle turned to Nash. "It's time to move out. You ready to finish the trip?"

"I'm fine. Let's get going."

"You still look a bit shaky," Carlyle said. "I better take over lead boat."

Nash laughed. "I can't wait to see what Marshall says, but go right ahead."

Carlyle gathered up his gear and stepped into the cockpit of Betts's raft.

"What's going on?" Betts said.

"What's it look like? You can't drive us back to North River with your hand like that." Carlyle grabbed the guide paddle and shoved his foot into the restraining strap.

"You're not licensed for this."

"You think some ranger's going to ticket me because I took over for an injured guide?"

"Fine. Just get us out of here. My hand's killing me."

Carlyle leaned out over the water, pulled them into the current, and maneuvered the raft slowly between a series of boulders. Five minutes later, the clouds lifted as they floated clear of Harris. Nearing the remains of the old trestle spanning the river, Carlyle kept the raft far from the concrete bridge pilings as the Hudson, near flood stage now, poured south.

"Looks like it's all coming back to you," Betts said.

Carlyle didn't take his eyes from the river. "Did you really think I'd forget everything I'd learned about this business?"

They came up on Greyhound Rapid at two thirty. The Hudson was over a hundred yards wide here. A rock wall bisected the current, creating a deep trench with a ferocious low-head dam on its downstream side. On days when they had strong crews, Carlyle and the other guides would surf the boil line over and over. They stopped playing this game when the teenage son of a TV anchor got tossed into the trench one afternoon and almost drowned.

Carlyle told his crew, "Because we've got to get sissy-face here to a doctor, we'll go round this thing today. Come back again when the river's boiling and I'll show you some real fun."

As Betts nursed his wound, Carlyle led Nash, Hernandez, and Marshall down the Hudson, past the now-abandoned Barton Mines, and out of the gorge.

Ten minutes later, Betts said, "Shit."

Carlyle spun around to check the rafts behind him. All looked fine. "What's wrong?"

"I dropped my knife." Blood seeped from his injured hand.

Marshall's four rafts pulled into a small cove near North River at 3:15. The state police helicopter that had been hovering over the convoy for the past ten minutes banked right and raced back toward the gorge. Carlyle could see Bognor, Pierce, two DEC forest rangers, and a half-dozen stone-faced state troopers standing just off the road. The rain had stopped, but a thick gray fog had begun to settle over the valley.

The cops who'd been on the river today shook hands with their five guides, gathered up their gear, and marched toward two sixteen-passenger government vans with blacked-out windows.

Before she left, the woman who'd saved Nash's life in Harris walked up to him. "I admire the way you took over that raft after the ordeal you went through."

"I'm fine now, but I don't know how to thank you."

"You could ask for my phone number for a start."

"Are you kidding me?" he said with a smile.

She pulled a card from her pack. "Just call. I'll be home tonight after seven."

A state police sergeant approached Marshall. "I'd like you to follow me. My boss wants you to provide a statement about what happened out there today."

"Who's going to watch our gear?" Marshall said.

The sergeant slowly looked around at the gathering of law-enforcement personnel and raised an eyebrow at Marshall. "I guarantee, no one's going to touch your stuff."

After Betts and Hernandez left for the lodge, Bognor, limping slightly, came over to Carlyle.

"How'd you all hear about the accident?" Carlyle said.

"That's was one of the best equipped outfits I've ever seen. One of the people in Nash's raft even had a satellite phone." Bognor stared at Carlyle. "You want to talk about it?"

Carlyle described the accident in Harris. "We almost lost Nash back there."

"How come you were you driving that raft when you pulled in just now?"

Carlyle told Bognor how Betts had cut his hand freeing the canoe from the river. "Don't tell Pierce I was working without a license. I've had enough grief for one day."

Bognor pulled out a notebook. "I've got a few more questions. You mind going over this once more?" They moved to a patch of open ground overlooking the valley. "Any idea why our suspect put that canoe right there?"

"It seems pretty obvious. He knows that Marshall always takes that route."

"How'd he get that thing into the gorge?"

Carlyle looked to his left, upstream, toward the mountains. "There's only one way he could have done it. He brought it down through the Narrows."

"What do you mean, brought it?"

"You've never back been in there, have you?"

"Ric, I'm five ten and weigh two-forty. Do I look like someone who would run that river?"

"He paddled the canoe through the gorge himself."

"When?"

"It had to be around dawn, before anyone else showed up."

"Are you serious?"

"Getting a canoe through that canyon when the river's this high is nearly impossible. But with almost no light, it's sheer madness. I've been on that river in some terrible conditions, but this stunt was off the charts."

"Goddamn."

"So now we know something else about our suspect—he's an expert boatman, so obsessed with his hatred of Marshall that he's willing to kill another guide and risk his own life if necessary."

Bognor glanced over his shoulder. "Could it be one of Marshall's guides?"

"I thought about that. Only Nash and Betts have that kind of skill. But neither of them had enough time to make the canoe run and get back in time for this trip.""Any idea how he got away once he finished with the canoe?"

"He must have bailed out somewhere in the backcountry," Carlyle said. "He could still be out there now, for all we know."

Bognor lit a cigarette. "You realize what this means?"

"He's not bottled up west of the Narrows like we thought. Terrain is irrelevant. He goes where he wants to."

Bognor closed his notebook. "Raines is going to have a stroke when she hears this."

Pierce and Marshall left a state police Crime Scene trailer and approached the two men. "Mind if we listen in?" Pierce said.

"Caleb," Bognor said, "This conversation will go a lot easier without your constant sarcasm."

Carlyle turned to Marshall. "I guess you realize that this guy knows everything about your operation. Which rafts you use, your boat order, what time you take off from Indian Lake. All of it."

"Ryan," Bognor said, "I hate to say this, but if Ric is correct, it may be time to close you down for good."

"Hold on a second, John," Carlyle said. "There may be a better way of handling this. We've learned a good deal about him in the past two weeks. When he gets anywhere near this river, he's almost impossible to stop. And we can't just wait for him to find us. That means we have to try another tactic."

"Okay, let's hear this bright new idea of yours," Pierce said.

"We flush him out of the woods."

"You're really not saying that we go in there after him, are you?" Bognor said.

"What other choice do we have?"

Pierce let the butt of his shotgun drop to the ground. "Wake up, will you? Thirty minutes after this operation begins, everyone within a hundred miles will know about it. Including the asshole we're looking for."

"But only two or three people will know where we're going." Carlyle pulled a topo map from his pack and unfolded it. "There's only three legitimate trails into the gorge east of Blue Ledges. We start at the top and work our way down."

"How many forest rangers will you need to find this guy?" Pierce said.

"I'm not planning on using any."

"You want to tell me, then, who's dumb enough to track this killer?"

"Wells and I will do it."

Pierce grabbed the map from Carlyle's hand. "You two are no match for that guy."

"Wells know this terrain better than anyone and he's just pissed off enough to try it."

"You think you can do what three different police agencies have been unable to?"

Carlyle reached over and took his map back from Pierce. "If you've got a better idea, either let us know what it is or stay out of our way."

Just before eight that evening, Carlyle found Beth sitting on the porch. A tiny lamp stood on a side table, an open book lay on her lap, and a cigarette lay smoldering in an ashtray. She had thrown on a hand-woven shawl that she'd bought in Taos last year.

Carlyle pulled out a chair next to her. "You haven't done that lately," he said.

"What?"

"Smoke."

"It was a long day."

He bent over and kissed her temple.

Beth said, "Are you okay?"

"Everything's fine." He would tell her later about Nash. "Can I take a look at the book?"

She passed the heavy volume toward him. "You may not like the image."

"Why not?"

"You once said you preferred realism."

Carlyle laughed. "I said that when we were dating. I was trying to impress you." He took the book from her hands. "You won't believe this. Even in this light, I can see it's Caravaggio."

"*The Conversion of St. Paul.*" Paul, wrapped in armor, a maroon cloak at his side, lay on his back beside an old man holding the bridle of a huge warhorse.

Carlyle stared at the painting for several minutes, its bold colors unmistakable even in the weak light. He looked outside at the shadows creeping across the garden and put the book back in her hands. "What's it supposed to mean?"

"I think Caravaggio's saying we can't trust reason, but emotions never lie."

"If everyone followed their gut, I'd never catch the madman who killed those two guides."

"Why not?"

"Everybody up north is trigger-happy."

Carlyle decided he had to tell Beth about his day. He described Nash's accident.

"Did anyone else get hurt?"

"Betts gashed his hand pulling the canoe out. That's all."

"You weren't in any danger?"

"No. But I had to drive our boat back to North River."

"How did it go?"

"You can't imagine how it feels to be in a raft when the river has some teeth in it, when it's fighting you every second."

Unable to sit still as he described his afternoon, Carlyle stood up, moved toward the window, and stared at the garden as the light faded. Furrows, deep and dead straight, stretched across it instead of weeds and brush. "Was someone working out there today?"

Beth picked up a wine glass. "I couldn't refuse his offer."

Carlyle kept his back to her. "Whose offer? What are you talking about?"

"Adrian's. He said he'd help us get ready for the spring."

"How long was he here?" Carlyle continued to study the expertly turned fields.

"Until about three."

"You said he'd left the area."

"He's got an apartment in town now."

Carlyle turned. "Listen to me, please. It's not safe to have him around us."

"Ric, there's nothing to worry about."

It was almost dark now. Carlyle put his glass on the table. "He probably thinks I'm responsible for booting him out of the program."

"How does that affect us?

"When graduate students get terminated, they can go a bit crazy. Some send menacing emails to their professors or phone in bomb threats to the university. One maniac in Utah stabbed his adviser as she was pushing her infant daughter in a stroller."

"Adrian's not capable of anything like that."

"Beth, let me explain something. The university employs a lawyer to do nothing but handle calls from faculty stalked by students, who can go berserk when they feel they've been mistreated by a professor. Why do you think I cancel my office hours at the end of the semester and suggest we leave town for a few days?"

"Adrian's really quite kind. He knows how busy you've been lately."

Carlyle turned to face her. "How can you be so certain this guy isn't dangerous?"

"You haven't been at home much. What was I supposed to do?"

"That's not fair."

Beth got up and walked into the kitchen. Carlyle watched as she put his dinner in the oven and, without looking back, went upstairs. A minute later the lights in her studio went on.

TWELVE

arlyle sat in a booth at the North Creek Diner at 7:20 on Saturday morning and watched the rain, driven by an unrelenting north wind, lash the shuttered store fronts that lined Main Street. If the temperature dropped another degree or two, the roads would ice up and the whitewater crowd, with no stomach for these conditions, would stay away from the river this weekend.

Leo Wells came through the front door ten minutes later. "You ever see anything like this?"

"Is it still illegal to shoot weathermen?" Carlyle said.

Wells stripped off his parka and gloves and slid into the booth. His deeply lined face, toughened by a decade in the mountains, looked drained. He was devoted to high-altitude rescue work, but it was an exhausting and solitary infatuation.

Carlyle had been to Wells's tiny, one-bedroom apartment once, several years ago. The place was filled with ice axes, crampons, first aid equipment, five pairs of mountaineering boots, high-tech flashlights, global positioning devices, a half-dozen portable weather radios, and enough camping gear to outfit an army platoon. Women who saw the place knew that Wells would never make room in his life for a family.

"What happened?" Carlyle said. "You look like shit."

"I thought you admired the Marlboro Man look."

"Seriously."

Wells began rapping the salt shaker against the table. "A couple of kids in a rowboat tried to run the low-head dam below Thompson's Falls. We've been out all night searching for them."

Carlyle rested his arms on the table. "You find anything?"

"Just the boat and two life vests. The bodies will probably wash up downstream in a day or so."

The waitress who took their order recognized Carlyle. "How soon before they catch that guy who's been killing guides?"

"Wish I could tell you, Ruth."

A four-man line crew from the local power company burst into the diner. They wore bright orange vests and carried heavy leather tool belts, thick felt gloves, and hardhats. One of them left his scrum to slap Wells's shoulder. "Leo, I heard about last night. You went into that wave below the dam to look for the bodies? That's insane."

Wells drained his first cup of coffee. "Tell that to the parents."

The lineman turned to Carlyle. "Your friend here's going to get killed one of these days if he's not careful. Keep an eye on him." He rejoined his crew.

"It's been nearly two weeks," Wells said. "You have any suspects yet?"

Carlyle pulled a small notebook from his backpack and placed it on the table. "I did background checks on everyone who's worked for the town the past five years. Three people—one on the highway crew and two in maintenance—have minor criminal records, but we haven't been able to connect them to this."

"Anything else turn up?"

"Marshall had a client a year ago who broke his leg in Soup Strainer."

"Did one of the guides make an error?"

"No, but the dude fractured his left femur and eventually lost his job."

"Why'd he show up on your radar?"

Carlyle watched the rain beat against the diner's windows. "He wrote some angry letters to the local paper blaming Marshall for his injury. I don't think he's our guy, though. Ryan's insurance company paid him to drop his suit."

"Anybody else on your list?"

"The fly-fishing crowd have spent big bucks trying to keep rafters off the river. I don't think they're desperate enough to try rough stuff, though."

"What about the paper mills? I heard Marshall's father took them to court, angling for exclusive rights to the water coming off the Indian Lake dam."

"If you're asking me if these people would play hardball to protect their operations, the answer's yes. They stand to lose millions."

Every time someone entered or left the diner, a blast of frigid air poured into the room. "So we've got nothing to go on so far," Wells said.

"Until that thing yesterday in Harris, everyone assumed that we had this guy confined to the Indian." Carlyle moved their coffee cups to one side, pulled a map from his pack, and placed it in front of Wells. "Our mistake was thinking that the gorge was outside his reach."

Carlyle pointed to the Hudson, a pale blue streak in the center of the page. It plunged due south and then east before flowing into the gorge, the vital link connecting the central Adirondack watershed to the ocean. "We neglected the surrounding territory."

"What did we miss?"

"The first trail that would give him access to the gorge itself."

Wells moved his hand slowly across the map. Carlyle shook his head. "Not south of the river. Look at the other side."

Wells pointed to a tiny dotted line running east and south through the backcountry. "Holy Christ."

"That's right. The Huntley Pond trail. It dead-ends at Blue Ledges, two hundred yards from the Narrows."

"How the hell did you find it?" Wells said.

"Are you kidding me? I've been staring at that map every day for the past two weeks."

Wells pulled the ADK guide to the Central Adirondacks from his jacket pocket. "It's no more than three miles each way. That means he can get to the river and back to the road in four hours."

"And once Marshall's rafts reach Blue Ledges, he's a sitting duck in the canyon."

"Why didn't I see it before?"

"Because you've been too busy trying to save people who think they're scaling Everest," Carlyle said.

"What happens now?"

The waitress put scrambled eggs and toast in front of Carlyle, pancakes and sausage before Wells. "You read the paper this morning, Leo?" she said.

"It's still in my car, but I have a hunch you're going to tell me what I missed."

"Marshall's father is evicting the families living on his land. He wants them gone by Christmas."

Wells put his knife and fork down. "What's that got to do with these murders?"

"Do I need to spell it out for you? It's why everyone around here hates his kid."

"You don't mean that," Wells said.

"I don't? Just ask anyone in here what they think about the little prick."

As they drove away from Riparius in Wells's truck, Carlyle stared at the derelict houses lining the road. The local manufacturing economy had been dying off for a century. When the lumber and paper mills finally collapsed fifty years ago, it tore the guts out of a half-dozen communities. Men who'd followed their fathers into the mills for generations, giving up decent pay in exchange for meager benefits, now spent their days running ski lifts or managing convenience stores. Their wives, the primary breadwinners, were employed as waitresses, daycare attendants, babysitters, and teachers' assistants. But two measly salaries still didn't cover the cost of rent, food, diapers, and cigarettes.

Wells shifted into low gear to climb a hill. "Marshall's father is creating second homes for millionaires, not jobs for ordinary people. He cares about protecting the damn trees, not the men and women who need work."

Twenty minutes later, their truck left the paved road and followed a gravel track through a forest of beech and red maple. Sunlight now washed over the windshield. Losing control for a moment as the back end fishtailed, Wells eased his vehicle through a sharp hairpin. They crossed the Boreas River and followed the valley road west and north. Six miles from the turnoff, nearly a half-hour from Riparius, Wells pulled over and stopped.

"You really want to go in here without backup?"

Carlyle opened his door and stepped from the truck. "We could call Pierce, but then we'd have to listen to him laugh at us all day."

The two men gathered up their gear and moved down the trail. A thick stand of jack pine marched across the hillside above them. Two crows, wings folded, dropped out of the sky. Clouds and light rain returned to conceal the sun. A sign nailed to a tree read *Blue Ledges, 2.3 Miles.* Somewhere just below them, a stream coursed through dense vegetation.

Carlyle stopped for a second and looked around. "Jesus, it's so beautiful."

Wells gave him a gentle nudge. "You ought to quit that desk job of yours and spend more time out here."

"And hang off a cliff like you? No, thanks."

They stepped across a narrow footbridge spanning the creek and were engulfed by thick vines bearing greedy, adolescent leaves. A carpet of pine needles and white mushrooms muffled their footsteps. "Watch yourself," Wells said. "You don't want to turn an ankle on these rocks."

Carlyle pushed his way through the undergrowth lining the trail that angled downhill toward Huntley Pond. They crossed a series of small streams seeping into the lake and made their way over slick rocks toward higher ground. An escarpment to their left kept the trail in semidarkness.

Just as they were about to reach the end of the pond, Wells tumbled to the ground. Carlyle rushed over to him and knelt down. "What happened?"

Wells rolled over on his side and pushed himself to his knees. "My boot got caught on something."

"You okay?"

"I smacked my right elbow on a rock."

Wells stood up. "It's nothing. Let's get going."

After a quarter-mile, the trail turned its back on the pond, headed southwest, and entered a grove of beech trees. When the wind picked up, their pale brown leaves filled the air and covered the ground. "It looks like a snowstorm," Carlyle said as he walked through the bright foliage.

"Old growth stays on during the winter until new shoots appear. I've been in white-out conditions in April."

Twenty minutes later, the two men found a dry patch of ground and stopped to rest. Wells said, "You have any idea why this guy's after Marshall?"

"This may surprise you, but I don't think he's out to murder anyone."

Wells nearly dropped his water bottle. "Two guides from the same outfit have died. How can you say that?"

"He's single-minded, obsessed maybe, but we really don't know yet what he wants."

"He's a monster, for Christ's sake."

Carlyle chose his words carefully. "He's got a grudge against Marshall, that's all we can be sure of."

"What more proof do you need that the guy's nuts?"

"We don't know that he's insane," Carlyle said. "He's trying to send us a message, but, like most angry people, he's not sure how to do it."

"Okay, so how in hell do you get inside the mind of a killer?"

"You don't. You can only try to predict where he'll strike next."

Wells fiddled with his bootlaces. "How's Marshall holding up?"

"He's getting hit from all sides. A local paper sent a reporter out to dig up some dirt on his father. They found that he owns a thousand-acre property in Connecticut with a fifteen-room house and a barn filled with thoroughbreds. You should see the hate mail Ryan got when that story came out."

"So why's Marshall living in an unheated bungalow when he's got a millionaire father?"

Carlyle looked at his watch. "We'd better get moving or we'll get stuck out here after dark."

The trail wound through a field of granite boulders, skirted the bottom of a cliff, and entered a wide, well-watered valley. Moss covered every rock, and tiny white mushrooms carpeted the ground. Carlyle pointed to a stream rushing off the mountain and checked his map. "That must be headed to Virgin Falls."

"So we're near Entrance."

"Less than a half-mile now."

An ovenbird, shrieking wildly, plunged through the canopy over their heads. Thick clouds moved across the sun as they walked toward a gap in the cliffs that would take them to the gorge. The creek to their right, filled with blue-gray snowmelt, had carved a wide trench through the valley floor.

It was almost noon. In two weeks, black flies would begin swarming from the undergrowth. Anyone out here without a head net would be covered in bleeding wounds.

After another thirty minutes, Carlyle and Wells broke through underbrush and found themselves staring down on Entrance Rapid. Upstream, the Hudson emerged from a narrow space between two cliffs, veered right, and plunged downhill. Whitewater, backwashing waves, and bone-shattering drop-offs filled the quarter-mile boulder garden.

The sun, directly overhead now, had burned through the cloud cover. Every collision between water and rock became a light show. The river was turgid green below the surface and incandescent white in the waves. Jack pine and red spruce covered the hillsides.

Wells, holding onto a thick limb, peered down on Entrance. "If I were him, this would be my next target."

Carlyle pulled binoculars from his pack and swept the valley floor with his lenses. "We're vulnerable here, that's for sure. The river's got to be two hundred yards wide. There's no way to set up a z-drag if we had a boat wrapped on those rocks."

"He could lay a trap here and be back in these trees in minutes."

"Once we started down Entrance, we'd never see it coming and there's no place to pull over."

"Is there any way you could protect yourselves?"

"This guy always tries something new," Carlyle said. "How could we prepare for that?"

They turned their backs on Entrance, climbed steadily for another fifteen minutes, and then hiked carefully down a narrow switchback to the river. Breaking through undergrowth, they found themselves on a sand beach. White cedar, their bright green leaves glowing in the sunlight, lined both banks of the river.

Carlyle shrugged off his pack and stared at Blue Ledges, a three-hundred-foot wall of granite, on the far shore. The cliff dropped straight to the floor of the gorge. A sheet of ice sixty feet high and several inches thick hung from the rock. He remembered that one April morning as his raft slid silently past this spot, a ten-foot chunk of ice separated from the bluff and, shattering as it fell, crashed into the river not fifty feet from his boat.

Carlyle watched the Hudson cascade down through Entrance and into the basin at the foot of Blue Ledges. In the other direction, downstream, he could see the river gather momentum, rise into one massive standing wave, veer right, and then plunge into the Narrows.

"If some clients knew this trail was here, they'd probably walk out rather than face the gorge."

Wells was sitting on a boulder with his back to the cliff across from them.

"Not interested in the scenery?" Carlyle said.

"I don't need to see it." Wells was silent for a minute. "My sister died in a place just like this."

Carlyle said nothing.

"I was sixteen. She didn't make it home one night. The police organized a search party. I spent two days walking through the woods behind our house. My parents, afraid of what we would find, stayed inside the whole time. They found her a week later. Someone raped and murdered her, then threw her body into an abandoned quarry."

Carlyle stared at the ground. "What happened to your parents?"

"It took my mother six months to leave her bedroom. My dad had a heart attack two years later." Wells picked at his lunch. "The guy got twenty years, plus five on probation. We got a life sentence."

Wells turned to look at Carlyle. "That's the problem with professors. You actually think you can explain why someone like my sister was murdered."

Carlyle watched a hawk circle overhead. "Don't you want at least some sort of answer?"

"I don't believe all those clever explanations for why people become compassionate or cruel. Shit happens no matter what you or I do to prevent it." Wells threw his lunch in his pack and stood up. "What are we doing out here, anyway?"

"There's got to be some evidence that will help us locate this guy."

"How do you know that?"

"DEC brought a dog to Cedar Ledges several days ago," Carlyle said. "The animal found the tool that he used to drag the tree to the river. It's called a peavey, a four-foot pole with a spike and a sharp curved hook."

"Why bring something like that to the river?" Wells said.

Carlyle stood up and brushed the sand off his rain jacket. "That's the way it was done seventy-five years ago, when nearly everyone was logging by hand."

"What exactly are you saying?"

"I think Blake was murdered by a person who feels compelled to act out rituals that are important to him in some way."

"You want to explain that?"

"Your father shave with a blade razor?"

"So what?"

"You use one?

"That doesn't prove anything," Wells said. "Our suspect is still a nut case."

"At least we can work on the assumption that this guy has some connection, however weird, to the logging industry."

Wells looked at his watch. "Time to get going."

"As long as we're here, might as well take a look around."

"For what?"

"If this guy's out for revenge, he probably can't stop himself from planning another attack." Carlyle paced the beach. "Blue Ledges is perfect. Steps from the gorge, a place he could watch boats drift by on their way toward his trap."

"As long as we get out by dark," Wells said.

Clambering over a series of boulders, Carlyle wandered downstream, deeper into the gorge. With only three feet between the cliff and the rocks lining the river, he soon ran out of space to walk.

The sun was high over his left shoulder. Scanning the hillside, he saw a dull blue object hanging from a limb near the ground. He slowly pushed his way uphill into the woods and found a carabineer suspended from a Scotch pine. Several large branches and a thin layer of earth had been thrown over a hastily buried object.

He bent down and carefully shifted the underbrush and dirt to one side. When he'd finished, he realized why the job of finding the person who'd been targeting Marshall had been so difficult.

He hiked back up the beach to Wells. "Grab your gear and follow me."

They walked back to the hanging carabineer. Carlyle pointed to a snub-nosed whitewater kayak painted camouflage green, brown, and gray.

"Holy shit." Wells bent down to get a better look.

"He must have paddled this thing down from Indian Lake. Give me a hand." The two men, one on either side of the boat, rocked it back and forth to remove the remaining leaves.

"Why put it here?"

"So he could hike in early some morning, do whatever he needed to do, and be off the river before anyone found him." Carlyle bent down to examine the kayak. "If he can run a boat through the gorge when the river's this high, nowhere is safe."

"There could be other boats like this one."

"Probably." Carlyle turned over the kayak and reached inside. "Jesus Christ." He held up a tool topped by a ten-inch spike on one side and a six-inch curved barb on the other.

"What in hell's that?"

"It's a peavey. Just like the one they found near Blake's body."

Wells took the device from Carlyle's hand. "Why did he bring it all the way in here?"

Carlyle stared at the waves filling the Narrows. "Some people get fixated on weapons, old knives, bayonets, or antique rifles. Often it's something they've inherited from a favorite relative. When the pressure on them becomes too great, these objects make them feel invulnerable."

"What's the connection with the peavey?"

"It may remind him of a disturbing event he can't get out of his mind."

Wells handed the tool back to Carlyle. "Some family thing?"

"Maybe. Whatever it is, this peavey is one way we can figure out what's going on in his mind."

"But why carry around something so awkward?"

"It could make him feel he's got some special power. Who knows, he may even believe he's defending a way of life he shares with that relative. I've been sifting through the records of online antique shops. It's a collector's item. Sooner or later, I may come across a paper trail that will lead us to anyone who's purchased one."

"What about the carabineer? Why hang it where someone is sure to see it?"

"He may believe no one would ever walk all the way down here. Or maybe he's just taunting us."

"You have any idea yet what the peavey and the attacks on Marshall tell you about what's going on?"

"It suggests, and I'm just guessing at this point, that our guy has deep roots in this community. If so, he may see the outside world as hostile and frightening."

"But these attacks on Marshall, what's that about really?"

"This guy probably thinks he's on some sort of crusade. That's how he may justify the deaths of Sanders and Blake."

Wells grabbed the front loop of the kayak and began dragging it toward the water.

"What the hell are you doing?" Carlyle said.

"I'm depriving our enemy of a vital asset."

"Leave it," Carlyle said. "I've got a better idea." He pulled a three-inch Spyderco knife from his pocket and punched four holes in the top of the kayak.

"Are you crazy?"

Carlyle stood up. "This should get his attention. He's a tightly wound guy. If he goes ballistic over this, he's more likely to make a mistake."

"You've been around Betts too long."

"Maybe it's about time we started fighting back."

It began to rain heavily as Carlyle and Wells retraced their steps through the beech forest. Water washed off the hills, and the trail quickly turned to mud. Tiny fluorescent green buds, like Christmas lights, sprouted from every branch.

After two hours of slow hiking across now-slick rocks, the two men broke free of the undergrowth. Carlyle dropped his backpack and gazed at the Sheriff Department's cruiser sitting just off the road, twenty yards east of the trailhead. "Look who's here. Captain America."

The door opened and Pierce, clutching a twelve gauge in his right hand, spilled out of the driver's seat. "Well, well, if it isn't Butch and Sundance." He walked across the road.

"Caleb," Wells said. "What are you doing out here?"

Pierce propped his shotgun against a tree. "Bognor and I are trying to make sure you two don't get your asses shot off. Why in hell's name can't you just let the authorities handle this investigation?"

"What are you talking about?" Carlyle said.

"How long have you boys been out there on the trail?" Pierce said.

"Four hours," Wells said.

"And you didn't hear or see anything unusual?"

"Caleb," Carlyle said, "for Christ's sake. Will you tell us what's going on?"

"It seems as though our friend has decided to begin terrorizing locals now. Some guy wearing a full black beard and a Paul Bunyan outfit, plaid shirt and leather boots, ambushed a teenager hiking alone on Kettle Mountain."

"Where's the kid now?"

"At the state police barracks in North River. His parents are on the way over there."

"Did he describe this person?"

"When the kid stopped crying, he said the beard was fake, but the axe was real."

"What'd he do to the child?"

"He tied him up with duct tape and left him lying ten yards off the trail."

"Is he hurt?"

"No, but this guy we're after has a real sick sense of humor. He gave the kid a water bottle and told him if he moved before an hour was up, he'd come back with the axe and his parents would have to pick up body parts all up and down the mountain."

Pierce got back in his car and rolled down the window. "One more thing. Bognor says to tell you DEC wants you in Albany Saturday morning. Some guy named Elliot is on the warpath."

THIRTEEN

After being kept waiting for twenty minutes, Carlyle and Bognor were ushered into a conference room on the eighth floor of DEC headquarters. It was 10 a.m. They found Karen Raines standing next to Abel Elliot.

Raines motioned for them to sit down. "Sheriff, the commissioner believes we need to make more progress in your investigation. He's asked Abel to evaluate the way you're handling the situation in Warrensburg."

"I understand what's going on, Karen," Bognor said. "Shit runs downhill. It's my turn to get called on the carpet."

"Not at all," Elliot said. "But before we begin, I'd like to ask Ric how things are going at the university."

"You're referring to my application for tenure."

"I just wanted you to know that if it doesn't go well, you should apply for a job in our Policy Enforcement Unit."

"I'm a criminologist, not a cop."

Elliot stood up, walked to the south-facing windows, and turned down the blinds. "Let's hope your investigation is successful, then."

Raines turned off her cell phone. "I think it's time to hear your report. Abel has a busy schedule today."

Carlyle described how he had proven that Sanders and Blake were murdered and that two earlier accidents were caused by the same person. "But we still haven't determined who has a grudge against Marshall."

"Your target could be a guide," Elliot said.

Carlyle pulled a small laptop from his briefcase. "That's the first thing I thought of." He paged through the relevant files. "Two hundred and seventy-five licensed guides have worked on the river since 1997. The majority were locals—carpenters, construction workers, electricians. People well known around town. I've also interviewed all the clerical and lodge staff, Marshall's and Burton's."

"Let's just skip the details and hear the results," Elliot said.

"If you want an answer," Bognor said, "you'll have to let Ric explain how he's gone about his work."

"Trust me, Sheriff," Elliot said. "The commissioner doesn't have time for background. He just wants a solution to this crisis."

"We both know your boss will make time if his department becomes the focus of a media blitz."

"What exactly do you mean by that?"

Bognor smiled. "It's pretty obvious. If the Johnston Mountain Project is delayed, everyone in this room will have to explain why the killer hasn't been brought to justice."

Elliot said. "Go on with your report, Ric."

"The people who run boats through the gorge aren't a bunch of yokels. We've had doctors, EMTs, paramedics, cops, and teachers working out there."

"So you've eliminated several obvious candidates," Elliot said. "What about the other suspects in your files?"

"I've gone through the CID database trying to determine if anyone with a guide license has a criminal background."

"Are you saying we've had felons working on that river?"

"Just hold on," Bognor said. "Have you ever spent any time in a rural upstate jurisdiction?"

Elliot turned to face Bognor. "What difference does that make?"

"Answer me. Have you even been north of Albany?"

"Sheriff, calm down," Raines said.

"I'll calm down when I get an answer."

"No, as a matter of fact, I haven't," Elliot said.

"Then you wouldn't understand how things work in an area with unemployment and poverty," Bognor said.

"You've made your point, Sheriff, but I'm sure Professor Carlyle has more to tell us."

Carlyle handed Elliot and Raines a two-page summary of his analysis. "Six people have been charged with petty theft, shoplifting, and reckless endangerment. Two others were found guilty of possessing cocaine or methamphetamines. Every one of those indictments was dismissed."

Without taking his eyes from the list, Elliot said, "Care to explain why outfitters continue hiring people like that?"

"Abel," Bognor said, "If I stopped every BMW cruising through my jurisdiction and had a high-strung drug-sniffing Doberman with me, my jail would be filled with downstate lawyers wearing double-breasted Armani suits."

"This is getting us nowhere," Raines said.

Elliot stared at Carlyle. "I want to know what your next move is."

"I'm going upstate early tomorrow morning. The person we're after has found another route into the gorge. I'm sure that's where he'll strike next."

"This so-called discovery of yours won't be enough to satisfy the commissioner," Elliot said. "He wants to see an end to these vicious incidents."

"We're also working through a list of suspects. It'll take a day or two to check them all out."

"I need to know how long," Elliot said.

"We can't give you a deadline."

Elliot let out an exasperated sigh. "You must have a profile of this maniac by now."

"We've found some of the tools he uses when he commits these crimes and where he hides out in the backcountry. We're also beginning to understand his habits, how he thinks, how he moves around out there, and how he's able to elude us."

"Cut the bullshit," Elliot said. "What'll it take to break this case open?"

Carlyle closed his case notes file. "If he makes just one more mistake, we may be able to take him down."

Elliot stood up. "You have two days. If there's no breakthrough, we'll tell the Bureau of Criminal Investigations to sweep through that region with SWAT teams. This case will end quickly when they take over."

"I wouldn't count on that," Carlyle said.

When Carlyle got home that afternoon, he made coffee and went out into the side yard. It had taken him and Beth three years to find this place. Two hundred acres of unspoiled woods surrounded the house. They could see two mountain ranges from their back porch, but he'd neglected his land this spring. Once the manhunt was over, he'd promised Beth that he would mend the fence near the road, find a way to revive the two giant mulberries bordering the pond, paint the shed, and prepare the garden for planting.

Three miles to the east, the Hudson plowed south toward the ocean. It was nearly an eighth of a mile wide now, a river the color of earth that heaved a hundred thousand cubic feet a second of fresh water toward New York City. A century ago, it had turned lumbermen and backwoods land speculators into magnates. Now, it did little more than move wood chips and rusted scrap metal from America's decaying heartland to Brazil and Pakistan.

Carlyle glanced up at the window toward Beth's studio. She'd been sleeping there for the past few days while she put the finishing touches to a new canvas.

"What are you working on?" he'd asked her last week.

"It's about that day."

"Does it do any good to keep going over it?"

"I'll never put it behind me until I turn my fear and rage into...into something else."

A year before they met, Beth had been attacked one evening while walking through Washington Park, a wooded oasis in the heart of Albany. Grabbed from behind, pleading for her life, she'd fought off a bearded man wearing a filthy red plaid shirt, brown trousers, and unlaced work boots.

His left hand wrapped around her throat, he'd pummeled her almost into unconsciousness. X-rays revealed a fractured right cheek and a broken wrist. The bruises on her face, arms, and chest took a month to disappear. She couldn't remember how long the beating had gone on, or why. After slamming her to the ground, her attacker had run off.

It took months to reclaim any traces of a normal life. A plastic surgeon needed two operations to cover the scar on her cheek. Her right wrist never fully healed. A psychiatrist, claiming she would recover more quickly without medication, refused a prescription for Xanax. Beth forked over a week's pay for a locksmith to make her apartment burglarproof. She stopped walking deserted streets alone, refused to teach night classes, seldom left home after dark, and paid for an unlisted phone number.

She described the details of the attack to Carlyle a month after they met. They were sitting in a coffee house along the river in Troy. It was late afternoon in November. Dark outside. The river gray and still above the dam.

"I kept a diary for a while, but the flashbacks just became more intense. Then I put my recent work in storage and started taking out my anger on the canvas." Rothko-like images, huge slabs of red, black, and yellow, quickly took over her studio.

Carlyle walked back to the house and began to make lunch. A few minutes later, she came down to the kitchen. "You're still here." She kissed his cheek.

He put his arm around her shoulders. "I didn't want to leave until you knew where I was going."

She sat down at the table and put a half-piece of toast on her plate. "How'd your meeting go this morning?"

"Some idiot in DEC thinks we're bungling the case."

She took an orange from a bowl and began to cut it in sections. "Are we safe?"

"You mean here, in this house?" She nodded. Carlyle wiped his hands on a napkin. "What are you afraid of?"

Beth pushed her plate away. "Haven't you seen the patrol cars cruising up and down our road?"

"I should have told you. When the press announced I was connected to the manhunt, I asked the local cops to watch the place."

"What else haven't you told me?"

Carlyle looked at his watch. "Do we have to do this now?"

"There's more, isn't there?" She got up and walked to the window facing the road.

"They have two people on rotating eight-hour shifts stationed in the house across the way."

"At the McMillans?"

"They moved to her mother's place until this is over.

"For God's sake."

"The police said it's best if we don't know what else they're doing."

She turned around and faced him. "But you won't admit that we're in danger?"

"It's just a routine precaution."

"Routine? How can you say that? Should I go somewhere until this is over?"

"I wouldn't let you stay here if I thought you were in danger."

She sat back down. "When are you leaving again?"

"Tomorrow at dawn. But I promise I'll be back by dark."

"Then what happens?"

"I'll start paying attention to this place. You won't have to ask Adrian to come back again."

The windows trembled as several helicopters, their rotors slashing through the thick afternoon air, cut through the valley on their way north. When the noise faded, she said, "Do they have anything to do with the manhunt?"

"DEC is moving forest rangers from across the state to staging posts around the gorge. The police have set up checkpoints on all roads leading to the river at every Northway exit ramp."

"And you still insist I have nothing to worry about?"

Working by the light of a single gas lantern, it took him forty-five minutes to assemble the equipment he would need for his next assault. When he was done, a lightweight wall hammer, a compact backcountry shovel, a sixty-foot piece of 9.2 mm canyon rope, a half-dozen snow anchors, a climber's harness, and two pulley sets sat on the workbench in his barn.

He stowed his gear, including a pair of Lund bear paws, in a high-volume external-frame rucksack. The four pieces of six-foot rebar now lying under canvas in his pickup would go on his shoulder. After studying the map and estimating how much snow remained on the trail, he estimated he would have to carry the forty-eight-pound load for two hours.

Because it made him feel invulnerable, he'd begun using his grandfather's gear, even the clothing the old man had left before he died. He tugged open the door of a large oak cupboard and began the transformation.

In the mirror, he saw what some would have called a ghost from the past, a lumberman with wind-scarred cheeks and a neatly trimmed handlebar mustache. The image did not reveal the hidden wounds that went along with a lifetime in the woods: a broken nose, fractured pelvis, and punctured lung. He was also missing the ring finger on his left hand.

His three-page, minute-by-minute plan for what would take place tomorrow required an eight-mile drive to the trailhead, a two-mile hike into the canyon, and at least two hours on-site. When it was all over, someone might guess how he'd set up this job, but by then it would be too late to prevent him from escaping.

The reporters had begun calling him a homicidal maniac, but they knew nothing about the grievances his people had faced here and did not understand the terrible things that would happen to these woods if his campaign failed.

Once he'd driven out Phillip Marshall and his cronies, Hamilton County would again belong to those who'd earned the right to live here. The forest would revive, logging camps would spring up, thousands of skilled men would be employed cutting timber, and boatmen would again run log rafts down the Hudson to Glens Falls. This region would be known for providing affordable land and decent jobs to working families, folks who wanted nothing more than to make a life in this frontier territory.

He shouldered his load, locked the house, and drove off in the dark toward the gorge.

FOURTEEN

At 8:00 a.m. Sunday morning, Carlyle and Wells stood facing each other in Bognor's office on the outskirts of Indian Lake. The room was littered with coffee cups, faxes, old case files, and maps of the gorge.

"You look terrible," Carlyle said. "What happened?"

"I've been up all night. A father and his two teenage sons got trapped on Cascade."

"They make it out okay?"

"One of the kids lost a toe to frostbite. The other kid is fine."

"Sorry I had to call so early."

Wells unzipped his jacket. "Forget it. What's the emergency?"

"The state police received a call just after dawn this morning. Two fishermen in a dory spotted him near the bottom of Harris."

"How do you know it's our guy?"

"He was wearing a top hat, canvas trousers, knee-high boots, and a calf-length leather coat. They also said he was smoking a corncob and had a black beard. Who else could it be?"

"Jesus."

"And he was carrying a weird axe in his right hand."

"This guy say anything to them?"

"Not a word," Carlyle said. "They assumed he was waiting for them to get out of his way. When they spotted the axe, they began rowing like crazy."

"What's he doing so far from the gorge?"

"It could only mean one thing—we've flushed him out of familiar territory."

"Why would he let himself be seen out in the open like that?"

"He may think he'll never get caught."

"Or maybe he's getting careless?"

"Him? Never. He's too disciplined for that…or it could be part of his plan."

"Is it finally time to bring in the cops?" Wells said.

"He'll just go to ground once the troops arrive. We need to figure out where he goes next."

Carlyle unfolded a large-scale map of the region running from Indian Lake to North River. "We've assumed the Huntley Point Trail was the only way he could get in there, that he would never attack Marshall in the gorge itself."

"Did we make a mistake?"

"Not really. Once the river turns east, the Black Mountain Range makes it all but impossible to get into the canyon."

"Where did we go wrong, then?" Wells said.

"What if the terrain is really no obstacle? What would happen then?"

"You can't have it both ways. Either it stops him or it doesn't."

"Drag that light over here." Wells brought a gooseneck lamp to the center of the table. "Look at the map again," Carlyle said.

Wells put his finger on the Hudson at Blue Ledges. He could see the Huntley Point Trail dropping down from the north-east, then the canyon walls enveloping the river. "There's no way for him to get in there."

"Really? Look farther east."

"What are you talking about? You've got a four-mile wall of rock, six or seven hundred feet high on both sides. And nothing but wilderness behind it."

"Keep going."

Wells slowly traced the Hudson from the Narrows to the Boreas. "The freight line to the mine at Tahawus crosses the Hudson just below Harris. Why didn't we see it?"

"Because it's been abandoned for over two decades and we just assumed the trestle was impassable. That's why we figured the gorge was invulnerable."

"That means we could get hit on either side of Harris."

"Right. He could hide his vehicle and be in and out in two hours and change. Or he may have a place to hide until we've given up looking for him."

"What makes you so sure Harris is his next target?" Wells said.

"He keeps moving downstream ahead of us. This is the first place east of the gorge where he can come and go whenever he wants."

"Are you saying we should bushwhack into the trestle?"

Carlyle got up and walked to a picture window overlooking the valley. "We have to find out if he can use it to attack us on both sides of the gorge. And he must have been planning something when those two guys spotted him."

Carlyle turned and faced Wells. "We may have overlooked something else. It's three miles from the trestle to the take-out at North River. There's plenty of unobstructed shoreline on both sides of the river. He could be planning almost anything along this stretch."

Carlyle drove slowly across the one-lane bridge spanning the Boreas, pulled his truck off the road to the right, and killed the engine.

Wells said, "You sure you don't want to let the state police know what we're doing?"

Carlyle opened up a thermos and handed Wells some coffee. "They'd only bring a SWAT team in an armored vehicle. He'd hear them coming a mile away and we'd never get near him."

"What happens if we do run into him?"

Carlyle looked through the windshield as a rabbit ran across the road. "We calmly explain that we're there to carry out a citizen's arrest. If he doesn't surrender, we run like hell."

"Be serious," Wells said. "I may get my ass shot off because of you."

Carlyle got out of the truck. "I promise to find a pretty young doctor to sew it back on."

After pulling on their backpacks, they began walking along the abandoned rail line, now almost completely overgrown by vines and thick bushes, that would take them to the gorge.

As soon as Carlyle entered the woods, the only sound he could hear was his feet striking the limestone chips between wooden ties. He felt hemmed in, cut off from the outside world. The tall pines and the granite cliff to his right blocked sunlight from reaching the valley floor. Ignoring the possibility that he and Wells were putting themselves in danger, Carlyle concentrated on moving south toward the river. Up ahead, the track snaked along the base of an escarpment, increasing his sense of isolation.

After a quarter mile, they stopped to look at the narrow, seething river on their left. The Boreas, boulder-strewn and only thirty yards wide, had carved a trench in the landscape from its source in a mountain lake twenty miles to the north. Once the snowmelt disappeared, it would again be a bone-dry ravine, though one day of heavy rain would convert the Boreas into a raging torrent again.

Wells said, "You mind telling me what our plan is today?"

"Every attack has been different. All we know so far is that he's patient and deliberate. That's not the portrait of a crazy person. I'm hoping that if we keep analyzing his methods, the puzzle will begin to make sense."

"If we don't stop him," Wells said, "could this crusade of his turn into a killing spree?"

"Every time we fail to stop him, he becomes more reckless."

"So how do we find out what's going on in his mind?"

Carlyle pushed a thick vine out of their way. "That Sherlock Holmes stuff, thinking like your enemy? It doesn't work. We can't anticipate what he's going to do because he probably has no idea himself. My guess is we'll catch him during one of his stunts. His need to get back at Marshall may push him over the edge, and if his rage overwhelms his caution, he may make a fatal error."

After another twenty minutes, they were again enveloped by the forest's semidarkness. Carlyle could see nothing but the serried ranks of Scotch pine and spruce to his right and the dull gleam of the rails stretching ahead of him. They had two miles to go before they would see the Hudson.

A mile and a half later, the track veered away from the river and through a stand of white birch, slender trees bent by age and wind, whose pale bark was peeling off like discarded snakeskin.

Just before noon, Carlyle heard the Hudson just ahead. Pushing aside a wall of vines, he broke free of the undergrowth. A single-span bridge supported by rough wooden girders and cross-ties embedded in eight huge concrete footings spanned the gorge. The Hudson, still swollen by the spring rains, piled up against the footings. Carlyle and Wells were standing on the edge of a steep embankment that plunged straight down to the river.

"Jesus," Wells said. "How far down do you think it is?"

"Fifty, sixty feet maybe."

The trestle was two hundred yards long and no more than eight feet wide. The rails, mounted on weather-resistant ties, were six feet apart. No more than eight inches lay between those rails and the edge of the bridge.

Carlyle retied his bootlaces and pulled a pair of binoculars from his backpack. He stood up, zipped his jacket, and stepped onto the first crosstie. The wood was weathered and cracked. Six inches of open space lay between the crossties. Below him, white-tipped wave trains battered the ancient steel supports of the span. With no handrails to grab hold of, he spread his arms wide to maintain his balance. "I'll be right back."

"What the hell you doing?"

"This may be our only chance to find out where we're vulnerable here." Carlyle took ten steps out over the gorge. "I can see all the way back to the top of Harris, and the shoreline on both sides. It's amazing."

"Be careful. One gust of wind could send you down on those rocks."

"I've got plenty of water underneath me."

"Does your wife know she married a madman?"

"You should come out here."

"Not on your life. I wear a harness bolted to rock when I do stuff like that."

Carlyle moved out and across the span. When he was thirty yards away from Wells, with nothing below him but the churning, boulder-filled Hudson, he paused.

Harris Rift, a half-mile set of continuous staircase rapids, each ledge leading to a set of white-tipped hydraulics, was to his right. Unable to stop himself, his feet inching across the wooden ties, Carlyle took another twenty steps farther out onto the trestle.

Balsam fir, hemlock, red spruce, and white cedar marched up the hillsides on both sides of the river. A thick line of gray and white clouds filled the sky to Carlyle's left.

Dozens of nearly inaccessible mountain lakes and trout-filled streams lay north and west of here, but only a single track led into the backcountry. South of the Hudson, the nearest trail out of the wilderness was four miles away.

Carlyle looked to his left. Two hundred yards downstream, the Hudson, wide and turbulent, disappeared into a gap between the cliffs. When he was a rookie, after he'd spent three or four hours fighting off the rapids, he could not wait to reach this bridge. On mornings when he was cold, bone-tired, and afraid of making a serious mistake, reaching the bottom of Harris Rift meant that he had finished brawling with rapids for the day, that he had proven his tenacity and skill on one of the toughest rivers in the country.

Carlyle was sure that his next meeting with Marshall's adversary would be near this bridge. Harris provided everything he needed: abundant tree cover, accessibility from both sides of the river, and, with the abandoned rail track, the perfect escape route.

With wind gusts rushing south through the valley, Carlyle turned around and made his way back to Wells. The two men moved back into the woods, sat on a large flat rock, and began to eat lunch.

"Okay, Spidey," Wells said. "You proved you've got cojones. What did you learn from that stunt?"

"This place is perfect. He'll show up here."

Facing the river, Carlyle saw a flash of red in the trees on the far side of the gorge. He brought the binoculars to his eyes and rotated the glasses slowly toward a stand of white pine a hundred yards to their right. "Pack up your lunch. We're moving out."

"I've just started. Give me a minute, will you?"

"Do it now." Carlyle stood up and, turning sideways to prevent himself from slipping on the loose gravel, made his way down the slope to the Hudson, where he began bushwhacking through the woods. After several minutes, he stopped, stepped out into the open, raised the binoculars again and scanned the hillside across the way. "Got glasses in your pack? Take a look right across from us. See the trees at one o'clock? Just to the left of that bare space in the woods, ten or fifteen feet up from the river."

Carlyle rested his elbows on a boulder and exhaled in order to steady the image. As he turned the binoculars' focus wheel, the pines faded into the background and a form emerged.

Someone was standing inside the tree line, just far enough from the river to conceal himself, a tall figure wearing a top hat and a calf-length coat. He had on a plaid shirt, gloves, and a black scarf knotted around his neck. Carlyle could also make out a pair of wire-rimmed spectacles and a long black beard. "Can you see what's in his right hand?"

"Holy shit. A peavey. You think he wants us to see him?"

Carlyle didn't take his eyes off their target. "I think he's sending us a message: You idiots will never catch me."

"What's with the goddamn costume?"

"It's not a costume, it's a mask, a way for him to assume a different identity, someone with skills he doesn't have."

"But why that particular get-up?"

"It's what loggers wore a hundred years ago. They told people they were dressed like aristocrats because they were doing a job no one else could do. Those men survived unimaginable conditions. He may be saying he's just as tough as they were." Carlyle stared at the figure on the far side of the valley. "This is worse than I thought."

"We've got a maniac standing a hundred yards across from us. How could it be worse?"

"The disguise intensifies his self-delusion. He may be switching personalities and losing contact with reality."

Suddenly, the figure across the way stepped into the sunlight and stared at them.

Wells said, "What's he doing?"

"Maybe daring us to stop him."

"How do we know he won't attack us?"

"Everything he's done so far suggests he's only after the Marshalls."

"You sure he's not going to come charging across that trestle and cut our throats with that thing?"

"He likes the game he's playing.

"So why's he tormenting us?"

"To show us who's in control."

When Carlyle looked across the gorge again, the figure had disappeared into the trees.

"He must have a place near here. We won't find him unless he wants us to."

"So how do we draw him out?"

Carlyle stood up and began walking up the hill toward the trestle. "The same way we did it before. With bait he absolutely can't resist."

At 3:00 p.m., Carlyle and Wells were back at the main road. Wells said, "Look to your left."

Two state troopers were moving toward them, both in combat fatigues and black boots. The one in front had on a lieutenant's bar with a nametag, "Morris." His backup, carrying a twelve gauge and a Glock, never took his eyes off the track and the surrounding woods.

Morris said, "We knew you'd pull another stunt like this."

The backup said, "Sir, I'd prefer we step away from the road. It would be safer if we moved out of the sun."

"How did you find out we were here?" Carlyle said.

"Abel Elliot told us to keep an eye on you. One of my men saw you leave Indian Lake this morning."

Wells glanced at the guy with the Glock and the shotgun. "What's with the armor?"

"You don't enter a virtual war zone without protection. I came to say you can stop this wild-goose chase of yours."

"Why's that?" Carlyle said.

"One of my men discovered fresh footprints and a spool of fishing line on the Indian where Sanders died."

"What makes you so sure it's fresh evidence?"

"A forensics team said the tracks were a day old."

"Where exactly did you find this stuff?"

"Just upstream of Guide's Hole. Right where Sanders went in."

"How does this affect your plans?"

"We're moving all personnel back there. If I know Elliot, he'll want you to move your operation upstream also."

Wells turned to Carlyle. "You want to tell him or should I?"

"Tell me what?" Morris said.

"We just spotted our guy near the trestle." Carlyle described their hike into the gorge and the person who emerged from the woods across from them.

Morris scowled. "What in hell makes you so certain I should reposition my men down to this sector?"

"This guy's still on the loose because he keeps moving to new territory. Trust me, Harris is his next target."

Morris dug a furrow in the ground with the heel of his boot. "Give me some solid evidence. Something I can take to my superiors."

"Tell him about the costumes," Wells said.

"He doesn't appear now without wearing a disguise," Carlyle said. "I think it's a sign that he's undergone a major psychotic break. And that may cause him to become reckless."

"You're goddamn lucky he didn't come across the bridge after you," Morris said.

"He wants to drive people away from the gorge, not bring them into it."

"Let's suppose for a second that you're right. That he's planning another attack. What would you do if you were in my place?"

"I'd have two crews, one at a staging area in North River and another in Riparius in case he eludes us. And a chopper ready to fly into the meadow just south of Harris."

"Are you sure of this?"

"I've been studying people like him for a decade and watching this guy night and day for over two weeks. I'm pretty certain that I've got a plan that will draw him into a trap."

When Carlyle got back to the house two hours later, he and Beth had dinner. "How did your work go today?" he said.

"It never gets any easier. You start the morning hoping to create something entirely wonderful. Then, after a half-dozen false starts, all your energy and optimism are gone." There was blue paint on her hair and glasses, tobacco stains on the fingers of her right hand.

Carlyle had watched her fall into a depression before. "How long before I can see what you've been working on?" he said.

"Not for another month. Maybe longer if it doesn't get any better."

Carlyle finished his coffee and cleared the table.

"When this business in Warrensburg is finished, we can get back to a normal life. Spend all day on the escarpment, have a picnic, just wander around." They had hiked or skied up there every week for the past three years, never growing tired of the trails that wound through the woods. In autumn, when yellow and red maple leaves lay thick under their boots, they walked for hours, saying little, content to simply be together.

Beth did the dishes. "Did you find your letter?"

Carlyle stared at his hands. "I saw it on the table in the hall when I came in."

Beth shut off the water. "What did they say?"

He pulled the letter from his pocket and read it again. "Just what you expect. The Provost thanks me for my service to my students and the university, but after reviewing my tenure application, he's decided not to renew my contract."

She sat down next to him and put her hand on his arm. "How can they do that?"

"I gave them no choice."

"You did everything they asked for, served on every committee they asked you to, and churned out papers like a madman."

"I appreciate the vote of confidence, but those people don't give a rat's ass about the faculty."

"What will we do now?"

"I've got a year to find another job. Don't worry; a criminologist can always get work in a town run by corrupt politicians."

Beth looked around the kitchen. "Will we have to leave this house?"

He took her hand. "Not unless you want to."

After Beth retreated upstairs to her studio, Carlyle finished cleaning the kitchen. He snuffed out the candles in the dining room and walked out to the front yard. As he approached the barn, a dark four-door sedan cruised slowly past their driveway.

Inside the barn, he threw his rafting gear, helmet, dry suit, pile jacket, two pair of socks, and river boots into a mesh bag. A Spyderco knife, throw bag, protein bar, and Blast whistle got tucked into a small waterproof satchel.

Outside the barn, he checked the gas gauge in his truck, entered the house, and locked the front door behind him.

The phone rang just as he turned out the lights in the kitchen.

"Carlyle? It's Ryan Marshall. Listen to this. I managed to line up a group to run the gorge tomorrow. Forty-eight people."

"Good. This will help keep your permit valid. You better use it before Raines decides she's had enough of you. Got a crew ready to go?"

"Betts, Nash, and two guys I borrowed from Burton. He says you still can't interview them."

"I won't even ask them what time it is." Carlyle hesitated for several seconds. "Either of them from that short list I gave you?"

"Both. Who are they anyway?"

"Guys I've heard are decent guides."

"I've got five boats and all the equipment sitting on the trailer outside my front door right now. But I can't do this without you. DEC and the state police say you're the reason I'm still in business."

"I'll be there at seven tomorrow morning." Marshall hung up. Carlyle stared at the woods surrounding his house.

Carlyle got a pot of coffee ready for the morning, shut off the lights, and wrote a note for Beth. He reminded himself to move those books down to the basement when he got home tomorrow.

FIFTEEN

Because traffic was backed up on the Northway, Carlyle drove straight to the put-in. He got out of his truck, pulled on his dry suit, grabbed his gear, and found Marshall at the top of the slope overlooking the basin. "Where's everyone?"

"Nash is down below, getting our crews prepped. Betts is taking a piss, and we're waiting on two more guides."

A rusted out '73 jeep, with a busted headlight and Bondo on both side panels, slid into a parking space. Two men Carlyle didn't recognize threw their rafting gear out the back hatch.

"These our other two guides?" Carlyle said.

"On the left, Al Sayers. The other's Dave Sutcliffe."

"You know anything about these two?"

"They're breathing and they come cheap."

"What else?"

"The tall dude, Sayers, works at the ski mountain. He's a gofer on the equipment crew. Sutcliffe's been around boats forever. But don't expect him to say much."

Betts appeared out of the woods wearing a new dry suit and a high-float life vest instead of his ragged squirt boat PFD.

Marshall punched Betts's life vest. "You expecting to swim today?"

"Don't give me that. The gauge climbed to nine feet last night.

Another hour from now, it'll hit flood stage. You sure you want to go through with this?"

"If you want to back out," Marshall said, "do it now."

"Have you looked at the river? It's fucking insane."

"When did you turn pussy?"

Betts looked over at Sutcliffe. "Hey, you think we should take these people through the gorge today?"

Sutcliffe shrugged. "These idiots pay good money to get scared shitless. Who am I to ruin their fun?"

"The Gorge is going to look like a washing machine," Betts said. "How are inexperienced people supposed to handle something like that?"

"You want to run back to mommy," Marshall said, "just let me know."

"Don't say I didn't warn you."

Marshall handed each guide a list of the people in their boats. "Listen up. I'm leading us through the gorge. Alex will be right behind me. Sutcliffe and Sayers follow him. Nash runs sweep, as usual."

Sayers stared at the meadow. "Where are the other outfitters?"

"It's Monday," Marshall said. "We're the only company that does weekdays."

"You're going out there with no backup?" Sayers said.

"You want police protection or something?"

"I was hoping you'd pay us before we took off. Your safety record's in the toilet right now."

"Do your job and you'll get paid, same as everyone." He looked over at Carlyle. "Who do you want to ride with?"

"Surprise me."

"You better go with me, then," Marshall said.

"Boss?" Sutcliffe said. "I'm a person short. He can come in my boat."

"Fine," Marshall said. "I'm sick of being spied on."

Carlyle and Sutcliffe grabbed their paddles and personal gear and began picking their way down the path toward the basin. "You sure you don't mind me looking over your shoulder?" Carlyle said.

"I did you a favor," Sutcliffe said. "You don't want to be trailblazing through these rapids today."

When they reached the basin, Sutcliffe marched up to a couple of burly guys sitting on his raft. "You two, up front. The rest of you, three on each side." He gave his clients the standard safety speech. "Any questions? Nobody's going to ask me anything? It's your funeral, then. Let's take off."

After each guide took his crew for a spin around the basin, Marshall raised his right arm, the signal that they were ready to go.

Sutcliffe yelled, "Forward one stroke!" The boat edged away from the trees surrounding the basin. "Stop. I'll take it now."

Current pouring through the wide-open sluice gate at the dam caught the raft and pushed it toward the Indian. They were twenty yards behind Marshall, but catching up fast.

The sun slipped behind a layer of gray clouds, turning the water a nasty shade of green. Carlyle looked to his left, toward the woods and the darkness beyond. The river, near flood stage for the first time this spring, hissed and groaned as it churned toward the Confluence.

"You're that professor I've been hearing about," Sutcliffe said. "The one out to catch our river ghost."

"That's me. Not that I've had any luck so far."

The Indian was supposed to be a warm-up for what lay ahead in the gorge, but juiced by the enormous spring snowmelt, today it was almost unrecognizable. Huge waves and boat-gulping hydraulics filled the river as it plowed through the canyon. A fierce wind whipped the current into a white froth that needled Carlyle's face with cold spray. Driven downstream by the dam release from Indian Lake, the convoy of five rafts took only thirty minutes to reach their usual rest stop halfway to the Confluence.

Sutcliffe passed Carlyle his water bottle. "You still hunting for that killer?"

"We're hoping this case will be over soon."

"Good luck with that."

Carlyle wiped his glasses. "Mind if I ask why you're out here today?"

"No one's willing to work for Marshall. They think he's jinxed."

"So why'd you sign up?"

"I can always use the cash."

Marshall soon took off, and Sutcliffe worked his boat into the current. Five minutes later, Marshall steered his raft into a slender chute on river right. Sutcliffe hesitated.

Carlyle eyed him. "We going to follow him?"

Sutcliffe never took his eyes off the river. "With the Indian like this? It's insane. But he's the boss." He slipped into the chute behind Marshall. Betts and Nash also followed them. Sayers did not, but stayed outside the chute picking out a broader route.

Although they were twenty yards behind the lead boat, Carlyle never lost sight of Marshall sitting high up on his back tube, his bright blue and yellow dry suit outlined against a backdrop of Scotch pines. Thirty seconds later, halfway down the chute, Marshall was wrenched from his boat and, arms flailing, somersaulted backwards into the Indian.

Although battered by waves and subsurface rocks, Marshall was able to grab the chicken line with his left hand as he was dragged downstream like a cowboy lashed to a Brahma bull.

Sutcliffe pulled up alongside Marshall's raft, and Carlyle yanked him from the river. Three minutes later, the convoy rafted up in calmer water fifty yards above Gooley Steps.

Carlyle eased Marshall into a sitting position. "What the hell happened?"

Marshall wrapped his right hand around a D-ring and gritted his teeth. "Didn't you see it?"

"See what?"

"That fishing line strung across the channel. Almost took my head off."

Carlyle turned around and stared at the waves pouring out of the chute. What was the booby trap doing this far up the river? He was certain that if there had been an ambush today, it would have been in Harris.

Nash grabbed Marshall under the arms, laid him across a thwart and covered him with a thermal blanket. "Where's it hurt?"

"My chest. It feels all busted up."

"Can you breathe okay?"

Marshall closed his eyes and inhaled. "Shit, no."

"Dizzy?"

"No."

Nash put his right hand on Marshall's side. "Take a deep one."

Marshall, pale but sweating despite the chilled air, groaned.

Nash stood up. "He's got two or three broken ribs."

"We've got to get him back to the basin," Betts said. "He needs a paramedic."

"Are you nuts?" Nash said. "We can't bushwhack two miles with him like this."

"You got a better idea?"

"We strap him to a backboard at Virgin," Nash said, "and I'll float him out in my boat."

Marshall attempted to sit up. "You can't be serious. I can't go through another three hours of this."

"We'll get you help as soon as we reach North River."

"Aren't you forgetting something?" Betts said. "How do we get his people out of here?"

"In the other four boats," Nash said.

Sutcliffe sat up higher and scanned the other rafts. "Where are you going to find eight empty spaces?"

Carlyle picked up his dry bag and stepped across to Marshall's boat. "We don't have time to argue. I'll take over for him."

"Are you serious?" Nash said. "With the river near flood stage?"

"How many times do I have to say this?" Carlyle slid his left foot under the restraining strap. "I've worked on the Hudson longer than any of you."

Betts lowered his voice. "DEC will go crazy if we let an unlicensed guide haul people through the gorge."

"We have no choice," Nash said. "If we try to walk Marshall out of here, he might dislocate a rib."

"Discussion over," Carlyle said. "Every second we stay here makes us open to another attack." He looked at the four guides standing around him, and then focused on Sayers. "Why didn't you follow us down the chute?"

Sayers put his fists on his hips and met Carlyle's gaze. "I've never gone that way before and it looked suicidal. What are you accusing me of?"

Carlyle looked at him a moment longer. "Just asking. Okay, here's what I want. Nash moves from the four spot to the one and leads us through the gorge."

Nash waved him off. "Are you forgetting what happened the last time you talked me into playing George Washington?"

Carlyle leaned back, testing the foot strap. "You're right, that wasn't fair. You take us down to Blue Ledges. I'll take us through the gorge."

"You're not serious, are you?" Betts said.

"If you think I'm joking, just watch me." Carlyle shoved Marshall's boat into the Indian and the raft picked up speed. "The really tough stuff is ahead of us, he told the people in his boat. If you want to change seats, let me know right now."

"Have you done this before?" the kid in the front seat said.

"Once or twice. You've got nothing to worry about except doing exactly what I tell you." He gave his crew the standard, "I know you can do this" speech and then let the Indian drag his raft toward Gooley Steps.

A boat moves so fast when a river is near flood stage that Carlyle could only rely on his experience and a set of automatic moves buried deep in his subconscious. He would not be thinking his way down the Hudson; this was a read-and-react situation.

Because of the almost constant rain the mountains had received this week, the most treacherous ledges were submerged today. Only an idiot could have scraped rock on the Indian. But as the gradient increased and the river narrowed, Carlyle's raft began to slide from wave to wave like a surfer coiled tightly inside a twenty-foot-high boil line.

For five or six minutes, Carlyle and his crew careened down through the Gooley Steps. If he allowed the boat to flip here, in a place where granite boulders plugged the current, someone might lose a couple of teeth—or worse—during a long, very cold swim.

When he finally reached the Confluence, Carlyle took several deep breaths. The experience of driving a raft through gut-churning rapids, where one was only seconds from a devastating accident, was almost hallucinogenic. Vital tasks, such as avoiding rocks that could rip the guts out of a boat, were all-consuming. The calculus of success here was simple. Either Carlyle made the right moves and his crew remained safe, or he let his attention wander and someone ended up in the river.

Just before they took off again, Nash said, "You sure you're okay?"

"Listen, when you do this river over a hundred times, it's in your DNA."

"Wait a couple of hours before you decide to relax."

Following Betts, Carlyle's raft barreled across the current. Cedar Ledges was supposed to be a warm-up for what lay ahead, but it shocked Carlyle. There were truck-sized holes everywhere, thunderous recirc engines that would hold onto his boat till the next millennium if he screwed up. But because he remembered every foot of this river, Carlyle kept them far away from places where a boat could wrap around a boulder.

Halfway down Cedar, Sayers caught up to Carlyle's raft. "Prettiest part of the trip, isn't it?" Carlyle said.

"It's all just lumber to me."

"You ever hike around here?"

"Why come all this way? I got trees where I live."

Twenty minutes later, Carlyle's raft picked up speed as it got pushed through a sweeping right-hand turn. "Pay attention now!" he shouted. "Entrance is just ahead."

As the Hudson churned south and east toward Blue Ledge basin, it crashed into a string of boulders and became a series of whitewater cauldrons, each one setting off a blast that reverberated through the canyon.

The river plummeted downhill. Surrounded by chest-high swells, they plowed past a series of white-tipped hydraulics. A line of boulders ahead turned the horizon into a ragged kaleidoscope of colors: deep green, white, and dark brown. Breathing deeply, Carlyle let himself slip into a rhythm, the reflexive process of threading a boat through a minefield. The procedure had an inexorable logic, a series of split-second calculations that got him through Entrance safely, but left him no time at all to be on the lookout for another surprise attack.

Just before noon, the convoy slid down into Blue Ledge Basin.

"We should take a break here," Nash said.

"Keep moving," Marshall said. "I've got to get off this river."

Nash said, "Everyone's exhausted. It's our last chance to rest up before the Boreas."

Marshall tried to sit up. "You heard what I said." He turned to Sayers and Sutcliffe. "What about you two?"

"You bought me for the day," Sayers said. "You call the shots."

Sutcliffe said, "I say we get it over with."

Nash turned to Betts. "You got an opinion?"

"Carlyle's in charge. Let him handle it."

"It's been a tough morning," Carlyle said. "No harm in stopping for a minute."

After the guides beached their boats opposite the ice-covered cliffs, Carlyle handed out snacks to his crew and then walked over to Nash. "Marshall okay?"

"He's got a chick stroking his forehead, probably wondering if he can get laid with broken ribs."

"I need to talk to him."

"What about?"

"I'll tell you later."

"You're welcome to him." Nash headed toward the woods.

Marshall, eyes closed, was leaning against a thwart in Nash's raft. "You going to make it?" Carlyle said.

"What choice do I have?"

"I need to talk to you."

"Are you serious? I can hardly breathe."

Carlyle leaned close to the injured guide. "If you don't answer me, we may not make it out of here."

Marshall coughed and, when his ribs flexed, groaned.

"I'll make it quick," Carlyle said. "Are you the only one who runs that chute on the Indian?"

"No one will go near it after what happened to Blake."

"You ever have an employee who's handy with a canoe?"

"What's this all about?"

"Just answer me."

"Good enough to run one through the gorge?"

"That's what I mean."

"Betts is too big to. Nash's specialty is kayaks. I've got no idea about Sutcliffe or Sayers."

"Any of them fixated on the backcountry? You know, survivalist types?"

"You mean like living off berries and mushrooms?"

"Right."

"They're beer and brats people, for Christ's sake."

"You know where they all live?"

"I'm not the type you invite over for dinner, in case you didn't notice."

"Anybody drive a really old pickup?"

"Guides are generally poor as shit. Why do you think they do this kind of work?"

"Anyone good with a fly rod?"

"You've got to be kidding. That's a rich man's hobby."

"Just answer me."

"Betts uses dynamite to catch his dinner. No one has time to tie flies."

"What about the two guides you hired today?"

"Sayers owns a few acres somewhere. Always short of money, like the rest of them."

"Sutcliffe?"

"He's local, too. Works part-time on the river. Keeps to himself. Will you stop asking me this shit?"

"That's enough for now. We'll get you out of here soon."

Carlyle motioned Nash over. "We're done."

Nash stared at the blue-gray cliffs hovering over the river. "You're doing great."

"You're not going to break my balls again?" Carlyle said. "What a surprise."

"I meant for a professor."

When it was time to move out, Carlyle brought his crew together. Sounding like a mother seal comforting her tiny white pups as the guys with clubs appeared, he said, "A hundred yards downstream, the river hooks right. Then it'll throw a half-dozen big waves at us. Ignore them. Keep your eyes fixed on the water and paddle like your girlfriend's husband is chasing you."

Carlyle checked their life vests, pushed his boat into the current ahead of the others, and let the river drag them toward the Narrows. They picked up speed. "As soon as we turn this corner, the current's going to try to slam us into a boulder on our left."

"What's it look like?" asked the guy in front of him.

"From where you're sitting, like one of Godzilla's turds."

The Narrows resembled an enormous washing machine on steroids. Tightly packed rows of white pine, ash, and maple plastered the sheer cliffs. As the river slithered over and around sub-surface boulders, it sounded like a child's anguished screams. The Hudson, dropping into the gorge at two hundred feet a minute, swallowed Carlyle's cries of "Forward! Forward!"

Ahead of them were six corkscrewing waves, each ten feet tall. The gorge had no room for all that water. It slammed into the walls of the canyon, reversed direction, and came barreling back at them.

The crew hesitated for an instant, and the boat immediately lost momentum and hung motionless at a forty-five-degree angle. In seconds, they would flip backwards and find themselves in near darkness, surrounded by paddles spinning like propeller blades, moving helplessly toward the next set of rapids.

Carlyle shouted, "Come on, damn it! Pull us over!" His refusal to let them capsize worked. The boat mounted the first crest, dropped into the trough, and rushed toward the next crest. Sheets of water as fine as mist, but hard as marbles lashed Carlyle's face. "Together now. Pull! Pull!"

They still had five waves ahead of them, a hundred yards of whitewater dropping almost vertically out of the gorge. Carlyle pushed his foot into the restraining strap, leaned out over the stern and, fists planted in the river, steered them toward the middle of that vortex. After ten seconds, time he measured only by his labored breathing, the raft freed itself from the Hudson's grip and slid into a large tree-lined eddy.

Water streaming from their helmets, the crew slapped hands, pounded their paddles against the sides of the raft, and grinned at each other like chimps in a banana plantation.

"Don't celebrate yet," Carlyle said. "There's three more miles of this ahead of us."

Because Carlyle had passed the point of exhaustion, his movements became almost robotic when they entered the Hudson again. He steered them around Big Nasty and through a seemingly endless series of turns in Mile Long Rapid.

A half-hour after they entered the gorge, they neared Givenny's. One-hundred-and-fifty yards of narrow channels and pounding waves lined the only safe route through the rapid. The river then funneled them toward Soup Strainer, the one hydraulic on the Hudson that scared even experienced guides.

"Slow down!" Carlyle yelled. "I need time to see what this sucker looks like." The current kept driving them toward the hydraulic, however. "All back two." The raft pivoted and slid across the lip of the big wave coming off Soup Strainer. "We made it," Carlyle said. "Now forward hard."

After ninety seconds of furious maneuvering, the boat juking left and right, Carlyle pulled into a large eddy just above Gun Sight Rapid, and the other rafts followed. They were five hundred yards from Harris.

Carlyle said to Nash, "I need a minute."

"It's your call. Just give us the word."

Pretending he was adjusting his foot strap, Carlyle thought about the past two weeks. The incident in Harris four days ago proved that Marshall's enemy was a highly skilled boatman, but he had managed to conceal his responsibility for the deaths of Sanders and Blake.

"You ready?" Nash said.

"Gimme another second. I've got to check these PFD's again."

"Come on, man. We're waiting on you."

"Okay, I'm set. Sayers, you want to take over now?"

"Screw you all. I'm done fucking around. There's an abandoned logging camp just beyond the trestle. I'll meet you all at the Boreas." Sayers pushed his boat downstream toward Harris.

"Sutcliffe," Carlyle said. "I guess it's your turn."

"Fine by me."

"You sure about this?" Carlyle said.

"It's not Niagara. Why the hell not?"

"What are you doing?" Nash said. "We don't know this guy."

"You heard Betts," Carlyle said. "It's my show today."

"For Christ's sake, tell me what's going on," Nash said.

"I'll explain when we get to North River."

"Keith," Betts said. "Let's listen to Carlyle for once."

"I can't just sit here any longer," Sutcliffe said. "See you gents later."

As the convoy prepared to move out, Sutcliffe grinned at Carlyle and turned his raft hard left, away from the route outfitters used, as he disappeared into the maelstrom.

"What the hell's he doing?" Betts said. "Nobody runs it that side. We'll be right under a sheer cliff the whole way down."

"Be quiet a minute," Carlyle said.

"Don't tell me to shut up," Betts said. "I've never even seen that side of Harris."

Carlyle stood in knee-deep water as he steadied his raft. There could be only one reason why Sutcliffe changed course from the path that Marshall and the other outfitters habitually took, the one Sayers had just followed.

"What's going on?" Betts said.

"Listen to me," Carlyle said. "I want you two to follow Sutcliffe."

"That's a kayak route," Nash said as they stared at the drop-off. "It's all holes and rocks."

"Trust me," Carlyle said. "I know what I'm doing here."

"You're crazy!" Nash yelled. "We'll all get trashed if we follow him."

"I'm through arguing with you," Carlyle said. "Just do as I say. I'll explain everything when I meet you."

"Where the hell are you going?" Betts said.

"To see what happened to Sayers." Carlyle tightened the straps of his life vest and turned to his crew. "Listen up. We've probably got a crew in trouble just downstream. You've got to pay attention here."

As Carlyle's boat approached the drop-off into Harris, one of the clients shouted, "You sure this is the right way?"

"Just trust me. Now, back left one. Stop." Their raft scraped the top of a submerged boulder and hesitated before plunging over the edge. "Hold on. Here we go."

As soon as he entered the rapid, Carlyle spotted Sayers's raft. It was upside down, impaled on a piece of rebar that had been driven like a harpoon clean through the boat's floor. The guide and his six-person crew, waves breaking over their heads, were clinging to the chicken line as the current did its best to sweep them down into Harris.

Carlyle had done half a dozen river-rescue courses, but never alongside raw, untested recruits. He knew that with no place to anchor midstream, he'd have only one chance to save Sayers's people. "All back! We don't want to crash into them."

His boat pulled up alongside the disabled craft. He reached over, slid a rescue line through a d-ring, and pulled his raft close. "Grab their life vests at the shoulder, lean back, and pull them out one at a time. Make sure no one slips under our raft. I can't hold on much longer."

When there were six people sitting on thwarts in the middle of his raft, Carlyle turned toward Sayers. "It looks like there's another piece of iron just thirty yards downstream. We've got to turn hard left as soon as I cast off. Grab the spare paddle and let's get out of here."

Carlyle's boat, its gunnels now only four inches above the river, cut across the current and began following the shoreline toward the trestle at the bottom of the rapid.

Ten minutes after he entered Harris Rift, Carlyle roared into an eddy at the mouth of the Boreas and found Sutcliffe's boat parked twenty yards upstream of the abandoned railroad trestle.

Betts yelled, "What the hell is going on?"

Carlyle looked over at Nash. "How's Marshall?"

"He'll make it," Nash said. "Just answer Betts."

Carlyle pulled his boat close to Sutcliffe's raft. "Where's your guide?"

A ranger sitting front left said, "When we got here, he jumped out and ran into the woods at the top of the slope. A minute later we heard an engine fire up. It sounded like an ATV."

"What's your name?" Carlyle said.

"Jason Williams, sir."

"Jason. You afraid of heights?"

"No, sir. I manage a skydiving club when I'm not doing stuff like this. I've got a couple hundred jumps in my book."

"Great. Run up to the trestle, cross it, and make your way back to the top of the rapid. If any other boats show up, tell them to run the left side of Harris, the same one we just did. You got that?"

"Yes, sir."

"Say everywhere else is booby-trapped. Someone will come get you in an hour."

Williams jumped from Sutcliffe's raft, scrambled up the slope, and made his way to the middle of the bridge. "You would not believe the view!" he shouted. "I can see the gorge and the mountains north of here. There's still snow on them!"

Carlyle shouted, "Forget the scenery! Just get going." Carlyle pointed to the people in Sutcliffe's boat. "I want all of you to move to our other rafts."

Betts said, "Wait a minute. How'd you know Harris would be booby-trapped?"

"I'll explain after we put Marshall in an ambulance at North River. Sutcliffe could be planning something else."

"Sutcliffe? He's the asshole responsible for all this?"

"It's him, all right. Now get going, but stay away from Bus Stop. We can't do that to Marshall."

Carlyle shoved his boat into the current and let the Hudson, now a relentless dark green surge, push them downstream. Worried about another attack, the four guides kept their rafts no more than twenty feet apart. The six rangers in Carlyle's boat sat grim and silent, staring at the woods and the abandoned railroad track as they rushed south through the valley. Thirty minutes later, when a chopper appeared over the beach at North River, Carlyle said, "You can relax. We're out of danger now."

Betts stood up in his boat. "There's police cruisers, ambulances, and cops with shotguns all over the put-in." Yellow tape kept a fifty-person crowd, mostly media, far from shore.

Caleb Pierce, careful to avoid the mud, made his way down the bank as Carlyle's raft hit gravel.

"How'd you hear what happened?" Carlyle said.

Pierce grabbed the front of Carlyle's raft. "That ranger, Williams, he had a cell phone. He made it sound like a war was going on out there."

"He tell you anything else?"

"Only that Sutcliffe ran out on them."

The rangers unloaded their gear, thanked Carlyle, and marched up to the road.

"Have they found him?" Carlyle said.

"We've got a dozen patrol cars searching a twenty-mile radius around the gorge," Pierce said. "That doesn't include the units stationed at Wevertown and Warrensburg. But nothing yet."

When the ambulance carrying Marshall had left, Bognor walked down the embankment and over to Carlyle. "How did you flush him out?"

Carlyle told Bognor about Sutcliffe's refusal to take the usual path through Harris. "He was clever enough to follow Marshall into the first trap, but he knew where to duck. When he abandoned his raft and crew for a getaway vehicle, that clinched it."

"I can't wait to get my hands on him," Pierce said.

Bognor turned to Pierce. "Give us a minute, would you?"

Bognor led Carlyle fifty yards up the road, away from the media, to where his cruiser was parked. The two men leaned against the vehicle, facing the river.

"Ric," Bognor said, "I know you've had a tough day, but I've got some bad news."

Carlyle slammed his fist into his own chest. "Is she okay?"

"She? Who?"

Carlyle let out a breath. "Sorry. I was worried about my wife. What, then?"

"They found Wells this morning."

"Found him? Where?"

"At the base of Mitchum Rock. He died trying to save an ice climber who'd been stranded overnight on a ledge. I'm really sorry."

Carlyle rested his hands on the cruiser. "He wanted to come with us today. I told him to stay with Search and Rescue."

"Come on, you're not responsible for his death."

"I can't believe it. We were together just yesterday. Where is he?"

"They're taking his body off the mountain in a couple of hours. Sorry to bring this up, but what about Sutcliffe?"

Carlyle said, "We need to bring our search team to the lodge. I have an idea where Sutcliffe's headed right now."

"Where?"

"Johnston Mountain. And I've got a pretty good idea why he's going there."

SIXTEEN

At five that afternoon, Bognor, Pierce, and Morris fought their way through a gauntlet of TV cameras and print reporters surrounding the lodge and locked themselves in Marshall's conference room.

Although sunset was still three hours away, the room was bathed in darkness. Two troopers stood outside the front door and a half dozen others were patrolling the woods surrounding Ryan Marshall's property.

Carlyle, who had changed out of his rafting gear, walked into the room and sat next to Bognor.

Bognor peered at him. "You look beat."

"I forgot what that river's like. My arms feel like I've been hauling sandbags around all day."

"Welcome to middle age."

"Beth will see this on tonight's news. If we don't catch Sutcliffe soon, my marriage may be over."

"They're calling you a hero."

"Who's saying that?"

"The rangers in your boat, that's who."

"Don't congratulate me yet." Carlyle stood up and poured himself a coffee. "Anyone hear how Marshall's doing?"

"The hospital's not talking," Bognor said. "The building's locked tight. No one gets near him without a damn good reason."

"Is his business closing down?" Carlyle asked.

"He's got no reservations and the State has pulled his license," Morris said. "There's nothing else for him to do."

"What about next season?"

"I heard that his father is talking about selling the business," Bognor said. "You ever think about becoming an outfitter?"

"Me? You must be out of your mind."

Someone banged on the Conference Room door.

"Caleb," Bognor said, "would you mind seeing who that is?"

When Pierce opened the door, Alan Metzger, the stringer for *North Country News,* pushed his media badge into his face. "Can you confirm the rumor that David Sutcliffe murdered those two guides?"

"How'd you get into the building?"

"Is it true that Sutcliffe's an eco-terrorist?"

"Are you looking to be arrested for trespass and harassment?"

"You have any idea at all where Sutcliffe's at?"

"Get the hell out of the lodge."

"Who's in the room behind you?"

"None of your business."

"Did he really set off a bomb in the gorge?"

Pierce turned to Bognor. "Sheriff, okay if I pepper spray him?"

"Caleb, watch it."

Pierce grabbed Metzger by the neck, shoved him into the corridor, and slammed the door.

"If you'd left this operation to us," Morris said, "we wouldn't have a killer on the loose now."

Bognor waved off the comment. "Right now, I want to know what we do next."

"Figure out how to narrow our search radius," Carlyle said.

Morris pulled out a map. "I've got cars patrolling all major roads from Albany to the Canadian border, as far east as the Mass. line and west to Syracuse. Both lanes of the Northway have been blockaded. Warren, Hamilton, and Essex are on lockdown."

"You can pull those cars back," Carlyle said.

"You mind telling me why that is?"

"I think he's going to stay put in Warren County."

"This going to be another one of your theories about how we deal with hardened criminals?" Pierce said.

"Let's look at what we know about Sutcliffe. First, he's never strayed outside this region. Second, the gorge is the only place where he feels safe."

"Which means exactly what?" Morris said.

"We've got to focus our search on an area where he has resources."

"I need specifics."

"I'm not done. Those antique tools and disguises may hold the key to finding him. That and why he seems obsessed with the logging community."

"Where are you going with all this?"

"While I was on the computer in Marshall's office, I discovered that Sutcliffe didn't have a criminal record. Then, on a hunch, I went back a hundred years and did a search on homicides in Hamilton County. There was something about the way our guy's been behaving that struck me as familiar."

Pierce shook his head. "Another history lesson?"

"This region's always been a fairly lawless place," Carlyle said. "But I hit pay dirt when I came across the records of the Pasco affair."

Grace Irwin walked into the conference room. "You all go on with what you're doing. Just ignore me."

"You can't just barge in here," Pierce said. "We've got a crisis on our hands."

"I won't be but a minute. Since this business is in the shitter now, I figured I'd just pick up my last paycheck."

Pierce stood up. "You can get your money after we capture Sutcliffe."

"Grace," Carlyle said, "sit down a minute, will you?"

She sat next to Carlyle, as far from Pierce as she could get.

"Did you know Dave Sutcliffe was Sam Pasco's grandson?"

She dropped her backpack on the table. "Are you shitting me?"

Morris was twisting the thick gold ring on his right hand. "Who's Sam Pasco and how is he connected to these crimes?"

"Every criminologist in New York State has studied the Pasco case," Carlyle said. He explained that Alvin (Sam) Pasco was born in Stony Creek in 1897, just ten miles from here. "Pasco and his brother-in-law, Joseph Woods, the trigger man, murdered his father, Leander, one night as the old man was coming home from a bar in Thurman."

"What happened to them?" Morris said.

"A jury found Woods guilty of murder. He was the first man from Warren County to die in the electric chair."

"And Pasco?" Bognor said.

"He served eleven years and was freed in 1926."

Pierce sat back down. "How in hell can you connect our case to something that took place eighty years ago?"

Carlyle looked down at his notes. "When Sam Pasco got out of prison, he came back here and married Alice Roberts. In 1929, they had a girl they named after her mother. Thirty years later, she married Robert Sutcliffe, a local farmer. Robert is David Sutcliffe's father."

Bognor looked at Carlyle sharply. "Robert Sutcliffe? Are you sure?"

"Sheriff," Grace said, "There isn't much to do around here but drink and nurse grievances. It's him."

"I'll be damned."

"Grace, tell them the rest of the story," Carlyle said.

"Alice and Robert Sutcliffe held a series of dead-end jobs. They were considered trash by people around here. But forty or so years ago, they bought a beat-up old cabin and six rocky acres on Johnston Mountain."

"You can guess what happened next," Carlyle said. "When Phillip Marshall and his partners bought up all that property on the mountain, they discovered that the Sutcliffe tract was right where they planned to put their base lodge. That's when their lawyers started pressuring David's parents to sell."

"It was brutal," Grace said. "They tried to hold on, but their neighbors, dreaming of what a buyout would bring, harassed them night and day for months."

"Dave's parents finally gave in, didn't they?" Carlyle said.

"Gave up is more like it," she said. "Losing their land broke them. Alice passed away in an asylum in Glens Falls. Her husband died of a heart attack in 2003. You wonder why people around here hate developers. Just get them talking about the Marshalls."

Morris pushed back his chair. "How can you be sure there's a connection between Sam Pasco and this current rampage?"

"It's all about the power of memory and revenge," Carlyle said. "After his time in prison, Sam Pasco became an outlaw. He poached his neighbors' trees, burned down their barns, killed their cattle, and destroyed their fences and phone lines."

"I hope they caught the bastard," Pierce said.

"It ended badly, all right. In 1934, he was convicted of stealing lumber and served time near the Canadian border. Then, in 1940, after a property dispute, he murdered his cousin, Orlie Eldridge, and ran off into the woods."

Carlyle turned in his chair to face Morris. "Pasco went on the run, living in caves and abandoned camps on Johnston Mountain and in the gorge. They finally traced him to a hideout just two miles from here. After Pasco ignored an order to surrender, a state trooper shot him."

Morris said, "So you think the grandson's been using the old man's death to strike back at the Marshalls."

"Subconsciously or not, Dave Sutcliffe may be relying on his grandfather's reputation to fuel his crusade against the company responsible for his parents' suffering."

"They're both nothing but murderers," Pierce said.

"I'm not supporting what Dave did," Grace said, "but folks who have nothing would rather die than lose their land."

"Give me a break," Pierce said. "David Sutcliffe couldn't even have known his grandfather."

"But his father must have talked about him," Carlyle said. "People were afraid of Pasco, but they admired his refusal to buckle under to outsiders. Add to that the injustices suffered by his parents, and it's more than enough to drive him over the edge."

Morris stood up and put his notes in a briefcase. "It's time to end this discussion. My Special Operations Response Team is primed and ready. I'm turning this manhunt over to them."

"Not so fast," Bognor said. "My office still has jurisdiction in this county."

"You think you and Pierce can handle Sutcliffe?"

"All right, then, suppose you tell us what your plan is for capturing him."

"We'll establish a Command and Control center here at the lodge," Morris said. "Once we locate Sutcliffe, I'll have two teams dropped into the target area."

Bognor shifted in his chair, "Ric, you want to show the Lieutenant the flaw in his line of reasoning?"

Carlyle leaned forward. "Nobody knows this terrain like Sutcliffe does. And I wouldn't be surprised if the locals keep him informed about your plans."

"If my men don't take him down immediately, then they'll flush him out of wherever he's hiding."

"He could be on the run for months," Carlyle said. "Are you prepared to wait until he attacks someone else?"

"Carlyle," Pierce said. "We're not dealing with textbooks here. It's a firepower problem now. Let the pros deal with it."

"Listen to me for a minute," Carlyle said as he walked to the map tacked to the wall. "Almost everyone around here lives in one of three valleys. This means we can concentrate our search in a few crucial areas."

Carlyle explained that primary and secondary roads further divided the region into quadrangles, each approximately four miles long. "I assume your men are already guarding the bridges spanning the Hudson at the Glen, Riparius, and North Creek."

Morris nodded.

"Then Sutcliffe will be forced to stay on this side of the river."

"Terrain is irrelevant under modern combat conditions," Morris said. "We put men and assets where we need them."

Carlyle looked over at Grace. "You want to show the lieutenant the problem his men are going to have on Johnston Mountain?"

"If we had the Israelis working for us," she said, "I'd say go for it. Seeing it's state troopers, my gut tells me someone on our side is going to get killed if they take on Sutcliffe straight up."

"That's enough" Morris said. "Will someone please get her—"

"Wait a second," Bognor said. "Grace, why are you so sure we're in for trouble?"

"David's momma was a frightened little thing. Your fancy doctors would probably call her paranoid. She made sure her husband built their place in such a way that they wouldn't have any trespassers."

"What exactly does that mean?" Morris said.

Grace pointed to the map on the wall. "You've got a three-quarter-mile hike in from the road. The spruce is thick as grass in there. You really think Sutcliffe will let you waltz in and shoot him like a dog?"

"If he's booby-trapped the trail," Bognor said, "You'll have to sweep every foot of ground between the road and the house."

"You don't think we've thought of that?" Morris said.

"The last bit," Grace said, "is real steep. Then, just before you see their place, the trail ends in a large meadow. When they cross that, your men will be out in the open."

"What about the house?" Carlyle said.

"It sits on a small rise at the far side of that field, right up against a cliff face. You can't be sneaking up behind him."

"If Sutcliffe decides to take a stand," Bognor said, "he could hold out for hours, maybe days."

Morris said, "I've got two airborne assault teams and twenty troopers sitting at a command post just down the road. Some of these men have been battle-tested in Iraq or Afghanistan. He doesn't stand a chance."

"You're forgetting something," Carlyle said. Surrender wasn't an option for Sam Pasco and it won't be for his grandson. Do you really want some Rambo conducting guerrilla warfare for months on end in these hills? I think there's another way to handle this."

"You've got one minute."

"I'll try to talk him down off that mountain."

"That's insane," Morris said. "They'll have my scalp if I put a civilian in harm's way."

"Lieutenant," Bognor said, "Carlyle has spent the past month studying the way Sutcliffe thinks and behaves."

"Sutcliffe's a psychopath. You can't negotiate with that type."

"He may be delusional, but I may be able to break through to him if you give me some time, Carlyle said."

Morris shook his head. "Not a chance."

Bognor said, "If you go in there without Carlyle, you're risking a major bloodbath. Are you willing to take responsibility for that?"

Morris began tapping his finger on the desk. "If I agree to allow Carlyle to negotiate with him, will you accept my conditions?"

"Let's hear them."

"My men will cordon off the mountain and surround the cabin. Carlyle will have three minutes to lure Sutcliffe out of that cabin. But if he gives any sign of resistance, we will take him down. Is that clear?"

Grace picked up her backpack and stood up. "It may be too late for negotiations."

"What do you mean?" Morris said.

"Just before I walked in here, I told Betts I saw Sutcliffe's van parked outside of Giuseppe's Pizza."

"I thought you said Alex was in the gear shed," Bognor said.

"Not anymore. Twenty minutes ago, he drove out of the parking lot like his hair was on fire."

"For heaven's sake," Pierce said. "Why didn't you say something?"

"You jumped all over me when I walked in here. What the hell was I supposed to do, talk reason to you?"

SEVENTEEN

Betts was lying on his side in the van, his hands and ankles bound with nylon cord. His head rested on a pile of oil-soaked rags. Every time Sutcliffe's vehicle hit a crack in the pavement, the business end of a lug wrench ground into his ribs. "God damn it, where are you taking me?"

"You'll see soon enough," Sutcliffe said. "But if you don't shut up and lay still, I'm going to tape your fucking mouth. And forget about kicking out a window; that would really piss me off."

"Any chance you can loosen these ropes? My shoulders are killing me."

Sutcliffe laughed. "If you hadn't tried to stop me in town, you wouldn't be hog-tied now."

A siren, like the cry of a stranded gull, echoed through the valley.

"The cops will find you," Betts said.

"For your sake, they better not." Sutcliffe's van turned onto a narrow unpaved Forest Service road and stopped. "You and me are going for a little hike. If you try to get away, this peavey will be the last thing you ever see."

"I'm trussed up like a pig. How the hell am I supposed to escape?"

Sutcliffe wrenched open the side door of the van, dragged Betts out, and dropped a rope over his head.

"What are you going to do with me?"

"Be quiet. Your job is to do what I tell you. Now get moving."

Sutcliffe pulled the peavey and a shotgun from the front seat and slipped his arms into a large army-issue rucksack.

"What have you got in that thing?" Betts said.

"None of your damn business."

With Betts in front and Sutcliffe watching him from behind, the two men marched along a plank boardwalk that meandered through a stagnant bog at the foot of Johnston Mountain.

White cedar surrounded the marsh. Fern, cattail, and water plantain carpeted the damp ground. Pickerel weed floated in the murky water. The smell of rotting vegetation, a mixture of dead leaves and decaying logs, filled the air.

"Fantastic, huh?" Sutcliffe said.

"You out of your fucking mind?"

"This is a special place. I used to hunt this swamp as a kid."

"You really expect me to say I'm having a lovely time?"

"Another comment like that and you'll be fish food."

Betts kept his eyes fixed on the boardwalk. "You mind telling me why you killed Sanders and Blake?"

"They weren't supposed to get hurt."

"Then who were you gunning for?"

"Marshall."

"Why are you so pissed at him?"

"You don't remember what happened last April when I flipped a boat in the Narrows, do you?"

"For Christ's sake, that was a year ago."

Sutcliffe hesitated a moment. "When we got back to the lodge, Marshall told everyone—you, Nash, Blake, Sanders, and a Forest Service ranger—to meet him in the gear shed."

"I have no idea what you're talking about."

"Marshall picked up a guide paddle and said to me, 'Have you completely forgotten how to use one of these things? I don't know how Burton puts up with you.' He said he couldn't believe why he'd ever hired me. I had to stand there like some stupid, snot-nosed kid and take it from that spoiled little bastard."

"It's coming back now."

"Good. Then maybe you also remember that he told me to pick up my gear, get in my van, and go home to think about the stupid mistake I'd made. When I drove out of the lot, you all were staring at me."

"You don't go berserk because some moron hurts your feelings."

"No? I never even got a chance to say there was nothing I could do to prevent what happened."

Betts tried to loosen the rope around his neck. "Everyone hates it when Marshall pulls shit like that. No one takes it seriously. But because you couldn't put that story out of your mind, two guys are dead. How fucked is that?"

Without warning, Sutcliffe threw Betts on his side, pressed his head to the mud, and brought the peavey's metal spike close to his ear. "I suggest you shut up."

Betts went limp. "I get it. Just let go. Just let go."

"Stand up and get moving."

Following a series of switchbacks, they hiked through thick stands of sugar maple and hemlock. A stream engorged with snowmelt poured down the side of the mountain. White birch, victims of the '96 blow-down lay on the ground like abandoned elephant tusks.

"Are you going to tell me where we're going?" Betts said.

"You see those notches in the trees? Just follow them and stop asking questions."

At twenty-five hundred feet, now breathing heavily, they broke from the undergrowth. Red spruce, with needles so foul even deer won't touch them, encircled the two men. Ahead stood a grove of paper birch, its outer layers peeling away like dead skin.

Sirens wailed in the distance. "They're headed our way," Betts said.

"Get your ass moving. It'll be dark soon."

Twenty minutes later, they reached the summit of Johnston Mountain, a bare expanse of eroded granite boulders.

"Look at that view," Sutcliffe said. The streetlights of Warrensburg, like miniature paper lanterns, glowed in the distance. To the east and south, Lake George cut through the landscape like a thick scar. A helicopter, its powerful searchlight sweeping through the evening sky, moved back and forth over the mountain.

"I don't see anything but shitty little trees, tiny scrub bushes, and slimy green rocks."

"You're an ignorant jerk. This is a special place."

"Maybe to you. For me, it's just useless and ugly."

Sutcliffe glanced at his watch. "It's 6:15." We've only got another hour of daylight. Get going." Turning south, he prodded Betts down a little-used trail that would take them off the summit. Twenty minutes later, Sutcliffe said, "We're nearly there."

"Where?"

"You have no idea, do you?"

"Not a clue."

"We're a quarter mile from where Marshall's lodge is going up."

"Why drag me all the way up here?"

"Stop right there and turn around."

Using the metal spike of the peavey like an axe, Sutcliffe lopped off the lower branches of a small pine.

"What are you going to do with me?" Betts said.

Sutcliffe pushed Betts against the tree and kicked his feet out from underneath him. When Betts was on the ground, Sutcliffe wrapped duct tape around his ankles and tied him to the trunk. Then he picked up his rucksack and turned toward the trail.

"Where are you going?" Betts said.

"I've got another job to do before this is all over."

"You can't leave me like this."

"Stop your damn whining. I'll make sure someone finds you before the bears do."

Betts struggled against the ropes. "You're not going to escape this time. The cops will be crawling over this place any minute."

"Maybe so, but I'll be done by then."

Ten minutes later, Sutcliffe rounded a bend in the trail and spotted a little boy walking toward him.

He looked to be four years old. His hair was sun-bleached blond. He wore gray-striped bib overalls, a long-sleeved cotton shirt, and tiny ankle-high work boots. A pinecone was nestled in his left hand. He stopped when he saw Sutcliffe.

Sutcliffe laid his peavey and shotgun just off the trail and bent down on one knee. "Hi there."

The child stared at the ground and said nothing.

"My name's David. What's yours?"

"Adam."

"Why are you out here by yourself, Adam?"

"We're out looking for mushrooms and stuff."

Sutcliffe reached out and shook the boy's hand. "Where are they? Your mom and dad?"

"Right back there. They let me walk ahead because I'm grown up now."

Sutcliffe turned to his left and saw the parents coming down the trail. The man, limping slightly, was tall and fair, thin as an alder, with a reddish blond beard. He walked up to his son. "Who's your friend, Adam?"

The woman smiled at Sutcliffe but put an arm around her child's shoulder. Although no more than five feet tall and barely a hundred pounds, she looked brick-strong and weathered, as though she'd done hard labor all her life. Dreadlocked, she wore wire-rimmed glasses, a dark red spaghetti strap halter top, wraparound skirt, and a pair of worn trail boots. Her face was sunburned, her eyes agate green.

"I hope you don't mind me talking to your boy."

"I would never stop him from meeting strangers," she said.

The man said, "I'm Jeff. She's Lisa."

"You staying nearby?" Sutcliffe said.

"In an abandoned cabin not far from here," Lisa said. "We can't afford Lake George. Land is cheap on the mountain and no one's bothered us so far."

"My people lived around on this mountain for three generations," Sutcliffe said.

The child looked up at his mother. "Can he have supper with us?"

"Ask your papa."

"Can he?"

"Sure, if he wants." The father was taller than Sutcliffe and more than a decade younger, with long, ropey arms and hands coarsened from working in the woods. He smiled at Sutcliffe. "Let me show you the way."

Sutcliffe picked up his shotgun and the peavey. The four of them walked down the trail for another ten minutes and turned off the path. Across a meadow, at the base of a cliff, a cabin was tucked in among second-growth spruce and silver birch. Sutcliffe's former home, almost invisible from the road, looked as if it had been there for a hundred years.

The place could not have been more than twelve hundred square feet. It had a steeply pitched, dark-green metal roof. Three chipped concrete steps led up to a covered porch supported by four log posts. An ancient cane rocker and a rough wood bench stood near the front door. The shingled siding, gone gray years ago, was cracked and weathered. Narrow double-hung windows stood at both ends of the house. A low-slung dormer and a stone chimney dominated the tiny second story of the cabin.

While Lisa worked over the wood-burning stove and the child built a series of slender towers made of wooden blocks, her husband told Sutcliffe their story. "We've lived in this cabin for nearly two months. I work in a lumberyard, she's doing carpentry. We plan on getting animals soon, a goat and one or two sheep. She'll make soap and cheese to sell at the farmers market. I'll trade for logs once we own a team of horses."

Lisa brought plates of vegetables and rice to the table. "You know the mountain well?"

Sutcliffe took off his boots and set them by the door. "My parents worked six acres for nearly a quarter-century and never managed to save a dime. You sure you want to try making a living here?"

Jeff pulled on a sweater and put a log in the stove. "We're young and have lots of time."

"We've put in a garden," Lisa said. "When we can afford it, we'll have a contractor dig a well. Hauling water gets old pretty quickly."

A leather couch, its seams stretched and worn to shreds, sat against one wall. Above it was a shelf of books on sustainable agriculture, Eastern religions, women's health, the history of Ireland, and basic woodworking techniques. Glass jars containing spices, herbs, and dried vegetables filled a small pantry near the sink. The couple had replaced the ladder to the loft, which Sutcliffe had climbed a thousand times, with a rough plank circular staircase. In one corner of the single downstairs room sat the child's playthings—a six-car wooden toy train; miniature cars; assorted dump trucks, graders, and front-end loaders; and a half-dozen painted metal warriors standing alongside a gray plastic castle.

When it grew dark, Jeff lit two large candles and placed one on a table and the other near the door.

Sutcliffe said, "How about some real light in here?"

"Sure," Jeff said. "If you say so." He hung a small kerosene lantern from a beam running down the center of the room and touched a match to the wick. "Better?"

"That's good," Sutcliffe said.

Lisa carried the drowsy child up to bed, read him a story, then came downstairs. She sat next to her husband and began folding clothes.

The boy cried out once in his sleep, then was still.

Sutcliffe said, "Mind if I say something?"

Jeff stood and turned up the lamp. "Sure, go ahead."

Sutcliffe leaned forward. "The soil around here is nothing but powdered granite. There's only a three-month growing season. Everyone who's tried farming has failed."

"We don't need a whole lot to survive," Jeff said.

"My parents were like that," Sutcliffe said. "They had no money and no education, but they thought this land would provide for their children. Someone took it all away from them."

Lisa began putting the child's toys away. "How did they survive?"

"He roofed houses, drilled wells, and cut trees. She cleaned homes, watched children, and cared for old folks."

The lantern began to dim. Jeff unhooked it and refilled it from a two-gallon can he took from a low kitchen cabinet.

Lisa stared at the knife hanging from Sutcliffe's belt. "You work on the river?"

"I did."

Lisa moved close to her husband. "We've been listening to the radio. You're the one they're looking for, aren't you?"

Sutcliffe got up and locked the front door. "Don't be afraid. I'll be gone in a few minutes."

"Why are they saying those things about you?" Lisa said.

Sutcliffe walked back to the sofa. "I didn't mean for anyone to die. I was just trying to save this area from ruin."

"What do you mean?" Jeff said.

"All that talk about a ski resort? It's a lie. A company's planning to work the garnet mine running under this mountain. They'll drain water from the Hudson to separate the ore from the tailings. The trout will die, and chemicals, arsenic especially, will leach into the ground. In ten years, the river will be dead."

"How do you know all this?"

"I've spent the past two years watching their engineers doing mineral tests and laying out stakes for roads and holding ponds."

"You've got proof?" Jeff said.

"The corporation's plans are in the assessor's office."

It was full dark outside now and quiet as death.

The child awoke. "Papa, I'm afraid," he called out from upstairs. "Go to sleep, Adam," Jeff said. "Everything's fine."

"I'll go up," the woman said.

A helicopter rose over a nearby ridge, its rotors shattering the night air. It hovered two hundred feet above the cabin, its powerful downdraft buffeting small trees and rattling the front windows. The candles flickered and went dark. A powerful searchlight swept back and forth across the clearing before the chopper moved off into the darkness.

Sutcliffe stood up. "Get the child. Bring him down and you all sit against the back wall. Stay away from the windows." He walked toward the front door. "Don't worry. This will all be over soon."

EIGHTEEN

At 7:05 p.m., Carlyle led Bognor, Morris, and Grace out the front door of the inn. A convoy of vehicles—four patrol cars, two twelve-passenger vans with blacked out windows, and an armored personnel carrier, its engine growling—stood near the road.

When they reached the parking lot, Morris said, "How can you be sure Sutcliffe's headed for his parents' home?"

"It represents everything he's lost," Carlyle said. "He'll go back again before he makes a break for it."

"You better be right," Morris said. "I lose my job if we screw this up."

Grace said, "Let me show you how to find his place."

"We'll find it all right," Morris said.

"His neighbors tore out all the road signs when Marshall evicted them," she said. "There's nothing but unmarked trails now."

Morris started walking toward his car. "Don't worry. We've got satellite images of the place."

Grace looked up at the sky. "Fog thick as wool usually rolls in at night. You'll be going in blind."

"You think the state police are that incompetent?"

"No, sir. I would never say that after the way you handled that Bucky Phillips thing. Just turn right at the first unmarked intersection. A bit farther on, you'll find a red mailbox with the name Sutcliffe on it. The trail begins there."

"Let's move then," Morris said. "I don't want a firefight on my hands after dark."

At 7:22 p.m., the convoy reached the place Grace had described. Between the road and a path running through the woods was a quarter acre of open ground surrounded on all sides by sixty-foot blue spruce.

Morris said, "We've got less than a half hour of daylight now. Let's get moving."

"If you'd taken Sutcliffe out earlier," Pierce said, "we wouldn't be doing this now."

"Caleb," Bognor said, "It's time for you to stand down."

"Remember," Carlyle said, "First, I get a crack at negotiation."

"You'll get three minutes," Morris said. "If he's not in cuffs by then, my men will take over."

"A siege will only end in a bloodbath."

"That's my final offer."

"We don't even know if he's armed," Carlyle said.

"Let's get going," Pierce said. "This is an assault, not a powwow."

Bognor gave him a hard look. "Caleb, if Ric gets into any trouble, the state police will handle it."

"At least let me cover him in case he walks into an ambush."

"Fine," Morris said. "Tell us when you're in position."

Pierce draped a 30-06 across his shoulder, bent low to the ground, and ran into the woods.

"Bad idea," Carlyle said. "He's trigger-happy."

"Don't worry, I'll have one of my men jerk his chain, if necessary."

With Carlyle in the lead, the three men crossed open ground and headed for the trees. In seconds, they were making their way up a narrow, rutted trail.

Carlyle turned around after several minutes. "Sheriff, it gets pretty steep just ahead. You sure you want to keep going?"

"I'm fine. Let me just rest for a second."

"Take all the time you want."

Bognor removed his hat and wiped his forehead with his sleeve. "Any idea what you're going to say to him?"

Carlyle drank from his water bottle. "I'll try to make him understand my aim is to avoid a shooting war."

"How do you do that in three minutes?"

"I'll pretend I'm being paid like a lawyer."

"Your wife know what you're doing here?"

"You kidding? I'll be lucky if she doesn't leave me when she finds out what went on today."

"You can always go back to the university once this is finished."

"No, that life's over with. I wasn't meant for a desk job."

"Come on, you two," Morris said. "My officers are wondering why we've stopped."

The three men, moving slowly when they encountered uneven ground, continued up the mountain. As daylight faded, they found themselves in deepening shadow.

"You sure we're on the right trail?" Bognor said.

"There's only one way up the west side of this hill," Morris said.

"How do we know Sutcliffe will let us get close enough to talk?" Bognor said. "For all we know, he may be watching us right now."

Morris shook his head. "That's pretty unlikely. I've got twenty-four troopers armed with assault rifles and stun guns. Four are watching us, the rest getting ready to surround that cabin."

They stopped just inside the tree line. A small field lay between them and a cabin sitting on a small rise fifty feet up the hill.

Morris spoke into a walkie-talkie. "We're in position. Hold your fire and wait for my orders."

Bognor stepped close to Carlyle. "You don't have to do this."

"I've spent a decade trying to figure out why people like Sutcliffe go on a rampage. It's final exam time." He slipped off his backpack, handed his flashlight to Bognor, took a quick drink from his water bottle, and retied his bootlaces. "I'm ready."

Carlyle grabbed a small bullhorn from Morris and took half a dozen steps into the open. "Sutcliffe. It's Ric Carlyle. May I approach?"

Sutcliffe cracked the door. "How many are out there with you?"

"Just Bognor and Morris, but there's troopers all around."

"Why'd they send you?"

"I told them I understood what the Marshalls had done to your family."

"You know nothing about us."

"I know that a cop killed your grandfather when he was trying to surrender."

Sutcliffe edged through the door but kept to the shadows. "Come on up, but keep your hands in the air."

Carlyle crossed the meadow, mounted the porch steps, and stood facing Sutcliffe. The two men were three feet apart.

"That's far enough," Sutcliffe said. "Now spread your arms wide."

"Why?"

"I need a shield." You carrying a gun?"

Carlyle opened his jacket. "Satisfied?"

"I still need to pat you down." Sutcliffe ran his hands over Carlyle's torso. "Why in hell should I trust you?"

"I know that what Marshall did to the people who lived here was wrong."

"Cut the drama. What do you want?"

"Where's Betts?"

"He's tied to a tree a thousand yards east of here. You can have him any time you want."

"We better go inside to talk."

Sutcliffe shook his head. "Can't do that. There's a couple and a young child in there."

"You've got hostages?"

"I'm not holding them against their will."

Carlyle turned toward the woods and raised the bullhorn. "Don't fire. We've got people inside." He said to Sutcliffe, "Step away from the cabin, please."

"Why in hell would I do that?"

"The state police are afraid I'll get killed in the crossfire."

Sutcliffe took a step away from the cabin, but continued to stare at the tree line. "You gonna put me in your book? The one about how you captured a terrorist?"

"There's no book. I'm just trying to make sure no one dies today."

"No matter what you do, I'm going to prison for the rest of my life."

"That may be, but we can't end this standoff while you've got hostages."

"What'd you have in mind?"

"Let them go now."

"I'm not holding them. See for yourself."

Carlyle raised the bullhorn again. "We're going into the cabin."

"Ric, that's out!"

"There's no other way." Carlyle followed Sutcliffe through the open door and found the two adults crouched against the back wall with a child between them. "You guys okay?"

Jeff and Lisa glanced at Sutcliffe, but said nothing.

"See, they trust me," Sutcliffe said.

"They're scared to death. Let this be between the two of us."

"You've got an army behind you. I've just got these hippies."

Adam opened his eyes but didn't move. When the woman began crying, her husband put his arm around her shoulder.

"I'd never hurt these kids."

"The cops don't know that," Carlyle said.

"Why would I just give up my only bargaining chip?"

"You don't need them anymore."

"Why the hell not?"

Carlyle took off his jacket and draped it across the back of a chair. "Because you've got me for a hostage now."

"This a trick?"

"You better do it before I change my mind."

"All right, smartass. You've got yourself a deal." Sutcliffe, shotgun in hand, cracked the door. "Make it quick. I don't want flash-bangs landing in here."

Carlyle helped the two adults to their feet. "When you get outside, put your hands in the air, and walk straight down the hill toward the trees."

Sutcliffe said, "Watch over that little boy now."

Carlyle, his hands up, edged out onto the porch. "The hostages are coming out. Hold your fire."

Without looking back, the two adults and the child left the cabin and disappeared into the dim light. Carlyle slammed the door shut behind them.

Sutcliffe grabbed him by the arm. "Sit down against the wall over there and face the door."

"You going to tie me up?"

"Not if you do as I say." Sutcliffe picked up a chair, jammed it under the doorknob, and turned down the lantern.

"You didn't have to do that."

"No? Your friends probably have night scopes trained on me."

"They won't try anything as long as I'm alive."

"How can I be certain they're not waiting for some signal to come busting in here? Which reminds me, did they put a mike on you?"

Carlyle unbuttoned his shirt. "Satisfied?" He looked around the room. "So is this where you grew up?"

"You trying to make some connection with the perp? Is that what this conversation is about?"

"I'm just trying to end this standoff without blood all over the walls. You've got legitimate gripes, but they don't have to mean you or anyone else has to die over them."

Sutcliffe said, "Is Bognor or Morris in charge out there?"

"Morris is holding all the cards."

"Then I'm fucked."

"That's not true. He wants to see this thing end peacefully."

"How do we do that?

"What if I can get Phillip Marshall to preserve the cabin?"

"Don't be an idiot. Once I'm in prison, his bulldozers will make this place disappear."

"How can I convince you to put down that shotgun?"

"Let me go on TV. I want everyone to know what the mine project will do to this land."

"They'll never agree to that."

"This is pointless, then."

"Let me finish. If you surrender, you'll get a lawyer. He'll work with the press to set up an interview."

Morris's voice came through a bullhorn. "Carlyle, your time's running out."

"I've got to let them know I'm safe," Carlyle said.

"Okay, but do it quick."

Carlyle opened the door. "Give us a couple more minutes."

"This can't go on much longer," Morris said.

Carlyle turned to face Sutcliffe. "You heard what he said."

"You've got to hold them off."

"Why?"

"None of your business."

"There's no way out of here."

"We'll see about that."

"You've got to surrender."

"My grandfather tried to negotiate, but they shot him dead."

"You'll get a chance to explain all that."

"You expect me to swallow that equal-justice-for-all bullshit?"

"No, but at least you can have your say on TV. What else can you do?"

"You think I'm trapped don't you?" Sutcliffe edged away from the wall and crawled toward the table in the center of the room. He grabbed his pack and pulled out the top hat and long coat that Carlyle had seen at the trestle.

"What in hell are you doing?"

"If I've got to die, might as well go out the way Sam did."

"If you do that, they'll shoot you."

"Don't be so sure about that. In a couple of minutes, it'll be dark enough so that if we're standing next to each other on the porch, they'll hold their fire."

"Are you nuts?"

"You really expect people like Sam and me to obey laws made in Albany?"

"Sam's been dead for half a century."

"Shut the hell up." Sutcliffe stood up and was reaching for the peavey with his left hand when a bullet blew out the window, missed Sutcliffe's neck by inches, and embedded itself in the wall.

Sutcliffe, his coat covered in splintered glass, dropped to the floor, and crept toward the back wall of the cabin. "You asked me to trust you."

"Stay down. Let me talk to them."

"Not on your life."

"I swear, I don't know how that happened."

"It was probably Pierce. That asshole's been waiting all his life for a chance to become a hero."

"For God's sake. We've got to end this before one or both of us get killed."

"You got that right." Sutcliffe crawled to a cupboard and pulled a kerosene can from the bottom shelf. He leapt up for a moment to grab the lantern and quickly ducked. There was no further gunfire. He then crawled across the cabin, grabbed Carlyle's arm, and pulled him toward the door. "Hold your fire! Your boy's coming out!"

"This is crazy. Nothing will stop them now."

Sutcliffe opened the door and shoved Carlyle onto the porch.

Carlyle said, "It doesn't have to end this way."

"If you don't get out of here, I'm going to shoot you myself."

"You're a damn fool."

"Get going!"

Carlyle ran down the stairs and across the rocky ground toward the tree line where Bognor was waiting for him.

"Who fired the shot?" Carlyle said.

"Guess."

Lisa said, "He wasn't going to hurt us."

Morris said, "Listen, one of my men will take a statement and then drive your family into town. Now you'd best get out of here."

"We have nowhere to go," Lisa said.

Bognor handed her a card. "There's a phone number here. Tell the woman who answers I said to put you up tonight."

"Who is she?" Lisa said.

"My wife. She'll take care of you."

Just then, two state police troopers left the woods. Pierce, his hands cuffed behind his back, was between them.

Bognor took Pierce's firearm from its holster. "I never gave you an order to fire."

"You all were just standing around. I thought he was going to kill Carlyle."

Morris turned to Bognor. "We'll bring your deputy to the county jail in Warrensburg. You can decide what to charge him with."

"Just get him out of my sight."

When Pierce had been led away, Morris spoke into his walkie-talkie. "Get ready. We're moving in one minute."

Carlyle said, "Don't do that."

Bognor said, "Ric, it's over."

"What's he's carrying?" Morris asked.

"A shotgun. And that damned peavey."

"Anyone else in there?"

"Just him."

"That's it, then."

"He may still change his mind."

"It'll be dark any minute. I can't risk waiting."

As the three men stared at the cabin, one of Morris's deputies ran up. "Lieutenant, our infrared sensors suggest the structure's on fire."

Just then, clouds of dark gray smoke began pouring from the roof.

A harsh orange light began to envelop the front room of the cabin. The windows began to crack and, one by one, fell from their frames.

Carlyle ran toward the cabin. Twenty yards away, he raised his arm to ward off the heat from the flames and began to cough.

Morris grabbed his shoulder and pulled him back. "There could be explosives in there."

Suddenly the second floor of the structure caved in. The front wall buckled and tumbled into the burning ruins. The porch, now engulfed by flames, collapsed. Cinders and soot drifted into the trees surrounding the property.

Morris's men walked out of the woods and watched the house disintegrate. They stood silently as the blackened timbers burned through the first floor and collapsed into the basement. What was left, a red-hot inferno that resembled an active volcano, continued to glow in the dark.

It took less than thirty minutes for the cabin to burn to the ground. When it was over, the only thing left standing was a cast iron stove, the fireplace, and the chimney.

"My men will rope off the perimeter," Morris said. "The Fire Department can deal with it when they arrive."

"We can't just leave him like this," Carlyle said.

Bognor put a hand on Carlyle's shoulder. "Ric, there's nothing more we can do now."

An hour later, after everyone else had left the inn, Bognor found Carlyle in the conference room of the lodge. "After all of Morris's complaints about your shielding Sutcliffe, he admitted it probably saved lives."

"Not everyone's."

"You think he would have surrendered?"

"I don't think he was willing to face the rest of his life in prison."

"Morris wants me to charge Pierce with attempted murder."

"His attorney will try to plea bargain, but at least he won't be your problem any longer."

Bognor got up and walked to the door. "One more thing. Phillip Marshall wants to see you."

"He can call me."

"Tonight."

"Are you kidding? I've been up since before dawn."

"Just see him before you leave town."

"You know what this is about?"

"No, but it seemed urgent. He asked that you stop by the hospital."

Carlyle stood up. "When will I see you again, John?"

"The State's going to hold an investigation on Monday. Come over for dinner after."

"I'd like that."

The two men shook hands and walked outside.

"The damn helicopter's finally gone," Bognor said.

"It'll probably be back in the morning."

Bognor stopped walking. "That was a pretty neat move you made this morning, luring Sutcliffe out into the open like that."

"I was pretty sure his next target was Harris Rift."

"I meant taking the almost insane chance to trap your suspect by putting him in a raft."

Carlyle turned his head to the left and squinted at Bognor. "Sheriff, do you really think I'd jeopardize the lives of all those people by pulling a stunt like that?"

Bognor returned Carlyle's gaze for a few moments, then smiled and shook his head. "No, I guess you wouldn't go that far, would you?"

Carlyle backed his truck away from the inn and drove slowly out of the lot. When he reached the road, he turned east, crossed the concrete span over the raging Hudson, and headed toward the hospital in Glens Falls.

NINETEEN

Carlyle spent two hours in a corner room of the hospital with Ryan Marshall, Marshall's father, and two attorneys from a white-shoe Albany law firm. After he explained the details of the contract he was offering Carlyle, Phillip Marshall said, "You won't get a better deal anywhere."

Carlyle looked at Ryan. "This work for you?"

Phillip said, "Ryan's moving on. He knows it's time."

Carlyle kept his eyes on Ryan, who glared back at Carlyle and then at everyone else in the room. "Nobody's giving me much choice, including your DEC pals."

Carlyle put the twelve-page document in his briefcase. "Let me clear this with my wife. If she approves, I'll sign it and fax a copy back to you."

"You've got twenty-four hours. Then we open it up to the highest offer."

At midnight, Carlyle called Beth to say he was too tired to deal with the traffic on the Northway and would take a motel room for the night. The next morning, his shoulders and back riddled with fatigue, he threw his gear in his truck and left for home.

Lake George, luminous in the morning sunlight, brought back his time as a guide. When he'd finally learned everything he needed to know about the job, he realized he would never have to fear the Hudson again. From then on, the work brought him astonishing happiness. Yesterday, the sight of the six huge standing waves in the Narrows, each capable of flipping his raft end over end, shattered his emotional defenses and made him realize what a gift his years on the river had been. Bitterly cold water made his body ache with possibility and the smallest changes in ambient light made him feel as though he was seeing the gorge for the first time. Once or twice a season, when he made a perfect move in the most difficult rapids, he felt as though he would never again have anything to fear.

Nearing the city an hour later, Carlyle looked to his right and spotted the four hulking granite towers that dominated the university campus. Once he signed the contract Phillip Marshall had offered him, he would find a publisher for his book, clear out his office, put his papers in storage, and begin searching for a new line of work.

Running a gauntlet of high-rise apartments, warehouses, abandoned factories, and railroad yards, Carlyle followed the highway east and south around the city. Anxious to get home, he hurried past shopping malls plastered across the suburban landscape. At eight-thirty, he turned into his tree-lined driveway.

The lights in the house were on, the front door unlocked. In the kitchen, he found yellow daffodils in a vase and a map of Italy on the table, the Amalfi Coast outlined in red. Upstairs, Beth's studio door was open, and an image of delicate blue and white flowers sat on an easel. Every curtain in their bedroom was pulled aside, light everywhere. A note on his pillow: *Eggs and toast in the oven. I'm in the garden. Come join me. Love, B.*

Carlyle crossed the yard to the barn, slid open the heavy timber door, and switched on a bank of fluorescent lights. The room was bitterly cold—the dense, brittle, inert cold of a structure built atop a concrete slab. His tools lay untouched and in perfect order on the workbench. He dumped his still-damp rafting gear on a chair and shut off the lights.

He left the barn and walked toward the garden. Beth was bent over a row of irises, their tall, elegant stalks and stunning violet-blue petals still wet from last night's rain.

"I'm home."

She stood up. "You surprised me." She was wearing the wide-brimmed straw sun hat he'd bought her in Venice two years ago, one of his long-sleeved cotton shirts, light gray slacks, and a pair of brown, open-toed garden shoes.

"How long have you been out here?" he said.

"A couple of hours, at least. I love it this time of the morning. Quiet and cool. The birds are going nuts and I can't think about anything but how I'm going to capture all this on canvas."

Carlyle wrapped his arms around her shoulders. "Sorry I called so late. It was chaos at the lodge until the press and the police left. Then I had to stop and see the Marshalls."

"It was all over the news. Let's go inside." She scooped up a trowel and pruning shears, put them in a wicker basket, and walked beside him toward the house.

"I thought you were done risking your life."

"Marshall was hurt. They needed someone to lead them out of the gorge. End of story."

"But did you have to help the police capture Sutcliffe?"

"There would have been a massacre if I'd let a SWAT team storm his cabin."

"You wanted to save lives. I can understand that part of it. But it's what you've always done -- put yourself in danger just to prove that you're not afraid of anything."

"I can't promise it'll never happen again." He stood up and went to the stove. "On the way down here, I realized I needed to ask you something."

"I know what you're going to say. Adrian's gone."

"For good?"

"Yes."

"I asked you when all this began not to let him near us."

"He was only around for a couple of hours at a time."

"What was he doing here?"

She stood in front of him and looked him in the eyes. "You were a hundred miles away in the mountains, hours from the nearest phone, while a madman was terrorizing this region. I was afraid to be alone. Maybe I was doing the same thing you were in the gorge, facing my fears at last."

"Of being attacked again?"

"Of strangers, dark streets, long hallways, and unfamiliar surroundings.

Sunlight flooded the kitchen. Carlyle stood up and lowered the south-facing shades. "You ever think about going somewhere to escape this heat? Maybe getting a place in the mountains?"

"I won't sell this house."

"I wasn't suggesting that."

"Then how would we buy something up north?"

Carlyle sat down. "Marshall's father is fed up with supporting that rafting company. They asked me if I was interested in buying it."

"Buying what exactly?"

"Their entire operation on the Hudson. The rafts, the outfitter's license, all the equipment."

"Why would Ryan give it all up?"

"The deaths of Saunders and Blake have ruined that life for him."

"What did you say?"

"That I had to see if you'd be willing to move up there for three or four months every year."

"Where would we live?"

"The lodge has a five-room apartment on the third floor. It has a large glassed-in room facing north that would be perfect for a studio. There's a huge kitchen and a garden out back."

"What about my work?"

"There's a gallery in town that would go crazy if they could sell your stuff."

Beth stared at the trees surrounding their house. "You're going to run boats through the gorge again, aren't you?"

"No. I'll leave that to the young guys who need to prove how tough they are."

"Are you sure about that?"

"You can trust me on this one," Carlyle said.

ACKNOWLEDGEMENTS

I am grateful for the assistance of the staff of the following organizations: the Library at the Adirondack Experience: The Museum on Blue Mountain Lake, the Adirondack Research Room at the Saranac Lake Free Library, and the University at Albany Library.

This work would not have been completed without the assistance of many individuals: Robert D. Hare whose work on psychopaths and criminal behavior was most helpful; Louise Cowley, Chris Noël, Laurie Alberts, Ellen Lesser, and Robin Hemley of the Vermont College of Fine Arts for their friendship and unfailing encouragement; the guides at the Nantahala Outdoor Center and at Idaho River Journeys who taught me how to row an oar rig: Bob Wolfe who pulled me from Mile-Long Rapid in April, 2000; Drs. Barbara Kapuscinska and Peter Kelly who explained the physiology of drowning; Annie Stoltie, Editor of *Adirondack Life*, who gave me permission to quote from Kathryn E. O'Brien's article, "The Saga of Sam Pasco"; my intrepid editor Peter Gelfan who read many drafts of this novel; and the staff at Bublish.com who shepherded this manuscript into print.

I cannot adequately portray the enormous debt I owe my wife, Iris Berger, who shared more Class V rafting trips than she ever bargained for.

ABOUT THE AUTHOR

Ronald Berger has a PhD in British history from the University of Wisconsin-Madison and an MFA degree in creative writing from the Vermont College of Fine Arts. He is the author of *The Most Necessary Luxuries: The Mercers' Company of Coventry, 1550-1680* (Penn State University Press, 1993). He was a licensed whitewater raft guide on the Hudson River from 1992 to 1997. *The Gorge* is his first novel. He and his wife live in upstate New York.

Made in the USA
Middletown, DE
07 October 2020